Malcolm & Jack

(AND OTHER FAMOUS AMERICAN CRIMINALS)

Ted Pelton

SPUYTEN DUYVIL
New York City

Acknowledgments

"Famous American Criminals" appeared in *La Petite Zine* 7.
Excerpts from other parts of the novel have also appeared in different
forms in the online venues *BlazeVOX*, *WebdelSol* and *Potionmag*.

Early versions of the first two chapters came about as a result of par-
ticipation in an National Endowment for the Humanities Summer
Seminar for College Teachers at Baruch College in 1995. Most of the last
chapter was written during a fellowship at Vermont Studio Center in
2001. The author also received a Just Buffalo Writer-in-Residence Grant
during the composition of this novel, in 1999, and benefited from both an
National Endowment for the Arts Individual Fellowship in Fiction in
1994 and a sabbatical award from Medaille College in 2004.

Library of Congress Cataloging-in-Publication Data

Pelton, Ted.
Malcolm and Jack : (and other famous American criminals) / Ted Pelton.
p. cm.
ISBN-13: 978-1-933132-09-9
ISBN-10: 1-933132-09-4
1. X, Malcolm, 1925-1965--Fiction. 2. Kerouac, Jack, 1922-1969--Fiction. 3. Nineteen forties-
-Fiction. 4. Bohemianism--Fiction. 5. African Americans--Fiction. 6. United States--Fiction. I.
Title.
PS3616.E45M35 2006
813'.6--dc22
2005028366

Printed in Canada

When you teach a man to hate his lips, the lips that God gave him, the shape of the nose that God gave him, the texture of the hair that God gave him, the color of the skin that God gave him, you've committed the worst crime that a race of people can commit.

Malcolm X

I goofed throughout entire wartime and this is my confession.

Jack Kerouac

CERTAIN EVENTS DESCRIBED in what follows did actually occur. Lucien Carr killed David Kammerer in August, 1944, in New York City, as the Allied Armies fought their way from Normandy toward Paris. Billie Holiday was sentenced to a year in Alderson Federal Reformatory for Women in 1947. Malcolm X, then Little, according to his own autobiography, ran marijuana to jazz musicians via the railroad. While World War II was still raging, Wardell Pomeroy, an associate of Dr. Alfred Kinsey, was interviewing men and women to obtain sexual histories for Kinsey's famous study. Nonetheless, what follows is fundamentally a work of fiction, and the author has frequently departed from history to suit the needs of the form. No statement contained herein should be taken as a simple statement of fact.

THE PRESENT NEVER IMPROVES, THE PAST JUST GETS WORSE.

FAMOUS AMERICAN CRIMINALS

1.

New York City is a '40s town.

Arriving from elsewhere, not having visited for a long time, you notice it. Something happens, rare in an American city. Yes, New York sizzles with an electric current of the now; nonetheless, you find yourself transported back a lifetime ago, to when things were wilder, more unsure in certain ways than they are today. To when war broadcasts came over the radio, silencing rooms where dancers had just been swinging to big band. Rumbling conga drums, an echo of blaring brass, a veneer of loud, innocent fun. Spiffed-up and shiny, disguising the fact that it could all come suddenly to a stop, that death could enter the apartment or ballroom at any moment.

Does it happen to you today, walking around Midtown, that flitting visions of Katherine Hepburn and Spencer Tracy emerge from facades of buildings familiar from black and white movies? Go ahead, take the A-train. Disney may have swept the pornshops out of Times Square, but the serviceman will kiss the girl on V-J Day there eternally. Santa Claus lives on 34th Street. Bums hanging out on the street corner are poets and jazz musicians who'll someday be famous. After they're dead.

The wrong people are still making all the money. Just as when Malcolm X called himself Detroit Red and hustled for bread uptown.

Much of what we call the '60s was born in the 1940s. Racial unrest, questioning of dominant values by members of a surly, growing underground. But those times were also far more settled, comfortable, less wild—people playing along, desires more repressed than in any time since. (Until perhaps today.) Citizens treated more unequally, which helped create the wildness in the first place, or which provided the defining context by which certain behaviors were called wild.

North of the Park, Malcolm spoke about self-determination and taught the people of Harlem about Africa and the world. Earlier, he'd run both drugs and women, knew both the syndicate leaders and the horn-men. A train man for a while, too.

Jack Kerouac came to Columbia in the '40s and soon knew where to go to see Billie Holiday.

Malcolm knew Billie well enough to chat with her between her sets. Maybe she asked him to score her some smack. Jack would be looking for some sticks of tea. Malcolm was also a go-between for downtown white men and uptown black girls. And men. Jack's best friend was a poet at Columbia in crisis over his sexuality. Another friend was a downtown junkie. A third murdered a man named David Kammerer who'd made sexual advances towards him, dragging the body from where it fell, stabbed, in Riverside Park, down the bank into the Hudson. Head spinning, the murderer went to the junkie to ask him what he should do. "Get a good lawyer and turn yourself in," said the junkie, William Burroughs. The murderer, Lucien Carr, didn't like that answer and went uptown to wake up Jack. They had a beer and Jack watched him bury the knife. Eventually Lucien turned himself in (the papers called it an "honor slaying") and served four years. Malcolm served six and a half for a string of burglaries in '45. Billie was busted for heroin in '47 and served a year and a day. Jack had taken so much speed that he was hospitalized for thrombophlebitis in late '45. He was 23. Malcolm was 20. Billie was 30. At least she didn't have kids. Her parents had married young: it says in her autobiography that her father was nineteen, her mother sixteen, and Billie three. But Billie didn't write her own autobiography. Lied to the man who did. Claimed not to have even read it.

Malcolm read his—though he didn't write it. Kerouac wrote and wrote, pretending for a while that it wasn't autobiography, then giving up.

Bob Dylan sings in "The Ballad of Hattie Carroll," "*and took out the garbage on a whole other level.*" Poor Hattie Carroll was a maid in the kitchen. She lived 29 years and gave birth to ten children. And never sat once at the head of the table.

Kerouac's family was French-Canadian. He was born Jean-Louis Kerouac and they spoke French in his home. When his father was on his deathbed, he accused Jack of defiling his mother's house by bringing a Jew there—Allen Ginsberg. His father died and Kerouac began working seriously on his first novel. Malcolm was reading anything he could get his hands on: dictionary, Bible, settling finally to absorb the words of the prophet Elijah Muhammad of Chicago. Billie wasn't reading her contracts, when there were any, and losing most of her money to her handlers. Before she went on each night, they brought her the white gardenias she wore in her hair and the white junk she cooked up in a tuna fish can and shot into her feet. Before her return concert after getting out of jail, she stuck a hairpin into her head but continued the show—she lost so much blood that she collapsed by her third curtain call. There was no cotton to be picked on 52nd Street between Leon and Eddie's and the East River, said Artie Shaw, but it was a plantation any way you looked at it. There isn't evidence of either Malcolm or Jack ever shooting smack, but it was the drug of choice among jazz musicians. Lester Young, Charlie Parker, Dickie Wells, John Simmons, Carl Drinkard, Miles Davis, Jimmy Green, Stan Getz, Joe Guy, Don Byas, Bud Powell, Fats Navarro, Gerry Mulligan, Anita O'Day, Sylvia Sims, and others got hooked. Billie made nearly a quarter of a million dollars between 1944 and '47, but when she went to jail had next to nothing. God bless the child that's got his own. Men would buy her five and ten dollar bags and take one or two hundred. The D.A. recommended hospital rehab but the judge said Billie was a "criminal defendant," "convicted as a wrongdoer."

Some eventually did kick. Others didn't.

Jack got Benzedrine without having to go through dealers. You could buy an over-the-counter Benzedrine inhaler, break it open, roll up the speed-soaked paper inside and swallow it. Drug laws were in their infancy. Marijuana had only become federally prohibited in 1937. Opium had only been made illegal at the turn of the century, largely to hinder Chinese immigration. The full force of Puritan demonizing of drugs is actually a twentieth century phenomenon. The typical heroin addicts of the nineteenth century had been wounded Civil War soldiers, "hysterical" women. Addiction was treated clinically rather than criminally.

Legal or not, you had pale and wan needle-junkies, hyped up boys from the village, lean red-eyed vipers taking in the scene, Broadway actors blowing into clubs in tuxes. Coke was the gentlemen's drug, heroin was for junkies, disrespected. Billie disguised her addiction from vigilant sheriffs by drinking constantly. No junkie could possibly drink that much. She chugged double Scotches and gin spodiodis, photographed at table after table.

Look at the photos today and you can't tell if she's high. She wears lipstick, rouge and eye shadow, smiling for the camera in a low-cut gown, wearing a turban, a hat, or flowers in a straightened forehead wave. Her dressing room smelled of cooked hair before her shows.

In Spike Lee's *X*, we see Denzel Washington as young Malcolm getting an amateur lye-job, panicking when he finds out the water's been turned off, rushing to the bathroom, burying his head in the toilet bowl and flushing. Maybe this actually happened. Or maybe Malcolm got the detail from Lester Young, the man Billie called Prez—who named her Lady Day—who also told the story. Maybe it was such an apt metaphor everyone claimed it happened to them.

Jack? Football player: speedy, tagged a "climax runner" for Columbia, to be brought into the backfield in crucial situations. The school had endured a winless season the year before and hoped for much from Jack, who'd shown flashes of spectacular play in one season of prep school action at Horace Mann. Then he hurt his leg.

1940. Allen Ginsberg's friends were shocked to see the Communist poet hanging around, then rooming with this Joe College guy. Jack looked like someone you'd find during the summer in uniform checking your oil—and who you'd trust to do it. Polite, a safe date for your kid sister. But at night Jack was hitting the streets. Later, he ditched a tour in the Army he'd enlisted for, told a Navy psychiatrist he just couldn't accept any form of discipline. *Ain't that the truth*, you'd hear in Three Deuces, the Famous Door, Onyx Club, 1942, '43. *They wouldn't even let me light up a goddamn cigarette!* Detroit Red did it anyway, played crazy, told his Army psychiatrist at the recruiting station that he wanted to organize niggers to steal weapons to kill Southern crackers. *Daddy-o, don't you tell anybody about this, but you and I is from up north here.* Military commanders didn't think it a good idea to give either one of them a gun.

His family would think he's crazy listening to that nigger music, but Jack don't care, Jack just wants to swing and delight to that sound: fast, fast, fast. And Red, them's bad people, and you're the baddest of 'em. You gonna be dead before you've worn out your first shaving razor. Red don't care. What's Red got to live for? Jack's got it all in front of him and Red tries to stay in front of it all or else it'll catch up.

Jack works only enough in the docks to make enough money to quit and have fun again. Maybe start traveling. Not that that takes much money. Hang out at Pier 19, East River, or out in front of the rope store on South Street—all the supply men go there—and you'll find a ship to go out on. It's still like Herman Melville a hundred years later. Or stick out your thumb on any kind of road and you'll get picked up if you look like Jack. People'll drive you home and feed you pie and ice cream. *On the Road* á la mode. Fundamentally, people are good, if only they'd just let themselves be good once in a while, free themselves of the grind that keeps them churning in their yokes day after day under the hot sun; it's dull and dreary life-boredom that turns a man or a woman against themselves and against each other and instead of enjoying their sweet loving with one another they live miserable small lives where they turn the soil over but never see the fruited rainbow of what they've wrought on the earth in their all too brief time.

Red is listening. He figures Jack's got at least a ten on him, maybe more.

"Know where a cat can get some tea around here?" says Jack.

2.

Red knows. And smack and ups and snow and here to your daddy's farm in Omaha.

"I love talking to black people, man," says Jack. "Man, I wish I was black. To see you cats sliding along in your zoots like you don't have a care in the world. Crazy! That's a feeling white people just don't have, they're so worried about being the same as everybody else, never really living because of a fear of being seen as different or queer or a loser in some jive-ass success story no one believes in because no one can, it doesn't allow you room to breathe! The richest white man in the world is still a poor copy of the image he thinks he's supposed to be. Black cats don't bend their knees to these false gods. Did I come into this world through the womb of my mother the earth just so I could talk and write like everybody else?"

"I'll show you the man," says Red. *What's this hype?* he thinks, at a shallow level. He can't say what he feels. Never in his life has he said what he feels. Does he even know? Has he ever even told himself? There's a bubbling pot of anger in his stomach, but it's rare that it rises to his placid face. He nods coolly to the bartender, who's been awaiting his cue without ever looking over directly. A bottle is brought over and two shotglasses filled brimming. Jack and Red toss them back and hit the street.

"Walk on the other side," says Red through smiling white teeth. "When I turn the corner, have a cigarette, and when you're done come down to the end of the street and knock on the yellow door."

They experience it differently, act on it differently, have it respond to different respective histories, it alternately confirms or replaces their experiences—but Malcolm and Jack both listen to, dance to, feel jazz. Both let it draw up into them like an ink that changes the color by which their souls (not their skins) are defined. Both live moment to moment. Said Malcolm: *My whole life has been a chronology of changes.*

Red hates Jack, sees him as a category. He knows Jack sees him as a category and hates being seen as something invisible.

Jack digs Red, but sees him as a category. But to be fair to Jack he knows what it means to be seen as a category, knows he too often sees within categories, knows that no one is really seen for who they are as long as the categories pertain in their vision, and wants desperately to get rid of categories: it's something he thinks about every day.

Outside it's drizzling, but too lightly to clear the humidity on this hot night. As Jack is smoking, feigning nonchalance, there staggers by a drunk. He stops before Jack and tries to straighten up, bringing a hand up toward his head, which Jack first takes as a threatening gesture before realizing it's an attempted salute.

"Evening, soldier," the man slurs.

Jack smiles painfully and squares his shoulders, arms at his sides.

"As you were," the man says and moves on, still almost falling over. Jack watches him for a moment, still standing rigid, then turns in the other direction.

Red hears the knock and opens the door. Jack slips inside, his shirt collar turned up. They go up three flights of stairs, Jack following long-legged Red who takes the steps two at a time.

The room at the top of the building is papered with faded old deco roses blooming beneath a patina of nicotine brown. The air is close, almost wet, the smell of sweat barely masked though doused in *eau de toilette* and a burning stick of incense.

He and Red are the only men inside.

"Would you like to meet a lady?" Red asks.

There are two here to be met, an older and a younger. The older, a matron, steps forward.

"Would the gentleman like something to drink?" she asks.

Another lounges behind on a sofa, a dark beauty with black curls falling down each shoulder onto plump breasts, barely hidden in a man's silk dressing gown. Jack is caught by the sight of her bush peeking out beneath the hem.

"Uh," Jack starts, but he can't think of what to say.

"What do you like in a woman, Jack?" asks Red. "Do you like our Samantha?"

Jack looks admiringly at Samantha. She wears heavy rouge and orange eyeshadow. She's not as young as she first appeared. But as she rises from the sofa he sees wide hips that were made for loving. Her large round bottom bounces and sways, making Jack aware of a radio playing Ellington's band in the next room. She's got more curves than the Yankees pitching staff.

Jack bounces a little on the balls of his feet, then pulls Malcolm aside.

"I want it naked," he says.

"She don't have to do much to get naked, my man."

"No, you don't understand." He lowers his voice, noticing both the older and younger woman, while now slowly retreating into the room with radio, are still keeping ears toward the two men, straining to hear Jack whisper his particular perversion. He leans close to Red's ear.

"I'm sick of rubbers. First the Navy, then my old lady. I want it naked. And I don't want to have to worry about getting the clap."

Red stands away. "Sure. Anything you want. Our girls are clean as Martha Washington. Twenty dollars."

"Oh, wait, man, you don't know who you're talking to," laughs Jack. "I'd be lucky to have seven bucks on me." He pulls out his wallet and opens to a five and two singles. "And if this is some creep joint, you picked the wrong fella."

"Naw, we don't steal from nobody. Ain't you and I friends?" Red's voice gets high. "But seven dollars? What do you expect for that kind of money?" He laughs, then frowns, then smiles, again the beautiful white teeth. It's all theatre. "I like you, my man. Other cats, they be already out of here, they be soft as cheesecake. But you know what you like and go after it. I like that. You wait right here, I'll sweet talk the lady for you."

It's happened so quickly Jack is surprised he's just agreed to spend his last few dollars on a woman. More theatre from the wings: Samantha says in a loud voice, "I'm a strictly-twenty-dollar call girl." Then after something inaudible from Red: "Does he have any nickels in his jacket for the subway?" Again, more unintelligible honeyed words, to both women, now all with lowered voices. Then Red returns with the younger woman.

"Jack, meet Samantha." She has unloosened her jacket to reveal her breasts, large mounds peaking in swollen brown areolas nearly the size of his palms. These are some tits!

Jack sees this vision of beauty, of his need and desire, of the glorious playground of her flesh, and he wants to say something cool and clever but it comes out instead: "OK, baby. We're gonna have us a party!"

Red reaches across and closes her jacket. "Twelve dollars, my man."

"Twelve? You said seven."

17

"That's seven for the slice of heaven," says Red, "And five and no jive for your master of ceremonies."

"You saw I only got seven."

"Come on, I know you got more. Something set aside for a rainy day?"

"Just some change—enough to get home."

"Home? What you wanna go there for? Samantha here will take you anywhere you want to go."

Jack searches the pockets of his baseball jacket and finds about forty cents. He wants to think of a clever way of keeping it but he can't. He gives Red every cent he has.

"OK? Are we square?"

"Man." Red indulges in a theatrical frown, then relents. "OK, man. But you owe us. You're one lucky man tonight."

"Yessir. I know it," Jack smiles, turning and putting his arm around Samantha. "Now I want to learn all about the secrets of your crazy loving soul, honey."

"She'll show you the way," says Red. "Won't you now, Samantha?"

Samantha issues a less than convincing, "Mm-hmm."

Still, she takes Jack's arm and they head down the hall.

Malcolm winks at the older woman, Eunice. Malcolm gives her the two dollars and pockets the five.

"What the hell you doing with that?" says Eunice. "What you mean even bringing a seven dollar man up here?"

"Well, what the hell else are you gonna put on your table, Mom? War's over. Town ain't jumping like it used to. These are lean times, and you ain't got nothing without me come along tonight."

"We need a different exchange here, Red. You ain't the one on your back."

Red laughs. "Neither's you, Mom. And I don't guess much of this money was going to the one that is if I give it all to you."

"You can take your runny little ass outta here, Red. I'm tired of putting up with your sassy tongue. And don't call me momma. I ain't none of your momma."

"Aw, Mom, that's no way to talk to the man what's bringing in customers and what's gonna make you rich. I'm just saving you time, giving you the service up front."

Eunice growls. "827," she says bitterly, like swallowing medicine.

"Combinated?"

"None of your tongue now. I play straight so I can win straight and never see the likes of you again."

"Mom, you're just begging to ask me to chicken dinner. You ain't fooling nobody."

"I ain't no fool for nobody, neither, Red."

Red taps the pocket where he's put the bill lightly with his fingertips.

They're both quiet for a moment, and this silence erases everything, all the static of the moment, so there's no guise to anything. Just like that, blank slate. Last call past, lights on. The hour of confessions.

"Maybe we're all the fools," says Red.

3.

What else might he say?

Who can tell? This is the silent Red, the even more silent Malcolm, the Malcolm described by the later, vocal Malcolm as deluded, prisoner of a false consciousness, a black man's stunted life in the white devil's world, intoxicated by alcohol, drugs and sex. This is the Malcolm who talks a smooth line, steals whatever ain't chained, sells whatever gets the green. But this language is lost in that moment.

How many have never spoken?

Eunice seems to see what's on his mind but can't find words. "Maybe so. Maybe we're the biggest fools of the world." The war is over, and the changes that were supposed to be coming, where are they?

Malcolm would speak, speak well, speak movingly, made the opportunity for himself to speak a language now familiar to us, one which made an example of his earlier self, made it an object, something pre-Malcolm, not-Malcolm. By any means necessary. I'm not against violence in self-defense. We didn't land on Plymouth Rock, Plymouth Rock landed on us. I don't know if I could start a race war; I don't know if I'd want to stop one. The violence of the white man against himself is just chickens coming home to roost. What is logical to the oppressor isn't logical to the oppressed. No, I am not an American. We ourselves can best solve our problems.

Much of this Malcolm must have already been alive in his earlier incarnation. He was transformed in jail by his reading and the teachings of Elijah Muhammad, but a foundation must already have been laid. He knew about black nationalism from his father, Earl, a Garveyite. One day, Earl preached, black artists would provide a black Madonna and a black Christ for the proper education of African-American children. He was not cowed into submission by the threats of white hate groups in Lansing, Michigan, even though public lynchings were a staple of American society in the pre-war years. One survivor of these lynchings, James Cameron, would later found the Black Holocaust Museum in Milwaukee, which today documents the crimes that took 30,000 lives during this era which denied due process to black men, for whom the accusation of having committed a crime was too often their death warrant. These lynchings were not done secretly. They could be advertised in the local paper, ballyhooed if there was fear of not a large enough crowd. Coming upon a hanged body in the square of a small town in Indiana one morning, a county coroner prepared to cut him down in preparation for burial. A white-hooded man rode up on his farm horse: "Touch that man before noon and you'll join him. We need to set an example." Earl Little was cut in half on the Lansing railroad tracks. Malcolm's mother Louise told her children the story again and again.

James Cameron had been living in Indiana. He was 16, hanging out with two older boys. He wanted to act cool so when they decided to pull an armed robbery, he stuck with them. They went up a dark, well-known path through some woods by a cornfield to a lover's lane and there found a white couple in a car, embracing. The oldest of the three boys pulled the man out through the driver's side and threatened him with a gun. They started fighting. In the distance, James heard police sirens. He knew this man from town and no longer wanted a part in this. He took off back down the lane. About halfway down the road he heard shots. The flashing lights of a police car came in off the road in the direction he was running. James turned into the corn, made his way out past the squad car, ran home; he lied to his mother when she asked if he was in trouble. Then the police came and though she filled the room with screaming they arrested James along with the other two. The three spent a few hours in the precinct, then were bussed to the township jail. James overheard a radio broadcast say that three black men had killed a white man. The man was dead! From the flagpole outside the precinct, the bloody shirt of the dead man pulleyed upward into the night.

Cars began to pull up outside the jail, honking horns. Men came out shouting. James looked down from the window on the third floor of the jail. Headlights and torches illuminated the crowd. They began chanting, *give them up!* A group of men stormed into the prison past the few guards, who didn't want to get in a shootout with so many people. *Give them up!* Many of the people they recognized, might even have called friends. *Where are they!* James had backed into the corner of his cell, but they came and took the three of them and walked them into the town square. One end of the rope snaked out and twisted itself on a tree limb. Two others followed. The men hanged the first two as James watched. He tried to tell them he'd had nothing to do with the shooting. But it was all deranged—he couldn't speak anymore and the giant tree upon which the other two boys were hanged branched out blackly above his head like a hungry spider, the clouds above massing wildly. They put the noose around his neck.

It was then a voice came out of the sky, the voice of heaven—a sweet female voice, soft, soothing and quieting the din of the mob. The voice told the crowd that James hadn't done what they were accusing him of, that he was innocent. An invisible arm extended out of the heavens and touched his shoulder. It guided him down from the tree and the crowd dispersed. Some members of the mob apologized to him as they led him away from the square.

"It's some weird shit," says Red. "But I don't want to be nobody's fool."

Eunice looks at him. She unscrews the lid of a jar of Bromo Seltzer and puts a spoonful in a glass of water.

Red watches her take the fizzing glass to her lips and slowly gulp it down.

"But that's not all, Mom. Like I say, it's weird. But I've always felt I was destined for something. Some sort of, I don't know, revelation. You know, like the cats in the Bible."

"The Bible?" Eunice almost chokes on the last swallow. "That ain't no weirdness," she says, but doesn't say anymore. It may be she's being set up.

"Well, I can't imagine it not being weird, Mom. I can't quite explain it. But I feel I was put here for some reason, I can't say what it is."

Eunice isn't sure of what he wants from her. "I know you're not a bad man, Red. You just get crazy sometimes, but down deep you're probably good."

"Naw, I ain't good. I feel like I'm gonna bust with hate." Tears begin in his eyes.

Suddenly, Eunice's defenses come down and she feels like hugging this dangerous man, so newly vulnerable. She touches his shoulder. "That's okay, son. Let it out."

Malcolm fights back the urge, stiffening at the feel of her hand. Words come instead. "I didn't fight in no war. Now everybody's home and the world's supposed to have changed. But I ain't seen no change, and I know you ain't either, except for it's harder to make a buck."

"That's the truth."

"But that wasn't none of my war and this ain't none of my peace neither. Lots of my boys came back in boxes. Lots of 'em. For what? White man still owns everything and is always gonna. Fools are the only ones think that's gonna change. Don't make no sense. You think the way they treat us has changed in the least?"

"No rightminded person think that, Red. Not if they got eyes in their heads."

"That's what I'm saying. I feel like I got eyes not just for myself but for everyone I see around me, like I'm seeing through eyes they don't know they got. And I'm all the time trying to keep that side of me shut off. It don't help pay the man."

"No it don't."

"My father was a preacher. Did you know that? He was killed by the white man. He was killed by the white man because he told the truth to his face."

"Your daddy's still deep inside you, child. Your daddy ain't never gonna keep still."

"Then I'm going to end up just like him."

"That's not for certain, Red. We can't never know the reason what we're here for."

Red laughs. "We're sure talking some jive here, ain't we?"

"Ain't jive if it's from yourself, Red. I just never heard this side of you before. You a regular John the Baptist." Having stifled it this far, Eunice lets go her own laugh and it's big and loud. It shakes her like a wind blowing through her body. "John the Baptist," she says again between breaths.

"Ain't I worked some kind a miracle tonight finding the only white man in Manhattan that ain't getting any?"

"You sure are, honey," laughs Eunice. "Saint Red, you sure are."

4.

Red leaves to go set some sleep. He walks down the nearly vacant Harlem street. Toward him stumbles the man who saluted Jack earlier, now the worse for wear, head down, steps short. Red is to the inside of the sidewalk and as the man comes closer something impels him to cock back his arm and, timed perfectly as the man passes without glancing upward, throw an elbow square to his jaw. There's an audible crack in the air and a second thud as the man reels away and his head smashes full into the top of a parking meter. His eyes roll back into their sockets and he's out cold. Red never breaks stride. To run might alert someone.

A man walking a nearly empty sidewalk, another crumpled in a heap in the gutter—nothing notable here. Harlem awakes to a new day.

Throughout the city, truck engines are cranked into motion to make their gray early morning deliveries. They load at the downtown harbors and bring the goods uptown. At the enormous green coffee warehouse down on Houston Street there's always been bums laying about, alcoholics, criminals who when the morning doors get opened scurry out of the light. But these past few months there's been a new type of cat—hipsters are carelessly sleeping off their long nights in mounds of beans while lorries back in and out to the four stories of half-moon doors, loading. Half the time it is nearly empty, as the cargo gets trucked to West Side roasting factories. So it's a good place to crash until, one day without warning, shipments start coming in, stir the cats from their sleep lest they get buried in tons of green coffee. The sky outside now a light gray, workmen heavily dosed with caffeine work to take back the streets. Gray men awake to lead their gray lives. But within gray you don't see gray. A whole Technicolor consumer future unfolds before them and their pregnant new brides. Televisions, electric mixers and home freezers, two car garages on tree-lined drives in the suburbs, stores filled with cheerful music putting them at ease while they make their purchases—music you don't listen to, nor made to be listened to, creating an ethereal, consumer heaven—these fulfill the vision. And large, well-heeled police armies form to keep it secure.

Louis Armstrong writes a letter to President Eisenhower asking him to consider legalizing marijuana. To the knowledge of scholars of this period, Eisenhower never responds.

1.

Where has JAZZ gone, free-flow, development of ideas, the life it brought into the arts and the questions it gave the U.S. just when it needed them, post-1945 into the fifties, a time not necessarily more repressive than today, but similarly defined by its fondness for insisting on codes of proper behavior? Kerouac's right, the "story of America" has always been simulated freedom, everybody "doing what they think they're supposed to do." We are still always short of truly free speech—and I'm not talking about sexual representations or artistic boundaries or PC speech codes, but something more in-bred and fearsome, like saying "I'm an atheist" in Congress, or "I'm a pacifist," or "I'm a socialist," as any sort of public act. The hangover of being labelled *Red* or much further back, godless, *heretic* by your Puritan neighbor-authorities makes these the thoughts that are really restricted. So that today most of the citizenry of this great experimental nation can't even conceive of what it would be like to rebel without already arguing with the everywhere prevailing notion that we need and simply can't survive without *Capital*, *War*, and *God*.

2.

They met later at an after-hours place uptown in Harlem, but earlier that summer night in 1946 both Jack and Malcolm were at Lady's show, working their respective ways through the crowd to their seats at the enormous Town Hall auditorium on West 43rd.

Now, a year later, 1947, Billie sits in her jail cell.

Lady Day.

I'm gonna see my lover tonight. It's movie night. She's white, so we don't get to see too much of one another usually, being in different parts of the jail. But I'll get to see her tonight and it'll be closer than when we're in the fields.

It's about the only thing I look forward to here. It's been about the only use this place has had for me. I suppose I do a lot more knitting now than I used to, and I've given some people some nice sweaters and knit caps. I'm also off junk, but that's no thanks to anyone here. The rehabilitation fucking program they got here? Sure they gave me the cure—shut the bitch up in a room and let her sweat and scream it out, cold turkey. Besides, I was off that two years ago anyway, until the cops kept hassling me so much. I went to one of the finest hospitals in the world and got an actual cure, with expert attention and at great expense—$2,000 worth! But no sooner than I'm out those motherfuckers are following me here, there, around the corner for a lipstick, everywhere I go, just waiting, just begging like old wolves. Hope they're all satisfied now, them and their goddamn friends up in the so-called confidential hospital. If that's the confidential $2,000 buys you, next time I'll go cheap to the blabbermouth hospital.

Naw, Cloris—that's her name—she's been about the only good thing to happen to me in I don't know how long. She makes me feel good. I ain't saying more than that, but you can guess what I mean. I guess I've changed quite a bit because of her. Time was, if a woman made a pass at me I'd have made a pass back—with my fist. Naw, I ain't ashamed. You got to take love where you can get it. And unlikely? Shit, you don't know the half of it! I've always considered myself a race woman, doing what's right. So, taking up with a woman, okay, but a white woman?

She's kind of like me in a lot of ways, though. Not in

physical stature. No, there we're about as different as night and day. She's short, but real strong, got strong hands and muscles in her forearms, broad shoulders for someone her size. Wiry, the kind you like to have on your side in a fight because there's no quit in her. Tender, though, soft in her way. That's how I mean she's like me. Hard too. You can't live a life like Cloris has lived, or like I've lived, and not get somewhat hard. But like me, Cloris has kept a place within her that's still . . . well, I don't know how just to put it. Pure, I guess. Like God made her, with a big heart.

Goddamn—don't I sound like the hick girl from the cornfields!

I guess I've just been lonely. Alderson Federal Women's Penitentiary. Welcome, ladies, I hope you like our facilities. Yeah, real fucking nice. About as friendly around here as church is to drunks. I'm not allowed mail from anyone but immediate relatives, and I ain't got none of them, so I just sit and stare as the others get letters and pictures and what not. They tell me I've got bags of mail I can read once I get out of here, but I ain't seen none of it. It ain't allowed. That's the rules. Miss Helen, the warden, at least we're all supposed to call her Miss Helen, but I just call her Helen and she don't seem to mind, she's okay. But rules are rules. She did allow me to get a telegram from this old couple in Sweden who were fans of mine, and to take a phone call that came in from them, and listen to them tell me how much they liked my voice—it's good to hear that again sometimes. They also sent $1,000 which I never saw.

But I wouldn't want to anyway. I never asked nobody for charity. Not Ingrid and Johannesburg or whatever the hell their names were, nor Miss Warden Helen Hironomous, nor no one else.

Anyway, Cloris never asked me for anything—yeah,

that's for sure. She's not the asking type. Just takes. But nothing I didn't want to give. Nor did she just want to get me to sing, to say, "Billie Holiday used to sing to me all the time when I was up in Alderson." She likes my music, but she never asks me that and I'm glad of it. I couldn't sing in this jailhouse, not even out on the farm, on the grounds, nowhere, not as long as I'm here. I sing my feelings, and I need to feel like singing if I'm going to sing, and being in this jail don't make me feel like singing no way, no how.

Not that I'd have much of a chance to sing for Cloris anyway—she's with hers and I'm with mine most of the time. There's six buildings on the grounds here. Two are white, two are colored, and then there's the dining hall with offices and what not upstairs, and a sixth building which has a library and movie room and the prison laundry and work-shop, the only building that ain't as a rule segregated. We even eat our evening meals at different times, whites at five, colored at six-fifteen. Then there's farm fields all around the buildings where they grow strawberries we never see again after we pick them and vegetables we do see but don't recall because by the time we see them again they've been boiled out of recognition. In the fields, black and white are kept separated, but we can get pretty close to one another some-times, when we've got to get the picking done, for instance. Then we can sidle over to one another a little bit on the sly, as long as we keep looking at what we're doing and don't rub nobody's faces in it.

But movie nights are the thing. The first time I met Cloris was a movie night. These are their way of giving us a little recreation here, to try to get us to relax a little, which it would take a lot more, but it's something anyway. They have some amateur nights too, but I stopped going to them on account of always being asked to sing. So movies are all I bother with. But I didn't expect nothing like this to happen. One night we're coming back from some damn thing, Bing Crosby as a singing priest, and I'm walking kind of by myself, in my own world, arms down at my sides, down this kind of half-lit hallway, when I feel the softest little touch on my hand. I don't know how anyone can touch so soft as that. Don't even feel it at first, I'm feeling it and know there's someone touching me, but it's like there's no line between touching and not touching, just a smooth blend. I get this chill—not a bad chill, but like I'm wearing a cool, flowered dress and get a breeze that just feels nice. Then we're holding hands. Just like that. She's kind of half behind me and we still ain't looked at one another. Just feels so nice walking holding hands like that. I don't remember holding hands like that since I was a little girl. And not much of it then.

Somehow, before even looking at her, I knew she was white and that we're gonna have to go off in different directions once we get past the main door. When we're almost there, I look back at her. I see this little woman, with her crooked teeth, but smiling, and sweetly, in her way.

It's two more days go by after that, that I'm walking down where I was working before in the laundry room and all of a sudden Cloris rushes in and grabs me, throws me into a closet with her. Her hands are all over me! She's got my dress down off my shoulders before I've even caught my breath. It's sudden and surprising, but I guess I must have been waiting for it, because I didn't push her away. She had my breasts in her hands and that felt so good. They'd been feeling so heavy, but it wasn't really something I could do anything about so I didn't even feel really how heavy they were until she took them in her hands and it was like my whole insides jumped. She was like a wild animal and I wasn't minding, her mouth kissing me all down my neck and bare arms. "Oh, you got some body, Billie Holiday," she's saying between kisses, and she keeps calling me that, the whole name, Billie Holiday.

It's funny. I know right then she's been hearing me talking to her in my songs. That's what wins me over. I mean, there was a point there when I caught myself, or could have caught myself, after the initial overflow of feeling, when I was about to or could have pushed her away. And then she started with the "Billie Holiday" stuff and it went to my head like champagne. I knew it right then. People come to you sometimes you never met and they act like they know you—and they do, they've been listening to your music. And usually you don't have the time to meet and talk with people like that. You do, but you don't really get to know them. Most you never get to know at all. It's like that. We've known each other a long time.

But I only really get to look at her a few minutes later, and then only for about a minute, as we lean back a little from one another and I kick over a pail and Cloris says, "Ssshh," but I start laughing, trying not to do it too loud, and then she starts too, trying to be serious but it being so ridiculous, two grown women with half their clothes off in a closet trying to stay quiet so they don't get called to the principal's office. But then we stop laughing and just look, getting ourselves presentable again. I see she has a kind of beauty. She's almost like a man. Small, like I said, but in fact like a plank, skinny but tight, practically no tits at all, just little nubs on top of firm lines of muscle and even kind of bow-legged, leaning now away from me in this narrow space like she was leaning on a lamppost smoking a cigarette, having stopped her rush to dress, like a man that don't care who might be coming down the street to hustle him off—he's just gonna stand there and enjoy himself and stare his fill until they physically push him down the road. Then she looks quickly out the door. She turns back in. "My name is Cloris. I'm a big fan of yours, Billie Holiday." She's got a Southern voice that lilts like you've been teasing yarns out of it with knitting hooks. I'm no fan of the south, but it's a young voice and sounds like a melody. She's only about 21 or 22. She's got dimples in her cheeks and straight blonde hair falling down to the tops of her shoulders. "I gotta go now," she says, "I was supposed to come down here and ask—" but she bites her lip at this and looks again outside, worried. Then she's out the door, "Bye bye, now."

I finish putting myself back together. It's a good thing we don't wear make-up in here or I'd be a mess.

I didn't even say a word to her.

An hour later I'm done down in the laundry and I get back to my cell. Then it's time to eat and I get through that and come back, I don't even know what I'm thinking as I'm doing all this. A million things at once, but nothing straight. It seems like only a few minutes have gone by but it's actually a couple hours, because suddenly it's time for them to lock us down for the night.

I hate that goddamned sound—metal clanking all through the jailhouse, bolts slam hard into locks and are fastened shut. A guard comes down the line checking each one, his shoes snapping down the concrete, louder, then softer again. It's like they want to go through some kind of evil concert to remind us we're prisoners and that there's no getting out until they open the doors up for us. This goes on no longer than it usually does, but tonight every second is like a sharp pain and I have to hold myself tight so I don't have to feel it. I always hated the motherfucking sound of a door slamming shut. Goddammit. It's almost as bad as when I first got here. I was all of a sudden going cold turkey in the prison ward and all the nurses or guards or whoever the hell were always in there looking at me and—SLAM!—I hear the doors for the first time, and it's all I can do—the need is like fire in my body that I can't put out and each slam is like someone cracking the bones that ain't burnt up yet with a hammer, so they crumble and I fall to pieces. And even that doesn't make it stop. I just want to jump out of my bed but they've got me strapped down.

I'd almost gotten that sound out of my head, and now I start hearing it again not only at night, because the actual sound of it I'm able to stand, but during the day, just a hard rush of memory and pain that hits me when I'm folding wash or putting soap in the big washer.

I remember, it was a different kind of door, a big wooden door, that slammed on me when I was a kid and they locked me up in the room at the last jailhouse I was in, where they put me when I was a kid. They shut me up in the room because I wanted to tell them what had happened to me, that I'd been raped, me only eleven years old, by a white man, that's why I was in trouble. But they kept telling me I was a liar, kept telling me it was all for my own good and I wasn't going to hear any of that. So finally they lock me in this room with this other girl who'd given them trouble.

I remember that man. I didn't know anything, being only a kid, and he invited me into his house and you know what happens next, and then he used to meet me like that on the way to school. I never got a proper education because of that, because of that man, Mr. Dick. And they say I made that man's name up too, but I didn't. How can you forget a name like Mr. Dick?

So I'm locked in this room with the other girl and I say to her finally when I'm calmed down enough, because she doesn't say anything the whole time I'm bawling my eyes out, I say to her, yell at her's more like it, "What, do you think you got problems?" and I call her some names, probably every name in the book I was so pissed off.

Still, she doesn't stir, so I go over to where she is lying on the bottom of a double bunk-bed, lying on her back with her head turned away to the wall, like Little Miss Superior who don't have to bother with what I'm saying. "You think you're better than me?" I say. Still nothing. So I nudge her shoulder and get the shock of my life, cause she's cold and dead!

I scream and go right for the door, but it's locked, which I knew but didn't think of just then. "Let me out of here! There's a dead girl in here!" I've always been creeped by dead people ever since my grandmother died when I was a little kid, right after she'd told me a story and I went to sleep, cause when I woke up she was dead right next to me and her arm was down across me and—oh, Lord!—I still get a shudder to tell it. But that's nothing compared to this. I was all cried out—they hadn't listened to me and just put me away so they wouldn't have to deal with me anymore, so no one was going to pay any attention to me no matter what I yelled or how I cried. But also, I was just past the point where I could take anything more. Have you ever been alone in a locked room with a dead person? If you had, you wouldn't soon forget it. I felt like death was starting to fill up the room and I couldn't get away from it, so I kept pounding and pounding on that door, and still they wouldn't come. It was a solid door, there wasn't gonna be any breaking it down. My hands got bloody pounding and pounding on that door.

Ah, fuck it, for all I care.

I remember the D.A. telling me, "The judge won't go after you. You're not a criminal, just someone with a problem. You're not a burden to society. You've got a successful career. You're not someone we need to get off the streets. We're going to get you into a hospital program and get you cleaned up." Yeah, yeah, yeah, okay, I say. I say all my lines, but then it doesn't go that way and the goddamn D.A. is all, "Oops, I'm sorry," and my black ass ends up here, hauling coal and laundry and picking fucking carrots.

That's the way it always goes. Doctors rat me out to the fuzz and club owners keep them on the take to keep quiet and when it all breaks down do any of them get hauled before a judge? Not on your life. Everyone's crooked. Just like these cops who won't even say hello to you in the street but then try to get you into a side room at the Hall of Justice and fuck your brains out.

Nothing surprises me anymore. Nothing. Everybody I've ever known has lied to me my whole life. Especially men. From Mr. Dick taking me inside his house before I was even a woman to the sisters in the home who after they locked me up with that dead girl made up with me by lying about it, saying it never happened and rapping my knuckles with a ruler every chance they got. They all lied. And when I told the truth they told me I was lying. They told me to repent. I never have seen much repenting going on, just a lot of holier than thous saying, "Repent!" Your so-called upstanding citizens.

Now I'm all mixed up at this Cloris thing. I'd pretty much gotten used to going through each day without thinking about anything, getting by day after day, and then all these feelings suddenly get sharp again. But intermingled with this the other feeling comes and ooh, my skin's all a-tingle. The greatest feeling in the world is to be taken in someone's arms, lifted up, having the weight come off your legs and floating in the air, knowing here's someone strong to look after me. I can't always do it all by myself.

I know we'll see each other again as we file into the movie room in our straight columns. We can make contact without anyone the wiser, without even a straight-on look, nor smiling, but both of us smiling on the inside. All of this invisible. My heart jumping in my chest, hot and cold at once. My hands sweating. Me—well, you don't need to know how old I am. But not exactly young as I used to be. But I still love love. We sit in the same spots as last time. She's over to my right and off in front of me. The lights go down. I hardly even see the picture, knowing she's looking over toward me and in my mind I'm looking at her. Neither one of us see the other one but it's like we're seeing each other plain. I feel my body like it's her hands feeling it again and there's goose-flesh all over my arms! And I know when we do see one another again and smile for real, it'll be like old red wine, warming us up, making us feel good.

And you know what she's in here for? I knew it from the start—I didn't hide anything from myself. She killed her own little baby, took him out to the ocean and drowned him. How can someone do something like that?

I know how. She was married to this Southern cocksucking bastard. Why do we women put up with these men and their bullshit? The man got drunk, beat her, apologized, got drunk again and the whole thing over again. Used to like to go out and leave Cloris alone. I don't get the whole story, but I can fill in the details. Here's this prick, don't even serve in the war because he supposed to be taking care of his family, but instead he's out every night leaving Cloris at home with the kid and if she says "Boo" he lays into her. He's the one I would've shot. Cut off his dick and throw it in the river.

But women get crazy over men. I've been there. They

treat you mean yet you keep coming back for it. It don't make no sense, to take all that shit. For love we take it, but what kind of love is that? And Cloris, I figure, one day she gets this idea in her head that before they had that child they were happy. Probably not true, probably never been any different, but she ain't thinking right. Even though she's just a girl still she's been banged upside the head so many times she don't know what right thinking is. Get lied to so many times, you start lying to yourself. So like in a trance, she takes her little boy out to the beach, pretending they're going swimming. And she takes him out and out, out in the deep water, maybe floating him out on a little raft. She's crying the whole time. What did that child ever do to her? Or maybe not—maybe she's just cold. It ain't even really in her mind, what she's doing, she's so poisoned by that man, so wants to please that angry bastard she should've known there ain't no pleasing. The boy wants to show he can swim and kicks his feet as his momma takes him further out. Spitting out water, but proud of himself. Must of been hard to see, too hard to even look at. They're out way over their heads. Cloris's a good swimmer, having been raised in these parts. She gets out far and pulls the raft away and lets the child go and starts taking off back to shore. Like that, snap! Has to be done fast because it can't even be thought about. Muscles working and working because she knows she's just gonna die if she even begins to stop and think about what she's doing. Not even dying, that's not what she's afraid of, but that she won't ever feel her man again, which is something she knows is gonna happen, and it makes her afraid, which makes her keep going. Hard, she swims back. Then she's been going so hard one of her hands hits sand and when she stands up the water only comes to her knees. That's when it hits her, in her chest. What has she done! She turns back and looks for her baby, but he ain't there. Jesus Lord, what have I done? She can hear him, she thinks, crying and splashing in the water, calling out for her, or she thinks she heard him while she was swimming, she looks around behind her, she can't be sure. She swims back out to where she had him. But he's nowhere around. She doesn't see any body, she looks all around and doesn't see any clothes, nothing. It's like the hand of God has plucked him up, that tiny little child.

Now how can I be involved with someone like that? I don't know, really. I guess I do understand her, though I don't really want to. A woman needs love, and there ain't a limit to what she'll do to get it if it ain't there. Or worse, if it used to be there and then ain't no more. Murder is nothing. Not to someone in that state. Believe me, I've been around that feeling.

Do I want to be involved with it again? When I realize I *know* Cloris, I start to think maybe this ain't the best person to be around if I'm trying to straighten out my life. I can get out early for good behavior, but with these types you never know what's gonna happen. The bad always outweighs the good with these types.

I was put in the laundry room because after my time kicking junk Helen didn't think I was in shape to work out on the farm. But I'm often left alone in the laundry—that's how Cloris was able to come to me. Maybe it's best to keep around other people, so that I'm not in that position anymore. Do my time without getting involved in such things, then get out of here, back to my real life. It might not even hurt me to get a little fresh air instead of that steamy laundry room.

So I request to go see Helen. It takes a few times of requesting this, and I keep worrying that something's going to happen again in the meantime, but then after a couple days they come and get me from the laundry and bring me up there to the main building.

She's got a nice office. Big oak desk, nice and polished, neater than I ever saw any man's office, all the files tucked into their little spots like they're supposed to be, almost like she's straightened them out for the occasion. She gives me respect, Helen does, for anything else you might want to say about her, I got no beefs. She's been straight with me since I got here.

"I want to work on the farm," I tell her.

"That's your prerogative," she says, "If that's what you want." She's stood up from behind her desk since the guard led me in the room, and she tells the guard she can go, and it's all very official and professional, but before we even sit down I say this.

"Why don't we sit down and talk?" she says to me.

Nice leather chair with brass pins all around the edge. Quality. I guess I notice all this because I've been in lots of offices with lots of men who've used their position to bully me around. But Helen's office gives me a different feeling. Proper and civilized. She seems every day to wear the same dark blue blazer and blue skirt and white blouse and her hair's pinned up, all official, but also sort of calming. I know I won't get any lies from her, she's a straight shooter.

"Why do you want to go out to the farm? You know, the work is very hard, much harder than in the laundry."

"I know. I'm just tired of being inside, is all."

"Are you feeling well?"

"Pretty well."

"It looks like you've gotten some weight back. You were all skin and bones when you came in here."

That's an angle. "I don't want to get all fat here, though. I think that some hard work would do me some good. Keep myself busy, take my mind off things."

"Well, there's plenty of women who'll trade places with you, if that's what you want. The laundry room is one of the most coveted assignments we have around here."

I don't need to say anymore, so I just nod and say, "Yes, ma'am." But she's looking at me hard, trying to figure out what's really going on. "Are you having any trouble here?" she asks.

"Oh, no ma'am." But she's a sharp one, that Helen. She knows there's more going on than I'm telling her. I guess you get a lot of experience with people doing what she does.

I get my wish and the next day I'm out in the fields. The real tough ones are out here, and I could be the Queen of Siam or a good-time hussy for all they care. And Lord, that Helen wasn't just whistling when she told me it was hard work. I don't think I've ever worked this hard since I was scrubbing the steps of rowhouses in Baltimore when I was a kid. I've always said I never wanted hard work like that again, and I've spent my life making sure I didn't ever have to do it. Well, in this life you can never say never. I asked for it this time. They have the black prisoners out in the field as soon as sun-up. We leave our cells and go out to eat before it's even light out, and we see the white prisoners filing into the dining hall as we've just left and are getting down to work.

It's back-breaking, because mostly what you do is tend to the fields, and I ain't never done any farm work before, so I didn't know all I was in for. If you're not out with a sack picking vegetables until your back feels like it's on fire, you're hoeing and raking and picking out rocks and wheeling the big wheelbarrow, and the only break comes when the water is carried out to you. It feels like you've done a whole day's work by the time it comes around for the first time, and it's only ten o'clock.

But hard work's got one thing going for it—once you get used to it, you don't think no more. Your thoughts just leave right out of your head. It's your back that gets your attention, your back and your shoulders and your hands. Your fingers get all dry and start to crack at the tips, and there's no manicurist to take care of your nails, which turn so ugly and dirty that you just cut them short and try to forget about them.

So I'm doing this for near a week when we go in for the mid-day supper and the other girls are talking about the kind of food they wish we had. This is West Virginia, and these are mostly southern girls, and they miss the good food they're used to cooking and eating.

"What I could go for right now," says one, "Is a pan of baked macaroni and cheese."

We ain't seen real cheese since we got here, just the stuff that they've remade up from powder, so that you get little pasty lumps of undissolved shit in with your food. Same with milk, which is all watered down and has that thin taste of powdered and a kind of bluish look to it. So when the baked macaroni and cheese is mentioned, there's a whole chorus of, "Yeah," and "Mmm-hmm," and "I can taste that now."

Another says, "I was thinking that when I get out of here, I'm going to go out and get a chicken and cook it for myself and eat the whole thing."

And to this, someone behind me says, "Yeah, but you're gonna have to fight Billie for that white meat."

I turn around and all of a sudden, before I'm even sure how to react, there's a bunch of girls crowded in between us to keep us from fighting.

They all know! I've heard there's no secrets in a jailhouse, and this proves it to me once and for all.

"You got a big mouth, you know that," I'm yelling at this girl past all the girls who've gotten between us, who are saying, "Easy, Billie," and, "She didn't mean nothing by it."

But I know what she means, and it's not good. They all know I've seen Helen, too, and who knows what they think I'm doing with all that. I've noticed when Cloris comes out with the other white women to start their working, usually off in another part of the farm, but almost always led past where we're working, and now I realize that as I see Cloris go past, they all see me see her and they've been saying things behind my back and watching me for signs.

What the hell for? It ain't like none of these bitches are Snow Fucking White. Some of them even flaunt it, hanging around with their girlfriends all day and hiding nothing. Who are any of them cunts to say the first word about what I do and who I do it with?

I ain't no sell out, neither. I got where I've gotten to through my own hard work, and I never kissed nobody's ass.

But here I've been ashamed of myself. I'm as much to blame as any of them. A little bit of pleasure in this miserable place, and right away I'm running away from it, like there's something wrong with me. Like there's something wrong with colored being with white. There ain't, not if it's two people who like one another. They should spend a night in Greenwich Village sometime if they think they know. But in some way I realize I've been letting them say what they say because I've been saying it in my own mind.

Well, no more. If that's what they want, that's what they'll get. Nobody talks about me behind my back. I ain't ashamed of myself. If they want something to talk about, I'll give them something to talk about. I'll be with my little tough girl Cloris if that's what I want.

Now out in the field it's all I think about. Her touches and kisses come back to me, and this time there's nothing bad about them. So her type is "trouble"—people are always saying that to me. Well, I'm stuck here for a year, I might as well enjoy myself. I'm going to take what I want, and let them say what they want because there'll be nothing to say.

The next morning, they lead those white girls past, and it's almost set up too perfect, because they walk right by us, closer than usual, and I'm positioned right to the nearest row by where they pass. I see them coming, and I see Cloris and she sees me. There's guards positioned at front and back of the row, but none near where she is in the middle of the line. I stand up straight and go right over to her and she stops there and I take her in my arms and everybody's dead still for a moment, but then there's all kinds of whooping and hollering because I plant Cloris with a great big kiss and she responds immediately, so that even with everyone around us there we just melt into one another, every bit of my body overcome with a wave of hot joy, and if the guards hadn't come right then to pull us apart we would have been humping each other right there on the ground.

3.

Almost a full hour after the show was set to start, a spotlight angles down on center stage, and Lady walks out from the wings. Wearing long white gloves, she stands in cirrus clouds of smoke to an avalanche of cheering, at which she smiles serenely, her posture regal at the stand-up microphone, touching it with one hand like the cheek of a lover. The piano starts a lonely intro and the audience shushes quickly so the only atmosphere is waiting, accompanied by a measured brush on the snare drum.

My man he beats me
My man mistreats me
Aw, but he completes me
So I love him
Yes he's a user
Every night a boozer
Some say he's a loser
But still I love him

Jack and Malcolm are in the audience. Do they know each other? There are different ways of knowing. Jack was that white boy smoking cigarettes constantly, for some reason not in uniform or dressed for work but talking, giggling, shouting impassioned, incomprehensible arguments in the late hours of bars or the foggy mornings of diners and automats. Good looking, exuding a beatific glow as he sinks into Billie's melody or enjoys the antics of his friends. But listening also for echoes of his own misery in the world, at times the only thing that makes him truly happy. As for Malcolm, he expends no excess energy unless he's dancing, and this is no dancing place. Slim cut suit and thin blue tie, orange hair parted neatly on the side, fingernails coated with clear polish. A smile and handshake for everyone he brushes past on the way to his seat, arranged by way of contacts in the business.

They likely never see each other in such a crowd. Or perhaps they do.

"Thank you very much, ladies and gentlemen," says Billie in a kewpie doll voice. Even tough broads are doing the cooing baby girl voice in the 1940s. "I've been requested to sing a tune. *I Cover the Waterfront.*"

Away from the city that hurts and mocks
I'm standing alone by the desolate docks

She bends a melody slowly, oh, so slowly. Other places, in the new music, bop, the bending is fast. At Clark Monroe's Uptown House (Billie had been married to and divorced from Clark's younger brother Jimmy a couple of years before), after hours at Minton's in Harlem where Thelonious Monk and Kenny "Klook" Clarke were part of Joe Guy's house band, at the Onyx Club, the Savoy, where Bird and Dizzy and Monk and Klook and Charlie Christian and Don Byas and Bud Powell jammed to the wee hours.

When it comes, when it really comes, it comes by means of accident, by means of a moment's diversion. Suddenly, feeling along a wall where there's always been just wall, where it's been a hundred thousand times, there's a door and the door's wide open, and it leads to whole new continents, back to Africa but also down to South America, to places we used to think of as familiar but suddenly in a new bright light totally changed. When I saw my friend Dizzy I used to say, "Hey," and he'd say, "Hey," and the world wasn't any different until we were playing our music, but now I say, "Hey-di-diddly-a-be-bop-smash," and he answers, "Oop-pop-a-dah," because the whole all of everything is something other than it used to be. And when we play, Klook-mop throwing in bombs and all doing the boogie right, t'ain't no crack but a solid fact we're doing something no one ever thought of before. Think of something and bring it and say, "Look, man," and then they try it and it's something else I hadn't thought of, and from them doing that I'm thinking of ten other things to do.

Was there a limit to how far we could go? How did the rest of the world operate? They, people, walk down the streets, go to their day jobs, have conversations, you must have seen them yourself. Who are they? Are they real, or just flashes and specks? Because when we see the cats at night, the ones who are really digging it with us, we have a sense of standing outside of ourselves and it's like we're no longer who we are. What used to be music was a hum of the familiar, and we dug that. But this is different. We've broken it open, played the magic notes that had been lost, secrets in the electric consumption wheel, and now the unseen substance of things lays glittering at our feet. It's being in there nice with the ice. It's all at once busting your conks.

"Hey, pull my coat on this—when she gonna do Strange Fruit!"

"Ssshhh. Put the clap on your trap, daddy-o. She ends the set with it. But yell out too much, she'll get sore and won't do it. I remember one time she mooned the audience cause she didn't like what she was hearing. Just turn around and bent over."

"Ha! Wish I'd been there that night!"

"Naw, you're here tonight, which is better. Watch her. She's gotta be almost in a trance when she does it. You watch her: she won't move, just crook her elbow a little bit. The light comes on her and the whole place shuts up. Then she really give out, man. She's the Lady. Lady Day."

Billie sang in whorehouses and hard-luck bars when she was just a kid. Singers would slide from table to table, then hike their skirts up. If a man tips a bill, he slides it to the edge of the table, and if she wants the real dough she's got to pick it without hands. Billie hated that lowrate shit.

"Lowrate? Who you? Some kinda Lady?"

"I ain't your maid and I ain't your whore," said Billie.

With Artie Shaw, Billie's the first black woman singer ever to tour with a white band. But they don't let her stay at the hotel, and they feed her in the kitchen. Plain damn hokum, that shit. Then, there's an incident at the *Lincoln* Hotel—and not in Birmingham or Chattanooga but in New

York City. They say Billie can't drink at the hotel bar because they've got some southern guests.

Lincoln—I thought he *freed* the slaves! Billie can't see for looking, she's so steamed. She charges into Artie's hotel room, not even knocking, and starts throwing things at him. He's generally not one to back down, but there's nothing Artie can do with an angry Miss Holiday. Billie storms out, takes off toward the lobby. Artie grabs people along the way as he's running after her, because Lady's a big gal and in this kind of mood Shirley Temple would have a better chance against King Kong. Lady gets to the lobby ahead of the rest and takes a stand-up ashtray and flings all the butts and ashes out of it all over the carpet, then wheels it around to stave off any attackers. All this time she's yelling, "I will drink wherever I want! I will eat wherever I want! I'll use any motherfucking elevator I want! You people ain't good enough to drink my piss! You can all just lick my ass!" Artie arrives puffing and red-faced, but the boys are trying hard not to crack smiles. And they're proud of her, too.

Artie soothes investors who threaten to back out. "Hey, do what you want. But I got the best band in the business and she's the only singer in the world who can keep up with them." He tells one story again and again. One time, he's got to make a telephone call to firm up a date so he leaves rehearsal, joking to Billie as he goes, "You take my part." So she starts doing it, singing like a clarinet. Artie stops in his tracks. He's never heard nothing like it.

But Billie is Billie. Some Jeff Davis at the bar might start acting up and where others would laugh it off, Lady will as likely as not call him a motherfucker—into the mike. That's just Billie. When you're that way, you do make some enemies.

On her deathbed, police say they found a small packet of

skag in her room. The nurses said she couldn't even lift her arm, much less cook and shoot up, so how do you think that got there? Now I can't say, but it always seemed like the police showing up was the start of problems for Billie, she always had more problems after they came than she had before. Here she is, in the hospital for the last time, flat out, *dying*, and the cops put guards on her room, place her under house arrest. She *dies* under house arrest. Has to die to keep from being dragged to court.

And as she's dying in that hospital, they find out she's got not a cent in the bank. All she's got is $750, fifteen $50 bills, and they're taped to her legs so no one can steal it from her.

"Thank you very much, ladies and gentlemen," she whispers as applause fades from the previous song. A single spotlight is on her alone. "I'd like to sing a song that was written especially for me. It's called 'Strange Fruit.'"

Southern trees bear a strange fruit
Blood on the leaves and blood at the root
Black bodies swaying in the Southern breeze
Strange fruit hanging from the poplar trees

This song is the slowest yet, a dirge. Faces turn red, drain pale, lips tighten, eyes well, breathing stops. Billie is stiff with the pain of the wife or sister or mother beneath the tree—but it's not her the people in this audience see any more in 1946 but the grainy images of Dachau, Belsen, Treblinka, Auschwitz. Piled bodies dumped in mass graves. Unnatural, emaciated, rag bodies. Local farmers had to have known what was going on but stayed in their routines, milking, throwing bales, sweeping the yard, speaking in drawl. Charred bodies, ghoulish, sexless bodies. It had to have gone on for years. The smell is something no human being can ignore, one you feel right down in your stomach. Eventually, do you put these things out of your mind, or do they always stay there while you debate how to ignore them? At what point is a decision made, or does acquiescence come gradually, incrementally? At some moment in the long decline, whatever the power of the mob you're in, isn't there a threshold you know—by instinct, by whatever is inside of us—*go no further*? Afterwards, at what point do you start to admit, *I was also there*?

Pastoral scene of the gallant south
The bulging eyes and the twisted mouth,
Scent of magnolias, sweet and fresh
Then the sudden smell of burning flesh

Some folks are shifting in their seats. The song isn't new by 1946, but this still isn't something people talk about— who did it, that is.

Only the Communist and Black presses are regularly reporting instances of lynching and bias crimes in the 1940s.

By 1947, accusations against Communists in the film industry lead to a blacklisted Hollywood Ten, a harbinger of the McCarthy paranoia to come.

Barney Josephson, owner of Cafe Society in the Village, New York's first interracial club, where Billie made her name among a lefty clientele during a standing engagement, 1939, is eventually persecuted for his political views and put out of business. Josephson was given the poem "Strange Fruit" by the author, Lewis Allan, a.k.a. Abel Meeropol, to pass to Billie.

After Julius and Ethel Rosenberg were executed, Meeropol and his wife adopted the Rosenbergs' two children, who were thereafter known by the names Michael and Robert Meeropol.

4.

Well, I shut everybody up alright, me and my goddamn grandstanding. I was never a bigger fool in my life. And I was a bigger fool because I let everyone know they had nothing to say to me when I didn't know all they did have to say.

For a while, no one said the first word to me. But now there was something different in the silence, too. Before, there was a distance, but also a measure of respect. I didn't think they all knew who I was the way they were before. But now I realized they had known, that they were keeping back what they were really feeling. Fine. I act don't-care-ish. It's hard to see Cloris right now, everybody's on the lookout. But we'll have our time. Meanwhile, though, the more I pay no mind, the more the air has a dead rat smell every time I come into a room. I get pissed off from time to time. One time I come into the general room and a whole bunch of them are sitting there saying nothing and I say, "You sure is a quiet bunch of motherfuckers." Still no one says nothing. It's my sisters who're doing this, gals I know. Not all personally, but I know their lives. They're who I sing about. They're in this jail hungering, hungering bad for love, just like me. And it ain't like they ain't helping themselves neither. So it's because Cloris's white. Bunch of bigots is all they are, fuck them, I'm thinking. I can give as well as I get. I get as cold as the fucking North Pole. They freeze me, I freeze them—we'll see who wins. Ain't no one gonna tell me shit.

Gerty is the gal I knit with. She's a little older, kind of sits off by herself most of the time. She only came in here after she'd already lived mostly a clean life. Had a little store, but got behind with it a little and tried to pass off some checks. They threw the book at her—added interest to the amount of the checks, got it up over the limit for Grand Theft and gave her ten years. A woman who already had grandchildren. So she's gotten used to life on the inside, figures she's not going to see much else the rest of her days. Just sits around and knits and to anyone who asks her and many that don't, she says knitting is the best way to pass your days. She does seamstress work in the jail to get out of field work.

The truth is I like company. Not going to beg for it, you understand, and I can take a hint, but Gerty's way never changed with me, and she's usually off on her own anyway, so it wasn't a problem to chat easy with her.

So on Sunday when we don't have to be out in the field we're both of us sitting there knit one pearl two and out of nowhere she spills it.

Yeah, Cloris killed her little baby alright, but she didn't tell me the whole story. The cunt. She didn't just give up. The police didn't search her out—she went to them! And she tells them some cockamamie story that some black man kidnapped her baby. She's got a black eye and bruise marks all over herself and she says some black man tried to rape her, and when she hit him back he got pissed off and took her baby, saying, "You never gonna see your baby alive again." How'd she get the marks? They say she took a rake and put it with the pointy end up, then closed her eyes and stepped on it, hard, let it smash her in the face. Is this for real? She does this a few more times, gives herself marks on her arms and back, then goes to the cops! Gives them a description of the man: black, tall, medium build, wooly hair, light-colored, kind of orange.

Descriptions start getting around.

"Nigger stole a white baby?"

"Yeah, he tried to rape the woman and when the woman fought him off, that's what he done!"

"Let me at him!"

Soon the white folks got a mob. They come down the

street into the lowland neighborhood where the black folks live, all of them carrying the newspaper that has the description in it. They got a police sketch and all. Of course there's no single person that description's gonna fit, because there ain't no one's done anything but Cloris, but the description fits any number of folks in a general way, and those white folks are gonna raid every house until they find out who it is.

The black men ain't gonna stand idle while hoodlums ransack their houses. These are good families. They've worked hard for what they've got, and they've got factory jobs, most of them, in the same factory the white men work in. Get paid shit, but they save—the young ones get married and live in their parents' houses til they're able to get out on their own. They're not gonna stand there and let the white men come and burn it down. They see the torches and they know what that means.

Gerty tells me all this, still knitting, just looking down, every once in a while lifting her eyes as if to look at me, but her eyes don't meet mine, just float in space, not really looking at anything. This allows the scene to form before us both, as if we're sitting above the town, pointing, gesturing, watching what happened. Gerty's eyes don't line up just right, so even when she looks at you, it's like she's looking off the other way, and your first reaction is to look to the side to see what she's staring at. But now these eyes hang like unrelated stars over the town, knowing and powerless.

The women beg and plead with their men: "Just be calm, let them come. They'll see we ain't got nothing to do with this." But the white men come and the black men want to stand up. "We're not going to be blamed for this." They start coming out of their houses, buttoning on their shirts over their undershirts, and women and kids are grabbing hold of them to try and keep them there but they still go out, some of them getting mad, some getting quiet and reassuring their wives and girls and kids, but there's screaming and yelling all over, like a war's about to start, and everybody's terrified.

As the white men get there, they come to a certain point on the old bricked street where the black folks are already making a line. They stop, and there's two groups face to face, about a car's length between them.

"Stand aside, boys," yells the main white man. "We're looking for a baby-snatcher boy with orange hair."

One of the black folks steps up. He's been trying to stop the ones that want to just fight. "Ain't none of them here, sir. We've all been checked out by the police."

"We are the police," yells someone in the white crowd, and there's laughter. Another white man says: "If you got nothing to hide, boy, why don't you just let us through?"

"No, sir, we got nothing to hide." He's trying to reason with the torches. "But this is a good neighborhood."

More laughter comes from the mob, evil laughter, like if this is a good neighborhood, how come it's full of coons? A white man sees the danger, too, and tries to make peace. They should continue the search, but starting something dangerous is just foolishness. "Maybe if we could go one house at a time," he offers. Someone answers: "But they might be hiding them. You know how they hide."

There's some young men who've never stopped laughing in the rear of the white crowd. Them and others are passing a bottle around.

"We don't want this to turn into something we'll regret later."

"Someone should have thought of that before they messed with a white woman and with our children."

"I've got three kids at home," yells out a voice. "I say we start and see how long they stay quiet." This gets considerable approval from the whites.

"The kid's probably in this one's house!" yells another. "Let's start in—they'll send him out soon enough if they know what's good for them!" Little by little you start to see things in the crowd, like the one or two carrying cans of coal oil.

"Where's that Simmons boy? He's a bad sort. Bet he's got something to do with it." This is a yellow boy who farms it a little on some of the bigger farms and gets drunk with the money, joyrides around, but he's never done anything real bad. But the crackers figure they're there for a reason, all this talk is just wasting good houseburning time, probably stalling so as to give the boy some time to get a head start. "They're all to blame if that's the case!" yells one of them.

The black folks are yelling amongst themselves with each comment from the whites—

"Ain't none of us here had anything to do with that."

"Mister Fred, you know me and my family and these here neighbors of mine—we'd have nothing to do with anything like this."

"Please, sirs, leave us be. We'll look with you if you want, just please please don't be crazy." Trying to address the white man who's been acting peacemaker. But he's rapidly lost favor.

"It ain't just one. You don't just have one bad apple in the barrel. That bad nigger apple's got a little nigger walnut brother and whole buncha little yellow banana monkey friends."

There's no leaders now. The space the two sides had squared off is no longer halved in the middle but exploding people in all directions, shouting and crying and there's no way you can even see what's going on in such a state. You just try to stay safe and keep your family together. Men are fighting and clubbing each other and you hear gunshots in the distance. Rocks smashing house windows and cars. It's not a big town, Coopersville. But some of the women in this very prison were there that day, Gerty tells me, if I want to check out the story. There's just a town square, a few streets of stores and shops, garages fixing cars and tractors, and outlying fields on the one side of town. Factory on the other, down by the water. The men's hands, white and black, are dirty from factory work, the way a man's hands get dirty, with deep cracks in them that've got dirt you just can't get out. You can always tell a laboring man's hands, that have been doing the kind of hard work I've been doing for two weeks for years. Lots of them are missing fingers. My mother's cousin Nathan used to need his wife Rennie to tie his shoes, but could still operate a drill press as well as any man at the factory. Had been doing it for years. His arms were part of the machine, his elbows like hinges, the whole action of him and machine like one if you saw them—down, up, bend, down, up, bend. Here's a man who sells shoes for a living door to door. You see him wearing good shoes, shiny, but that's only because that's the business he's in and he's got to make a good impression. He ain't got anything else that nice. Other folks are just getting by. There ain't many pairs of pants that ain't got stitched patches at the knees and backside. Women have one good dress, not new but clean, to wear on Sunday and the rest of the week they wear the coarse stuff, the tougher the better, with aprons across the front to keep them clean as best they can, yellowed from being bleached out so often.

I've worn some fine dresses in my time. Silk. Real diamonds sewn into the neckline. That dress cost $1,500. That's more than some of these people paid for their houses. But I know their lives. I come from Fell's Point, Baltimore, and it was bad when I was growing up—drugs, gangsters, chippies, you name it. Worse than Coopersville. I sang so I could avoid this life, and to get out of it.

You can fight it, but you can't lick it. One time I was playing a club with Basie's band and the first night I came out to rehearse, run through a couple numbers before we're to go on that night. The club's kind of dark and they got the spotlight on me and the manager starts yelling out from the back of the room in the middle of the song, "Wait! Stop!" We stop.

"What's up?" says Basie.

"That girl's awful yellow," says the manager. "From back here she looks white."

I know what that fucker's saying. He wants me to put on blackface before I come out to sing, so there's no mistake. I can bitch and moan, and believe me I do, but what can we do? We signed a contract to play and if I don't go on no one gets any money and Basie gets run from the south. He don't like it any more than I do and I can tell he's not going to make me do it, but I don't want hang up the Count. Yeah, some Count, and some Lady, too, who've got to tom it up to be acceptable to a bunch a goddamn crackers.

They're all coughing and crying now trying to get things out and keep from getting hurt, people are huddling together, holding each other so no one will foolishly run into a burning house and just make it worse than it already is. Some get their furniture out and flop down on their sofas in the street, stunned. Old ones' papers and younguns' dolls and teddybears and clothes and albums as much as they can get sit on dirt lawns and sidewalks, shifted out of the way of running and puddling water, get loaded up in cars which then try to wend their way around the piles of stuff and of people, and already have a smashed rear window. Families dazed, wondering how they got here, how they got to be a family in the first place. This woman met this man when his mother was sick, she cooked for him and after a while they were like family anyway, so they made it official. Over there, he met her when her sister got married and he was hired as a driver. They made good use of that old car for a summer and the next summer they were married themselves. There's a pregnant daughter across the way, too, knocked up just like her mother was at her age, only this boy's run off.

Someone realizes this—Mr. Wagner, who's got a gas station and used to give him pop bottles to scrub out.

"Where's Earlie?" he yells.

Earlie's hair ain't orange, but that's a technicality. It's like an air raid siren. Everybody pauses a second in the middle of what they're doing. Then they all go round to one house.

"He's gone off to Charleston to try to get on a ship. He left last week." It doesn't matter. They set that house on fire too. And keep going.

If you go today to Coopersville, Gerty tells me, you still see white and black. But the white is the motherfuckers living in their half of the town and the black is the burnt up and rusted out old garbage of what's left of where those poor folks used to live. Yeah, there's still some black folks there. They come in to work as cooks and maids and take the bus in.

Goddamn. Goddamn.

5.

For at least a full five minutes neither one of us says a word.

One of the details doesn't make sense. "If she blamed it on someone else, how come she's in here?"

"The cops didn't believe her in the end and worked on her till she confessed."

I don't even thank Gerty, though that's what I should have done. Straight off, I get up and go to a guard and ask to go see Helen. The guard doesn't give me a bit of lip but just turns around to lead me right out the building and over to her office.

What, did everybody except me know what was going on?

The guard brings me to Helen's secretary, who takes me inside. No sooner than she's out of the room then Helen lays into me—

"Listen, Miss Holiday. We have tried to be respectful of your status in the outside world. But, for the time you are here you must be treated the same as every other inmate. I don't know what kind of life you were used to leading in New York, but we are now in a United States Federal Penitentiary and I'll expect every person here to behave themselves according to codes of proper conduct."

I never took a harder sock to the jaw. I guess I'd never been so unprepared. I had let my guard down after what Gerty had told me. I knew I had done wrong, and meant to set out to putting it right. But the wrong had nothing to do with this that I was being chewed out for. Did Helen know who Cloris was? Of course, she had to, she was the Warden. So what was I to her for what I had done with Cloris? Did she put me in the same category as that bitch? I reeled for a minute, I really did. I had to shake my head like one of those cartoon animals after they've been bonked on the nog with a big mallet.

Helen breaks the silence. "Would you like me to find you something besides farm work?" Only she says it with this "what would the Princess like now" kind of voice.

Then it occurs to me. They let me come right in here. Helen's giving it to me right off the bat. But there's a guard right outside this door who'll come flying in here if I so much as boo. "More of her bad city ways," they'll say. "You can dress them up and put them on stage, but they're still animals down deep." I'm on the edge of a cliff here, and they're waiting for me to take the next step off, begging me to.

"What do you have?" I say, gripping the back of a chair but saying no more.

"Well, you gave up the laundry room. I guess you're stuck on fieldwork for another month, until we fertilize again." Her lips pucker up to to a point. "Otherwise . . . ."

I look at her.

"Otherwise, there's the pig sty."

She says this like a threat. If I don't watch out.

She's standing cross from me behind her desk, with one hand on her chair, as if to brace herself in case anything happens. Not fearful—you don't get to be a warden if you show any fear. Just prepared for whatever might happen. Sending me to the pigs is not what she intended.

Fuck her. "Put me in the pigsty."

"Billie!" Her face reddens and all of a sudden she's all concerned again. Fuck her.

"Helen, put me in the pig sty."

Now ain't that a kick in the ass? Last year I was a Hollywood actress. You might have seen the movie I was in, *New Orleans*. Probably not. That thing sank like a bad biscuit. I'd always wanted to be in a movie. I kept asking Joe

Glaser and anyone else who'd listen. Years of this. Lena Horne was in one. Lena's a sweet gal, but what's she got on me?

Finally they got one for me.

I was going to sing in it. I started thinking about buying some new clothes, but they say, "No, Billie, they'll outfit you once you get there. They got a whole wardrobe budget." A whole wardrobe budget! I'll be a fine lady on the screen, all done up and bigger than life! I'll get a gown of silver for the silver screen. I'm more than just a singing star, they'll all see.

Except it ain't like that. I figured I'd be in a club the people come to and would sing there. No, they've got me as a maid, lying on the floor, singing about my man that's left me. I ain't never been no one's maid.

And the Hollywood types, they let you know just who they think you are.

You want to know something? I've never gone back to the movies, not anymore while I was in that jail, nor when I got out. Fuck movies. People go to them and think what they're seeing means something. It don't mean shit.

No, really. What do I want to go to the movies for?

It's all just fantasy bullshit, and it ain't your fantasy, no how. What do they have to do with the way things really are?

Fuck movies.

"What kind of a town is this?" (yells Henry Fonda as Wyatt Earp in *My Darling Clementine*, 1946, to residents of the mismanaged hamlet of Tombstone, throwing a drunk out of the local tavern). "Serving liquor to Indians!"

DEAD MAN

<u>Characters</u>

David Kammerer, a large man in his early 30s with brown hair and a red beard.

Lucien Carr, an attractive blonde-haired, green-eyed man of small-average height, aged 19.

Young Lucien, a frail boy of fourteen.

Jack Kerouac, a rugged-looking, brown-haired man, aged 20.

Allen Ginsberg, aged 18, bespectacled, small-average height, with hair somewhat longer than the other men, uncombed.

Bill Burroughs, *tall, gaunt, 30.*

Edie Parker, dark-haired, slim but with a nice figure set off with a fashionable 1940s style dress, aged 20.

Celia Young, blonde, 19, a student.

Phil Andrews, *a dark-haired Naval cadet, aged 20.*

Recruiter, *40s, wearing a military uniform and buzz-cut.*

Doctor, *50s, in white lab coat.*

Man #1, Man #2, Man #3, three young men recruited for war-time service.

Bartender, *50s, graying but beefy.*

Extras in bar scene.

Sigmund Freud

Pantomime David/Dream David

The curtain opens on a stage constructed with a small partition in the back center—characters may easily pass in front of this, but it marks a division between right and left sides. Only the left side of the stage is lit. This is David's apartment. The walls are drab, paper peeling from them in spots, in other places some crude repairs have been made, some with painted pie tins. The only furniture in the room is a bed, a folding chair, a fan off in one corner, and a clothes horse draped with ironed slacks, shirts, ties and a suit jacket for daily wear. David will mostly address us while sitting on his bed. The right side of the stage is open space, in which the activities of David's monologues are played out. He at times will cross over to participate in the activities of his former life, while on the left he merely describes them.

Between scenes in what follows, the lights flick out for twenty seconds, then come back on for the new scene. For the finale, an extensive piece of tree scenery will need to be constructed, simultaneously utilized as a split-level, multi-angled stage for the final dance extravaganza.

David is dressed in Broadway show-style evening clothes, including a top hat and cane, at the start of the play, but he wears clothes badly. He is a large man, brawny, wears a beard he has made an effort to trim neatly: the effect should resemble that of a lumberjack trying to look like Fred Astaire. A pocket comb should be in evidence to restore hair that is mussed, but David uses it more than is necessary, as a nervous habit, with decreasing skill as the scenes play out. As he goes from side to side of the stage, he will remove and then attempt to put clothes back on, with the general effect toward dishevelment in the last scene, as befits the final action.

Scene One

David: Dead men tell no tales. Isn't that what they say?
Well, I guess I never have been one to follow rules.

At least I'm rid of that thing that plagued me while I was
on the earth. My BOD-ee. I was never meant to have a body
at all. And the one they dealt me—a cosmic joke! No chin.
Look.

[Stands in profile to the audience. Continues self-critical-
ly as if looking into a mirror. He tugs at his beard and combs
and recombs his hair.]

Well, you can't really see it now in all its proper horror.
My nose actually never was so big, and my complexion's
always been good. I'm tall, that's nice. I can dance. I'm no
Fred Astaire—no, that's for sure. But I could be known to
cut a dapper figure out in the world. It's not out of the question. To have Astaire's grace, fluidity, his ease—

[He forgets the mirror and tries a few softshoe dance
steps, ending by tapping the cane to the floor and then to the
crown of his top hat—he's not terribly ungraceful, but as he's
said, he's not Astaire. He ends by sitting on his bed.]

It's good to have stature, to have presence. Astaire isn't a
big man, but he has that anyway. Grace. Even with his reced-
ing hairline. And his pointy nose. His jutting chin. It just
shows you can overcome the adversities you've been dealt by
nature. If it had only been just that I was too tall. That
wouldn't be as bad. I could be lithe, willowy. Except that
that's not the body I was born with. Look at these muscles!
And believe me, you can't see now, but without this beard I

look like a Dodo bird. Big, boxy, and chinless.

So I grew a beard as soon as I was able. And when you've got a body like this, if you don't keep fit you just turn into two hundred pounds of flab. I liked the outdoors, I'm athletic, I could live with that. I got a job as a gymnastics teacher. Not that I even needed the money, with my family. I could have lived as a fixture in the drawing rooms of St. Louis society. Livestock! Wheat futures! Uggh—get me out of there!

No, that wasn't for me. St. Louis might think of itself as the real world, but I could see from the movies it wasn't. Or maybe it was the real world and I wanted to live in fantasy. New York, 42nd Street. After all, real life never did me any favors. Look, I grew this beard to cover up my chin, or lack of one, and what do I get? Again, laughter from the balcony. Red! Not quite Fire Engine Red, but not Strawberry Blonde either. The hair on my head the dingiest of browns, with hardly a red highlight, so you'd think I could put together a thin, nondescript beard, but no, not for David Kammerer, not for this joke of fortune. No—thick as a lumberjack's, red to match the plaid shirt.

I had it for a year when I was 19 and it was a novelty. Then one morning I looked in the mirror and saw what the rest of the world saw for the first time. God—shave it off! I reached for the razor so quickly I cut my finger.

There was blood. I just looked at it as it trickled down my fingers all the way to my wrist. It was a nasty cut and the blood branched out every which way, like my hand was encased in thorns. Lines of blood, so much blood I just looked at it, fascinated.

I probably knew then about Lucien. I'd just seen him in shorts in my class the previous morning.

[A spotlight appears on the side of stage, illuminating Young Lucien. David looks at him for a moment, then turns his head, at which point the spotlight disappears.]

It probably wasn't actually that day. But don't you think it makes for a more romantic story?

Indulge me.

Anyway, no sooner had I cut off my beard than I remembered, and saw, in gruesome detail, why I'd grown it to begin with. I didn't go back to work again for a week, until I had a reasonable start on another beard.

Oh, Lucien. You never cared about me at all.

[The spotlight comes up for just a moment on Young Lucien and quickly dies away. Lucien is in shorts and no shirt, a towel casually thrown over one shoulder. He is skinny, and has neither developed muscles nor hair on his chest.]

Scene Two

[As the lights go up, David is removing his jacket and tie.]

David: So why wasn't I in the war? How does a gym teacher get 4F?

I showed them straight out that I was a homo.

It worked like a charm! Really, you should have been there.

[The entire stage is now lit and David walks to the other side, where a long table is set up as men come before the draftboard. In the right rear corner is a screen, and what happens behind it cannot be seen by the audience. Three recruits are lined up opposite the table on a diagonal line. Seated at the table are a no-nonsense recruiter in uniform and a doctor, wearing a tie and white labcoat. Like David, the recruits are all dressed in t-shirts and dark pants. David assumes a position at the end of the line of recruits, furthest from the audience. The Army Recruiter rises from the table and walks up and down before the recruits.]

Recruiter: You men have been drafted to serve your nation in war. When the Japs attacked Pearl Harbor, millions of men volunteered—patriotic men who gave up their jobs and their families to serve their country in time of need. You were not among them. So you've got a strike against you already. You're all finks in my book.

Yeah, I know. Some of you feel insulted, like you've had good reasons to stay out of the action until now, like you're not just a bunch of sniveling cowards. Well I say you are. Have I hurt your feelings, ladies? Good. Cause you've got to get rid of feelings. A soldier doesn't have feelings, except for love of his country and hatred for the Nazis and the Japs. A soldier does what he's told, even if he's tired and dirty and wet and miserable. You don't know what it's like to be a soldier now, you bunch of lily-livers, but you will.

Now the doctor here's going to look you over to see if you're fighting material. I think you are. I've seen lots of lily-livers like you, and they didn't look any more like fighting men than you do now. But we changed them and we'll change you. You're scared, but we'll whip that out of you. There's nothing wrong with you that six weeks at Fort Dix won't cure.

Drop your pants. Doc?

[The doctor comes around to the front. All are expressionless except David, who wears a look of mixed bemusement and fear. They drop their pants before he does, then everyone begins to look his way. Slowly, as if in a tease, he slides down his pants to reveal hip garters, bloomers and stockings.]

Recruiter: So, a wise guy.

David: No, sir. I just like wearing these, sir. I'm normal in every other way. I want to serve my country.

Recruiter: Listen, you. Don't give me any of your funny stuff. And don't think you're going to bamboozle the U.S. Army with some faggot act.

David: Oh, no, sir. You've got me all wrong. I'm straight as an arrow. I just like the comfort of a woman's undergarment.

Recruiter: Why, I oughtta take you outside right now. If I wasn't doing my job right now, I'd show you a thing or two.

David: I'm not a homosexual, sir.

Recruiter: [interrupting] I don't care what you were, Mac. You're in the Army, now, and you're nothing but a grunt like the rest—

David: [continuing] The first time I sucked a cock it wasn't at all a pleasant experience. It caught in my throat and, well, that seemed to do something and the guy shot right then, and—

Recruiter: Shut the hell up!

[The doctor takes the recruiter by the arm and leads him a step to the front of the stage.]

Doctor: If I can have a word . . . . [The recruiter and doctor stand away and the doctor whispers.] Glenn, I believe I can determine whether or not he is a homosexual.

Recruiter: [Interested] Yeah? How's that?

Doctor: [Doubtful, now that recruiter wants more details] Yes, by, well, by taking him behind the screen and, uh . . .

[The other men in line are looking sidelong at David, who smiles weakly and sheepishly at first, then coquettishly, at which point the man closest to David inches away from him and the man next to him is bumped and speaks up. The last man in line is amused by the entire scene, which should be played broadly, for laughs.]

Man #2: Hey . . .

Doctor [still to Recruiter]: Well, by dilating the anus . . .

Recruiter: Jesus Christmas!

[At this point, Man #2 is behind the line and shouting.]

Man #2: Hey, I don't want to be in no barracks with no

guys like him.

Recruiter: [coming back to a central position and screaming to restore his authority] Shut up, all of you. Get back in line. [The men are cowed and return to their positions.] Okay, you, pretty boy, behind the screen.

[David goes behind the screen with the Doctor, holding his pants neatly over his arm. The men observe this and shuffle a little in line.]

Man #1: Uh, permission to speak, sir.

Recruiter: Permission denied! [He softens a little.] Listen, men. Don't get your skivvies in a bundle. No man that bends over for his buddy fights in Uncle Sam's Army.

[The Doctor suddenly leaps from behind the screen, flustered and shaking his arms.]

Doctor: Outrageous! The nerve!

[David appears from behind the screen more slowly. The doctor points to him.]

Doctor: You! [Turns to recruiter] This man . . . this man is a thoroughgoing pervert!

[There is a freeze to capture everyone's silent reaction: David's comic shrug, the Recruiter's outrage, the disgust of Men #1 and #2, and a doubled-over laugh from Man #3. Then the lights go out.]

Scene Three

[David has his pants pulled up and while he speaks his first lines in this scene puts on a dress shirt and tie. Instead of his evening tails, he takes the sport jacket from the clothes horse so that he is dressed in a 1940s era everyday suit by the middle of the scene. At the same time, low lights on the right side of the stage reveal Bill, a thin man in horn-rim glasses and a dingy armless undershirt, sitting at a small card table. He very slowly goes through the process of emptying a small paper packet, transferring what's inside to a spoon and cooking it up with match flames. Bill pays no attention to David until David walks over to that side of the stage.]

David: That was fun, wasn't it?

Actually, I should confess. It didn't really go quite like that.

Actually, it didn't go anything like that.

Actually, my mother had our family doctor write a letter to the draft board explaining that I'd been a lifelong and desperate sufferer of severe, chronic hay fever. So it was just a formality when I actually went to the draft board. I was out of the war before they even got around to inviting me.

It would have been far more interesting my way. But, OK, I'll give it straight and objective from now on. Straight truth for the straight world.

The truth? I'm pathetic. It's no wonder no one wants to be around me. I know why perfectly well why, believe me. I loathe myself. I know I get too angry. I absolutely loathe myself. But they don't have to be all so childish about it. I mean, all of a sudden no one can be found. And this just before Lucien and his friend Jack are supposed to be off to France. That's right, Occupied France. They plan to ship out on a merchant ship and out-run the Allies to Paris to be there when the city is liberated.

Oh, by the way, kids, there's a war on. [This is a cliche in 1944, and David gives it a sarcastic inflection.] Haven't you heard?

But instead they talk about rediscovering their French ancestors. Jack speaks some French, and it's true, it fits Lucien. His sneer, the pencil mustache he's been wearing lately. His studied ennui. He looks like a French con-man. Aloof and dead to the world, cold as ice before age 20, nursing a cocktail at Rick's Cafe in Casablanca.

Only we're talking about real Nazis, not movie Nazis.

They'll probably be able to pull it off, knowing them. But one day the charm's going to run out. They'll be way in over their heads and no one will be able to save them then. Their little games will all of a sudden turn deadly serious.

[Pauses, then recollects himself, speaking in a clipped, bitter voice.]

These are the kids, the children, that are giggling at me behind my back? Playacting little children. [Pauses, lets the anger go.] Is that what has me so worked up? Me, better educated and certainly more presentable than the lot of them. I have a master's degree and several classes toward a doctorate at Columbia University. By contrast, you should see the flophouse they live in on 118th Street. Clothes all over the house, bodies flopped all over the furniture and on the floor. I've arrived at eleven o'clock in the morning after an eight-hour shift downtown and found a dozen of them passed out all over the floor, no one able even to get up off the ground to open the door. Then they wake up and it's nothing but grunts and groans until they get coffee in them and then it's on about Dostoievsky and Nietzsche and Joyce and Yeats as if they're the only ones who've ever read books. Ogled incessantly by their cooing, half-dressed little bourgeois girlies, who meanwhile quietly pass back and forth copies of *Planning Your Marriage*. So rebellious, oh yeah. Sure. All of them in ten years will be salesmen with wives and broods of screaming little kids. It sneaks up on you, I've seen it happen. They don't have the discipline for graduate school. Believe in nothing and all of a sudden inertia puts you where you never thought you'd be, where you always swore you'd never end up. I tell them. But they don't listen to me. They're all "Artists." Which to them means acting like they're the only reason for the whole world to exist, as if there's no war, nothing outside New York City, no blackouts, and the only reason the city even exists is to provide them with their own personal playground. Hitler? Just a little stage-show, a red-faced villain for the common people, but not worth their time. A distraction for the masses who don't understand.

[David pauses a moment, then slowly begins to walk across to where Bill is seated. The lights come up on that side of the stage.]

David: I wish I could stop obsessing about all this. But I'm just as bad. I validate them. Bill is the only one I can really talk to, the only one my age. The three of us, Bill, Lucien, and I are all from St. Louis, so we have that in common, too. A shared hatred of the Midwest.

[He calls ahead.]

David: [Aloud, since there's no door] Knock knock.

[David stands outside Bill's portion of the stage while Bill, begins to put things out of sight, placing a newspaper carefully over his works. David speaks still to the audience while Bill prepares.]

David: Bill's is more of a flea-bag than my place even. This is what you get when you live in Greenwich Village. The floor here is sticky and smells like piss. Like alcoholic piss that you can still smell the wine in. This is where I come for solace? What a life.

Bill: Who goes there?

David: It's me.

Bill: Come.

[David walks into Bill's room.]

David: Bill, am I crazy?

David: [After a pause] I mean, I'm not crazy. They're avoiding me. Do you know anything about this? [Still no response from Bill and after a shorter pause than earlier David continues.] OK, I know I sound like a scratched record, the same things over and over, but I've been to Jew Ginsberg's house, nothing. Up around Columbia, over to the West End—nothing. Down to the docks where Jack and Lucien were supposedly going to ship out—nada. Back uptown to 118th Street. Subway here, subway there, never getting to sit down for all the goddamn soldiers and old ladies. Lucien's shacking up with that little tramp some-where.

Bill: Allegedly virginal.

David: Oh, yeah, like there's any of those left in New York City, naval screwing headquarters. There's more abortionists in this city than traffic cops. You know, every time a virgin goes past the lions out in front of the New York Public Library they roar. Haven't ever seen that happen, have you?

Bill: [Deadpan] No.

David: A virgin! That's how she thinks she'll trap Lu, but I've yet to see the lock he can't pick. The legendary swordsman. Or so I've heard. Over and over again. Are you stoned?

Bill: No. But I should be.

[Bill reaches over to the newspaper covering his works and returns to lighting matches under a spoon. David pays no attention—it doesn't matter whether Bill's high or not and David has known him long enough to know this.]

David: The worst thing, the absolutely worst, reprehensible behavior is that every time I show up anywhere, they've just left. That's malicious. They've told everybody they know, Hank over at the West End, you name it, to tell me they've just left if I ever ask about them. That's not paranoia, that's a fact. They've recruited the whole neighborhood to have their joke on me. They should be so lucky as to have someone to look out for them, keep them out of trouble. Many's the time they would have went to jail, all of them, if it wasn't for me there to defuse the situation. And they must have spies, too. Else, how would they know where I'm going to be and know to all clear out?

Bill: [By this point in the act of fixing] Sonar. A trick Jean-Louis picked up in the Navy.

David: What? Sonar? What are you talking about?

Bill: We might as well call it sonar. [Speaks in a labored drawl, eyes half shut] We know nothing about it. But one supposes a man picks up strange survival instincts during wartime. Any moment he feels his life is in danger. A clarity. Receptiveness. We're as close to being able to describe this as we are to knowing where all the past lives are. Common sense is ignorant.

David: [Looks at him with annoyance; Bill doesn't acknowledge.] Are you through? [Bill doesn't say anything.] I'm serious, Bill. [Takes off his jacket—he's suddenly feeling the heat.] Don't you have a better fan?

Bill: I detest advisors.

David: What? Bill, make sense.

Bill: An advisor is one who advises.

David: So you think I need advice, is that it? Like you're not partial to boys yourself. Don't think I don't know it. You don't fool me with Joan, even if you do fuck her. If you do. [Rolling up his sleeves] Jesus, did you have the oven on? That fan's piss poor. Christ, I don't even talk like this! [Bill still isn't responding] OK, OK. You want to get on me about climbing the marquee, is that it? But I was invited to that party. What am I supposed to do? Ethel invited me, too. You were there. I get there and I can hear them upstairs. They're only on the second floor. I ring the bell and it doesn't work. No one comes down. I'm ready to go to a party. I come home from work, change my clothes, dress up, and now I can't get in. What would you have done? I mean, if you were me, and able to get up there like I can? What?

[Bill is now slumped backward in his chair, his eyes closed. David continues to speak as he crosses back to the left part of the stage. Lights go out.]

Scene Four

[David has stopped dead in the middle of the stage as the lights go out. He retains his position and continues his speech after the interval between scenes. He takes out his comb and plays with it, but a general dishevelment has set in. He drags his coat and his shirt will start to become untucked as he puts his comb in and out of his pocket during this scene.]

David: It's like they treat me like I'm a crazy man. But anyone would have done what I did.

[The lights go up on the right side of the stage, where we see a second David in pantomime before a theatre marquee. The marquee advertises Bing Crosby and Barry Fitzgerald in *Going My Way*. Above it, on the second floor, there's a party going on. As David talks in his apartment on the left side of

the stage, the lookalike tries the bell of the apartment building, looks upstairs at the party, is not seen, tries the bell a
second and third time, each time mimicking shouting up but
being ignored, and finally realizes that there is a foothold on
the rear side of the apartment, toward the back of the stage,
about shoulder level. He begins to climb up. We see,
upstairs, besides some women we don't know, Edie, Jack,
Lucien, Allen, and Celia, Lucien's girlfriend. These and other
actions in the scene, by all characters, are done in pantomime.]

David: [In apartment, alternately sitting on the edge of
his bed and pacing nervously.] How is it that the only sane
one gets cast in the role of the crazy man? It was perfectly
sane to climb up the marquee. The doorbell was broken, the
door was locked, they were making too much noise upstairs
to hear me, and I was able to see a foothold on the side of
the building. I did teach physical education in St. Louis. This
was nothing compared to a gym rope or those obstacle
courses we used to set up. I could have shown them a thing
or two if I'd gone to boot camp. I'm a healthy man, in great
shape. It was nothing to get up there on the foothold and
reach over to the marquee. [The pantomime matches the
actions he describes.] I had to keep one arm on the wall to
keep my balance, but I could reach the middle of it. And they
still weren't paying any attention. Or at least that's what
they were pretending. I could hear Lucien, making some
inane point about *les actes gratuits*. That's what he'd call
being a heel—a gratuitous act, like it was a work of art.
Once, we were eating spaghetti at some Mom and Pop joint
and no sooner does the waitress leave after giving us our
plates than Lucien flips his off the table onto the ground. [In
the pantomime, Lucien is standing and telling a funny story

and all the others are listening and laughing.] Ginsberg and that idiot Jack start laughing. "What are you doing?" I yell at him. "Aw, don't get all bent out of shape. She's paid to clean up the place. What do you care?" This is what constitutes normal in their sick world. "Look at it on the floor there. It's art." Yeah, art in marinara sauce that some poor slob has to clean up after them. Spoiled brat. I work a security job, can't just go to every party and every bar at the drop of a hat. That's why I was late that night to begin with. I had to get off work, go home and change. I could have brought my evening clothes with me, but then I'd need to iron them, and a board. There was nothing that could be helped. So I suppose that all makes me crazy.

[David in the pantomime, trying to get a hold on the marquee, pulls off a piece and a few letters fall off and crash onto the ground. This gets the attention of the party revelers, who look over the edge and see David. They hoot him down off the building. He yells back at them, waving his arms. He goes to the door, but no one will come down to let him in. There is more yelling and drinks begin to hail down on him, while at the same time those who are throwing the drinks stay away from the edge so David can't see their faces.]

David: Animals! That's what they are. They showed their true colors that night. And not one would admit a thing. But they were all over me for climbing up there. Oh, yeah, David's always wrong. Stupid, blundering David. "What kind of idiot climbs up the side of a building to crash a party? Didn't he think anyone would notice? Leave it to Kammerer to not even know how to crash a party."

[In the pantomime, David realizes people on the street are looking at him. Then he notices the letters on the ground. He yells above once more, then half-runs away.]

David: I guess I don't really know how to crash a party.

[Lights go out.]

Scene Five

David: Finally, I run into Jack in front of the West End. He's all "I dunnos" and "what do ya knows." But I don't even let it phase me. I can play it that way.

[On the right side of the stage is Jack, whistling, arriving at the door of the West End bar. Inside, at a long table, sit the following characters:

Allen, wearing thick glasses, looking Bohemian, with wild dark hair that sticks out in every direction and an ivory cigarette holder that he gestures with even when not smoking. He looks to be the youngest of the group;

Lucien, like Allen wearing a jacket and tie, but with more elegance, with close cropped blonde hair and a lean and sneering face;

Jack, wearing a plain t-shirt, which reveals his thick, stocky physique. His appearance is clean, his hair neatly parted;

Edie, a pretty woman with medium-length dark hair combed up into a "Victory Roll" and wearing a low-cut, high-shouldered party dress;

Celia, like Edie, also dressed up to go out dancing. Her blonde hair is bobbed and her manner is that of a young college-girl sophisticate;

Phil, a Naval cadet who is the same age as the rest of them, but out of place in this group, made especially so by his dress-blues officer uniform, which would fit in most places, but not in this dive.

Behind the bar is the bartender, wearing a sleeveless undershirt. At the near end of his bar is a tub in which sits a block of ice. A fan is placed just behind it to blow cold air into the bar.

Extras should be older, ne'erdowell types, shady gangster figures. There is also a jukebox playing mainstream jazz, Big Bands and singers. David walks over to where Jack is waiting.]

David: Hey, Jack.

Jack: [Sheepishly] Well, hello Dave. Uh, I haven't seen you in a couple days.

David: Yeah. Hey, I thought you and Lucien were going to ship out to France.

Jack: [Brightening] We sally forth tomorrow morning, into the great unknown. Hey, you've made it just in time for our *bon voyage* party. *Bon voyage!* [Jack mimics toasting with a glass of champagne and pronounces the words with a loud but natural French accent.] *Bon voyage!* Come on in.

[They enter.]

Jack: [Inside, to table] *Bon voyage!*

All at table: Bon voyage! *Bon voyage!*

83

Allen: [Holding up a glass] Hey, get yourself a martini—it's the most alcohol you can get for the least amount of money!

David: Hello everybody.

[Most of them look askance. Lucien is standing, furthest from the door. Everyone else at the table is sitting. Jack and David stand inside the door.]

Celia: Hi, David.

Lucien: Hope you didn't hurt yourself the other night.

David: No. Why? How would I have?

Lucien: I just heard you had an adventure the other night.

Allen: [Laughing] He just wanted to see his name in lights.

Jack: A star, climbing his way to the heavens. [After saying this, he notices Edie with a soldier sitting closely next to her.]

Allen: His name in lights! Hollywood on the phone!

[Jack doesn't respond, though Allen looks his way.]

David: I don't know what you're all talking about.

Lucien: Who invited you here?

David: Jack did, just now, outside.

Celia: Oh, come on Lucien, it's alright.

Lucien: [To Jack, angrily] Did you invite him?

Jack: What? Yeah, yeah. Come on, Lu. Tomorrow we're out of New York, off the continent, bound for France. Sit down, everybody. What are you drinking?

Allen: Martinis! Everyone drinks martinis!

Edie: Just a beer for me. By the way, everyone, this is Phil. He's from Savannah, Georgia, and tomorrow he leaves for San Diego and then on to fight the Japs in the Pacific.

Phil: Hi everybody. Let me get this round, fella.

Celia: I like this guy already.

Allen: A generosity exceeding Lear's!

Lucien: Let's hope he ends up better.

Jack: Thanks anyway, I'll get it. Nothing's too much for our boys in uniform. Right, Edie?

Edie: [Turning back to Phil.] You have to be sure to write me once you're stationed.

Jack: [Annoyed] Edie, could I talk to you for a minute?

Edie: I'll be right back. [She gets up and joins Jack at the bar.]

Celia: So, do you think you'll be involved in taking back the Philippines?

Phil: I can't say, miss.

Celia: Can't or won't?

Lucien: Don't press him, Celie. You know what they say about loose lips.

[Celia gives Lucien a sarcastic pout and Lucien starts laughing. David looks painfully on their flirtation and breaks in.]

David: Hey, so what happened that you guys didn't take off already? I thought you were heading out on a ship two days ago.

[Meanwhile, Edie and Jack have their own conversation in low tones at the bar.]

Jack: So, you're not even going to wait until I'm out of town.

Edie: Don't be a baby. I'm just showing him a good time before he ships out. These boys don't see civilization for months at a time. We're just going to go out dancing.

Jack: Are you going to fuck him?

Edie: You're so crude. I don't see why I have to answer to you. You just take off at the drop of a hat. What am I supposed to do, wait for you while you're overseas? That only goes for soldiers.

Jack: I'm sleeping in my own bed tonight.

Edie: Fine. It'll be there.

Jack: You want to fight like some old married couple? I can do that. It's just that I know these guys.

Edie: Yeah, Jack, you know everything. Everything except how to relax and have fun. There's always something better somewhere else.

[Meanwhile, conversation continues at the table.]

Allen: Oh, that's a story. Tell him, Lucien.

Lucien: No.

Allen: [Waving Lucien's objection aside] They went downtown and found this supply ship bound for France and went in to sign on. But no one was on board. So they just help themselves to a meal from the galley. Roast beef! They just take it out of the cooler and are helping themselves, slicing it up, when in walks the first mate. Big, hairy, hulking thug of a guy, six foot four, two hundred pounds at least.

Lucien: Yeah, he looked just like Dave.

David: Thanks for the compliment.

Allen: He's about to kill Jack and Lucien.

Lucien: And Jack says, "Hey, could we take a quick cruise with you guys, maybe up to Albany, to see if we like it?"

Jack: [Overhears this] You were the one who said that!

Allen: The guy wanted to kill them!

Lucien: OK, so it didn't quite work out as planned. [Everyone laughs, and Lucien plays it this way; he isn't the butt of anyone's joke.] Hey, no sweat. I've seen a lot of these Navy guys, they're not all like King Kong today. We shall head out tomorrow afresh and find another boat, one more generous with their provisions, embarking for the bounteous vista of France. [He stands and raises his glass, shouting.] We shall see Paris—the Paris of Baudelaire and Rimbaud, of Lautréamont and Oscar Wilde . . .

Allen: Of Proust! Of Mallarmé!

David: Of Victor Hugo!

Lucien: Even so—this city of lights—we shall see it alight again! Liberated from 'neath the heel of Axis oppression!

Allen: Hurrah!

Lucien: Hurrah indeed!

Phil: [Confused] You guys aren't in any branch of the service, are you?

Edie: No, they're tourists. France is so lovely this time of year.

Celia: [Turning to Edie her own mocking sarcasm] Oh, I've read about the lovely wine country, and the fashions this past Spring were just marvelous. [To Lucien] Oh, bring me back *parfum. Chanel? S'il vous plâit?*

Lucien: *Mais oui, mademoiselle.*

[Jack brings a tray with drinks back to the table.]

Jack: Okay, so that was four martinis, two beers, and one glass of white wine.

Celia: [Taking the wine] Thank you, sailor.

Phil: Really—you guys are going to try to go to France?

Jack: There are lots of ships, and supplies can start going in there now. We can get on a merchant ship, we've got it all set up. I already had all my papers and this last week we got Lucien a Coast Guard pass, WSA waiver and a Union card. We'll have to hurry if we are to be there for the actual liberation of Paris, but the country should be pretty safe to travel in coming from the Normandy peninsula.

David: How do you know?

Jack: There's maps every day in *P.M.* and all the other papers. The ones in *P.M.* are really detailed. You can see for yourself.

Lucien: And Jack speaks French like a native, or at least a Canuck relative. He'll do the talking—

Jack: We'll be able to move pretty quickly—

Lucien: We'll pass for French—I'm going to pretend I'm his deaf and dumb brother.

Phil: So you guys are just sitting out the war.

David: I'm 4F.

Jack: I was in the Navy for awhile. We were up off the coast of Greenland, chopping through ice, not going anywhere or doing anything. No offense, but I just couldn't take it. Some men are soldiers, and they can take orders and live like that.

Phil: How did you get out?

Jack: I just couldn't follow orders. It's nothing I can do anything about, it's just in my constitution. They realized this and discharged me. But it was crazy being on this ship. I got jumped one night below decks by some Polack for my wallet. What the hell do you need money for out there?

Phil: Why'd he do it?

Jack: Damned if I know. Just driven crazy, like I was, I

guess, just flipping his lid from being locked up in a metal can at the top of the world doing nothing but peeling potatoes and hoping you don't hit a land mine or run into a U-Boat.

Phil: But you're missing what it's all about. It's not like everyone fighting loves what they're doing. It's about defeating the Nazis and the Japs. There's a higher purpose.

Jack: That's what I mean about thinking like a soldier. I couldn't do it. I'd be in the galley peeling potatoes or swabbing the deck and all I can think of is there's some other guy on the German boat, and either he'll get it or I'll get it, and I just didn't have anything against that guy. Yeah, I want to see Hitler defeated, but I just didn't have anything personally against that guy. OK, he's fighting for the Nazis, but he's just doing it because that's what everybody's doing in his country. It's what his friends are all doing and his father and everybody else is telling him he should be doing. You know, I wish I could think like a soldier. I don't like being like this. But I just couldn't follow the rules because they ask you to put your own mind on hold and pretend everything made sense when it didn't.

Phil: That's a pretty selfish attitude. Someone else will do it for you, huh?

Jack: I didn't say it wasn't selfish. But then again, I'm a writer. I want to make my contributions to society in other ways. Why can't I be free to do that if what we're fighting for is—Ow!

[Jack jumps away. Lucien's been burning his arm with a

cigarette.]

Jack: [Mad, but also laughing] You asshole!

Lucien: I just can't abide a speech of more than seven continuous sentences. If you can't make your point in five well-fashioned grammatical sentences, then you don't have a point. I even gave you a few free sentences, but you were too far gone.

Allen: Are you employing Aristotle's Rule of Abridgement and Consecution?

Lucien: The same. Mistranslated by St. Thomas Aquinas, this text is just becoming clear to modern scholars. I see you are up on your philology.

Celia: Sounds like Joe Aristotle from 93rd Street if you ask me.

Lucien: A research partner of Phil Ology at Columbia. I would think a Barnard girl like yourself would be up on all this.

Edie: Well, well, well, this is all very pleasant and enlightening, but Phil promised us a little dancing tonight, and we're meeting people over at the Flamingo.

Phil: [Rising to shake hands] I don't agree with what you all are doing, but Jack's right in a way. We are fighting for freedom.

Lucien: [Rising along with the others] And we don't

agree with what you're doing either, but we won't hold it against you.

Edie: [Aside to Jack] I'll make you breakfast before you go tomorrow morning.

Jack: [Aside] Six-thirty AM. We want to get an early start. [To all:] In fact, I think I should be going too. If we want to get out early tomorrow, I should get some sleep. I'll walk over with you guys.

Lucien: That's right, Ishmael. Since you will be choosing our ship, you best get a good night's sleep. I still have to sell some shrunken heads before morning if I'm to make the journey myself. No rest for us South Seas cannibals.

[After shaking hands all around and goodbyes, everyone adjourns from the table to leave except Lucien, David, and Allen, who is now the most visibly drunk of the group, swaying a little as he stands up. Before leaving, Celia turns to Lucien.]

Celia: [Aside to Lucien] I hope I'll get a chance to say goodbye to you.

Lucien: [Loudly] An assignation! [Aside:] I'll be at 118th Street at 5:30 AM.

Celia: You should sleep a little before you go.

Lucien: [Loudly] Sleep! The last refuge of a scoundrel! I shan't go there this evening! I will sleep aboard with my comrades at sea!

Phil: [Is glad to be leaving, though he remains polite to save face with Edie] It was nice to meet you all.

[Edie, Celia, Jack, and Phil exit. The remaining three sit back down, Allen putting his head across his arms on the table. David is looking rougher than when he first came in, but Lucien, while slurring more, looks the best of the three.]

David: Allen, maybe you should get home, too.

Lucien: Ah, the poet Ginsberg. *Ses ailes de géant l'empêchent de marcher.* [Badly mispronounced] He cannot walk, for he has the giant's wings. [To David:] Buy us a round, faggot. I'm broke.

David: I don't like the way you treat me.

Lucien: Then go away. Leave me five dollars.

Allen: [Righting himself at the table somewhat] Those things really go right to your head.

Lucien: Lazarus, back from the dead! So, Ginsberg, what did you think of our visitor this evening, the imperialist pawn?

David: [Angrily] I told you to stop that.

Lucien: Not you, dimwit. The cadet, what's his name, going off to war, the tool of nations. [Allen doesn't respond.] I'll give you a moment to think about it while I take a piss. [To David:] You stay here—there's only one toilet. [Exits through the back]

David: [Watches Lucien until he's out of sight, then signals to the bartender for two drinks. He looks doubtfully at Ginsberg.] Are you sure you're OK?

Allen: Yeah. [Breathes deeply, then opens his eyes wide to wake himself up.]
Yeah, I'm fine.

David: So what did you think of Phil? I kind of liked him. I hope he gets through it all OK.

Allen: I would have liked to have talked to him a little more seriously about what he's doing.

David: He seemed pretty committed. He's just been through cadet training.

Allen: So we would have needed an equal amount of time to depropagandize him. Give him some Spengler.

David: Spengler has all the answers, does he? What would Spengler say to me?

Allen: I don't think you need Spengler. I think you should undergo psychoanalysis.

David: Thanks a lot.

Allen: No, I don't mean it in that way. There must be a hidden cause of your obsession with Lucien. You do admit to an obsession with Lucien, don't you?

David: He's going to be right back.

Allen: Let me know when you see him coming. You've been behaving erratically, you have to admit. That stunt two nights ago.

David: I didn't do anything anybody else wouldn't have done if they were invited to a party and . . .

Allen: That's not what I'm talking about. You have to see that Lucien feels threatened by you. That everywhere he goes, you show up, and . . .

David: Here he comes.

Allen: Think about it. My father can recommend a good psychoanalyst.

David: [As Lucien nears the table] So, is that Bill's Spengler you've got there?

Allen: Lucien, you've got to read this book. [The drinks arrive.] Hey, don't I get one?

Lucien: David, why didn't you buy a drink for the Spenglerite poet? Are you anti-intellectual?

David: I'll get him one. [Sarcastically to Lucien] Is the men's room free now? [Goes to the bar]

Lucien: See that he's keeping the bartender occupied. [Takes out a small knife.] I've got to leave my mark.

Allen: Queequeg, his mark!

Lucien: As it were—a sign of our embarkation. [Presses hard into the table.] So, how am I going to shake the old man?

Allen: Maybe we should just skip out while he's at the bar.

Lucien: Let me just finish this. [Continues carving] There. "LC JK Bound for Paris 8/14/44." Shit, it's the 15th now, isn't it? Oh, well. OK, let's go. Let me just down this. [Drinks his drink and puts the knife back in his pocket] Here, drink this other one. Let not haste stand in the way of excess. [Hands Allen the other martini glass, spilling some of it]

Allen: Quick, here he comes. [The two get up and start for the door.]

David: [Seeing them as he turns from the bar] Hey! [They don't turn around and David runs over, setting the glass on the table in mid-stride, grabbing Lucien by the shoulder and spinning him around. Seeing them both standing together, we see how small Lucien and Allen are compared to David, who towers over them. His bearing is suddenly menacing.] OK, OK. I've had enough of this shit!

Lucien: We were just going to catch a breath outside.

Allen: [Weakly] The heat in here . . .

David: You were going to ditch me. You're always trying to ditch me. "Let's ditch Dave." It's like a sport for you guys. Well, Dave isn't getting ditched tonight. Dave is going to have something to say about it tonight. [He pulls Lucien back to the table by his collar like a rag doll and, one hand still on him, takes the drink down in one gulp.] There, I'm finished. I'll go with you.

Lucien: Really, Dave.

David: Fuck you, I'm sick of this shit. Yeah, I should go see a psychoanalyst. You're the ones who need a head-shrinker. Someone to teach you manners. "It's only Dave, fuck him."

Bartender: [Has reached under the bar for a baseball bat, which he pounds on the bar—the sound gets their attention.] Hey, none of that in here. Go on, beat it, all of you, you've had enough.

Lucien: [Scared, comes up with a proposal to ease tensions] Easy, Dave. Let's go over to Morningside Park. It'll be cooler over there. We can pick up a bottle on the way. . .

David: I don't think Allen needs to do any more drinking. [Threateningly] Do you, Allen?

Lucien: Come on, Dave. Don't be like that.

David: Oh, there's nothing wrong with me. [Pulls Lucien between him and the door and pushes him through the door, where Allen is still standing. The two crash and Allen is knocked over.]

Bartender: [Coming around from behind the bar] Break anything and I'll break your skulls to match.

David: [The only one not cowed by the bartender, angrily] Alright, we're going. Don't have a heart attack. [Pushes Lucien out the door ahead of him] Don't try anything funny, I'm right behind you. [They leave out the side entrance, in the middle of the stage, and turn out toward the back, exiting in the rear. Allen is still sitting on the ground as the bartender looks over at him, tapping the barrel of the bat with his free hand while gripping the handle with the other. Allen can't get up quickly, and smiles weakly at the bartender. Lights go out.]

Scene Six

[David looks a mess as he walks from stage forward across his room on the left side of the stage and flops on the bed. He turns on his back and, sitting up, notices he's not alone. Across from him on a simple wooden chair is a short, bearded man in a lab coat.]

David: Who are you?

Dr. Freud: [With an exaggeratedly thick German accent] I zink you know who I am.

David: [Angry, but not getting off the bed, as if stuck there] What are you doing here?

Dr. Freud: [Calmly] What do you zink I am doing here?

David: You're dead!

Dr. Freud: Zo are you.

99

David: What happened?

Dr. Freud: Vy don't you tell me vat you remember happening?

David: Can I tell you a dream instead? [We start to hear a Broadway show-style string orchestra swing up faintly, which rises in volume over the next few moments. The lights fade up on the right hand side of the stage.]

Dr. Freud: If zat is what you want.

[On the right side of the stage are Lucien and a David double. Lucien is wearing a boy's athletic outfit something like we saw him in earlier, except now he wears a white t-shirt with his shorts and sneakers. As well, upon his head is a bridal veil, swept back off his face. David is dressed more in full evening formal wear. He will move more gracefully in this scene than he has before—with a gliding ease that is styled on Astaire.

As the lights come up, the two are in tableau: David holding out his hand as an escort requesting a dance, Lucien's hand extended to rest upon David's, so that he may be led.

A simple park setting should be improvised on the right side of the stage. Also, as the band music quiets slightly so that he may hear the characters speak, we should hear a faint rumble from the rear, as of a river.

David is looking over toward the right side of the stage, though not noticing particularly what's going on there. Rather, what is happening there seems projected from his eyes. Dr. Freud keeps looking at his patient; the right side of the stage is behind him and he doesn't notice anything happening there.]

David: Lucien and I are in Morningside Park. He's beautiful. And the way he looks at me, he's never looked at me that way. Well, maybe he used to, when I first knew him back in St. Louis. Not quite the same, but with the open-faced look he used to have. Trusting. There's music—it's not coming from a band or anything, it's just there. Lucien looks so beautiful, like a Greek boy athlete, but a neophyte, his skin pale. Trusting me. Looking up into my eyes. The tune isn't one I've heard before, but seeing Lucien like this, I'm suddenly filled with song and I know all the words.

Dream David [Singing]:

On such a lovely
Night as this
Who is there that
Can resist?

[The Dream David sings these lines looking into Lucien's eyes, then begins to tap dance. It's not possible that one could tap-dance in a park, but no one involved is worried about this incongruity. The Dream David punctuates the next verses with a second burst of very accomplished tap-dancing. His voice is deep and rich.]

Dream David [Singing]:

When we met,
You were just a boy
But now you've taken my heart
As your toy

[The music changes to the chorus, and David takes Lucien and leads them waltzing around the park, singing romantically to him.]

Dream David [Singing]:

Oh, come with me
Darling, come with me
What will we have after tonight?
Come with me
Darling come with me
Be mine forever for one night

[The music shifts to an instrumental and the Dream David really starts to strut his stuff. Lucien hardly dances at all, but gazes admiringly at his partner: Dream David has left Lucien standing in the middle of the park as he twirls around the perimeter of the stage, arms outstretched, flipping back to front as if in a rotating orbit around Lucien, his sun. After several spectacular moves by Dream David, Lucien claps his hands close to his chest, girlishly. Dream David finishes his circling and joins Lucien's side.]

Dream David: [His arm around Lucien, swaying in rhythm to the music and singing]

Hard to get
I remember when
I hoped you'd think of me
Now and then

[As Dream David sings these verses, the tree behind them leans over and as the verse concludes, picks them up off the ground. It raises them to a central platform branch while around them many large branches reach outward in each direction.]

You have my heart
Now don't be shy
Cause without your love
I'll surely die
Come with me
Oh, darling, come with me
Together we can reach the heights
Come with me
Yes, darling, come with me
We can have forever in one night

[Dream David now grabs the branch immediately above their heads and hoists himself up in one quick leap. He dances gracefully over Lucien's head for a few bars, then skips across to a far branch and does an incredible tap routine, run-tapping up to the highest point of one side of the tree until he's nearly perpendicular to the ground until, reaching near the top, he back-flips onto his feet again and run-taps down to the platform where Lucien still stands in rapt astonishment. But Dream David doesn't stop there but goes right by him up the other side of the tree, run-tapping again up to the top branches, then back-flipping over again and, after clicking his heels, coming back down toward Lucien. Even this doesn't finish the dance: he grabs branches, goes hand over hand above Lucien's head and with his feet in mid-air, keeps tapping them together and against various branches and the main trunk, keeping up a steady rhythm. Meanwhile, Lucien reaches into his pocket and pulls out a pen-knife, and turning around to the main trunk, starts to carve a heart into the tree with his and David's initials. David finishes his swinging tap routine at one of highest branches, lands on a perpendicular limb, and again tap-races down to Lucien's arms. Lucien turns toward Dream-David as he approaches and Dream David hurls himself upon Lucien. The outstretched knife lands in Dream David's chest.]

Dream David: [Stabbed so suddenly and unexpectedly, he staggers slowly backward from Lucien. The music slows its tempo and breaks for the final line of the song, which comes from David word by word.]

We . . . have . . .

He looks down at his wound and puts his hand to his chest. Removing his hand, blood starts to pour from the wound, running down his shirt to his pantlegs and spilling to the ground. His voice is a drawn out, mellifluous, touching mixture of resignation and beatific joy, held for several seconds.]

For . . . ev . . . er

[The air having left his lungs, he whispers rather than sings the final word.]

To . . . night.

[Dead on his feet as he pronounces the last word, he plummets forward to the ground. Lucien falls to his knees and screams. The lights on the right side of the stage go out.]

David: [Wiping a tear from his eye and gathering himself, turning back to Dr. Freud] What do you think of that dream?

Dr. Freud: Vat do you mean vat do I think of zat dream? It's zee most preposterous zing I've ever heard.

David: I didn't think you would understand.

Dr. Freud: Maybe it's you who do not understand. I don't know vy you vant me here. I can't help you. Psychoanalysis can't help you. Psychoanalysis is for the living, not za dead. It vill not redeem you. The dead are useful for the analyst, not vice-versa. The dead, revealed, help absorb the zources of neuroses and cleanse the living. But you—I can do nothing for you. Zis is not the provinze of Zychoanalysis. I vould only lay greater crimes at your feet, maybe even crimes beyond those of vich you are actually guilty, because it doesn't matter, the dead are no concern of mine or my theories. You need art—or literature or grand opera or vatever—zese things are much more concerned with the possibilities of your redemption. I concern myself only with the living.

David: Even now?

Dr. Freud: Even now.

David: But what if you are merely a character in my drama?

Dr. Freud: Ah, but zat is not me. Zat is not a true representation of psychoanalysis. Zat is you, your version.

David: And any absolution I receive?

Dr. Freud: Is vat you give yourself.

David: Deserved or not?

Dr. Freud: Deserved or not.

[David rises from his bed and walks over to where Dr. Freud is sitting. He pulls Dr. Freud out of his chair and leans him over backward in a long kiss reminiscent of the serviceman kissing his girl in Times Square on V-J Day.]

Dr. Freud: [Readjusting himself and speaking only after a few moments] You can't really say you buy zis ending, can you?

[David walks a few steps away and looks out into a darkness that's fallen over his fantasy production. He stares blankly for several seconds. He remains frozen.]

Dr. Freud: Do you?

[The lights dim.]

—Poor Verlaine, 2 years
in the can, but could have
got a knife in the heart
        Jack Kerouac, "Rimbaud"

Nightsaints

1.

In his mad days hustling rough blue avenues of upper Manhattan, pulling jobs in Boston banker mansions,

    careening town to town through Northeast using bogus railroad ID, roll of reefers inside vest pocket,

    Red Little (woulda been "Little Red" because so young except he stood beanstalk six three)

    connected to nearly all the cats playing the best music in USA—jazzing, venturing, proposing in little ruminative joints or big county balloon-shine ballroom dances for white folks,

    like subtle buttered rum Ellington drummer Sonny Greer & string-horn juggler Ray Nance, also with Ellington, languorous swan-necked beautiful Dinah Washington,

    cool Lionel Hampton, the original vibe man, & his tenor saxes, Arnett Cobb, Illinois Jacquet, Dexter Gordon,

    swinging Joe Newman on trumpet, Alvin Hayse on trombone—& Billy Eckstine—the smoothest man alive

    then leading a band not fully appreciated until they broke up, including drunken athlete Bird, bespectacled child-genius Diz,

    & knew also honeywide ranging Ella Fitzgerald & the downest of the down bandleaders Cootie Williams & the Count, Basie himself as well as his cats, led by President Lester Young, & a diplomatic entourage from the land of groove—Harry Edison, Buddy Tate, Dicky Wells, Buck Clayton—

Yes, Red was down, Red was BEAT—
but America still had grown men donning Halloween

sheets, making Elm tree kangaroo courts in southern pastures,

split whites & colored into different cars once you dipped below the blue-gray string of north & south,

& had put the blanket with the sheet making these things silent—

oh, the enemy everywhere, the enemy everywhere—

everywhere the tyrannous bewigged majority which didn't even want you thinking certain thoughts.

Only a few hundred real flesh people left in the whole world, seemed like, not to mention the ones that weren't actively killing you,

owning everything & so killing you slowly—

the only way to make a real buck unless you played an instrument or declared yourself Uncle Sam fodder was by rigging the game,

siphoning off a little of that capital always flowing upwards to Beacon Hill & Park Avenue—

The Man didn't take too kindly to that,

though one advantage lay in the fact that he thought you incapable & this put him off guard—

so when Red showed his pass to Euroamerican conductors he was waved aboard quickly,

a certain number of nigras being needed to run a successful railroad from New York to Hartford,

Boston, Albany, Scranton, & Philadelphia, across to Pittsburgh & Cleveland south to Columbus & Cincinnati & east to DC.

To hear Red tell it, he was the first mobile dope man of the Eastern United States

in the first decade of all major drugs' illegality when dope meant not only good bucks but a kind of celebrity

cause whenever & wherever in history you look there's

109

*always people awaiting the arrival in town of the lovely
dopeman,*

*they take the money out of the teakettle saved for the
war bond,*

*the war right now being something someone else is
doing, but also a reason to really live because there might
not be a tomorrow, dig, & given a choice*

*do you want to die shoveling ashes out of someone's
fireplace, a Kraut bullet in your heart?*

Or test your own heart's limits, make it race & sing?

Red even gets supposed one of the band sometimes and
gets in free. But as if he didn't have enough to worry about,
lately some older brother has been asking what happened in
the back of the station with his little sister two weeks ago.

"Ain't you scared of these big corn-fed country boys you
crossing, Red?"

This is Alvin, whose home is Harlem—used to work the
same crew with Red on the railroad and now still porters
and is just heading home for a short rest. They're sitting
after-hours in a dining car.

"Shit, Alvin," says Red with a grin. "What are you asking me? You asking me not to love a woman? Gal's gonna be
loose, she gonna get my juice. What you think, I'm some
green boy like old Lima Bean?"

Lima Bean's new on the scene, and you never saw such a
greenhorn.

Alvin looks over in his direction but still talks to Red and
K-Rib: "Now how you think he got the name Lima Bean?"

"Not good with women, old Lima Bean."

"Shit, Lima Bean couldn't get laid if he was an egg."

Lima Bean's temples flex.

"Ain't that the case, though, Lima Bean?" says Alvin. "I mean, we brothers's doing all we can for you, but we can't do everything."

"We even fixed him up with Thelma," says Alvin.

"Hartford Thelma?"

Alvin nods gravely.

"And the boy didn't get nothin from Hartford Thelma? That is one SAD state of affairs."

"Hartford Thelma—*man*," says Red, shaking his head in amazement. "That gal's so big and loose she's got to seal herself up with candlewax before it's safe for her to walk around!"

"That is one big and loose gal," agrees K-Rib. "She went to the Grand Canyon and lay down next to it and no one could tell the two apart!"

"She keeps all my reefers for me when I'm in Hartford and when I want a hit I just light a match by her mouth and suck in the smoke from her twat."

"You stick your face in that bitch?" says Alvin, twisting his own face grotesquely.

"When she's fresh out of the bath there ain't nothing sweeter, my man."

"Hope you took your reefers out first before they got soaked."

"You don't have to worry about that."

"I don't know if we're going to be seeing much of Thelma anymore," says K-Rib.

"Why's that?"

"The Army wants her."

"The Army's already had her," laughs Alvin. "Yessir, many times."

"But they need to use her," says K-Rib, then pauses, measuring time before the punchline. "For an airplane hangar." He slaps the table and chortles.

"Naw," says Red. "I heard it wasn't for that. I heard they were going to tie scrub brushes on the insides of her thighs and give a good cleaning to the Empire State Building."

Alvin bends double with laughing as he chokes out, "That must be the reason."

"Spic and span," says Red, laughing too. "Top to bottom."

The laughter dies out. It's suddenly too quiet. It's something behind Red. He turns.

"Well, hello," the man says, looking at Red. "This is a coincidence."

It's a white man of about forty in a tan suit jacket and a medium-width red tie. His voice catches slightly from nervousness as he speaks. "Remember me?"

Red turns back to the others. He taps a cigarette out of his pack.

"Sorry, Mac. You got me confused with somebody else."

The guy nods, glancing at the rest of the table. "Yeah, okay," he says. "My mistake." He walks on.

"Nut job," says Red after the man leaves. "Probably one of those shell-shock cases."

And everyone knows Red's lying, hiding something. But also that it ain't cool to get too familiar and ask what. If Red don't want it known, don't cross him.

Only the new guy doesn't know the drill.

"He must have wanted to know about Hartford Thelma," says Lima Bean, voice breaking nervously. All heads turn toward him he chokes out the punchline. "He heard what we were saying and wants to get introduced."

Lima Bean laughs but no one else does. He stops.

Red looks at him. "That some kinda joke or something,

Bean?"

Lima Bean ducks his head. "Yeah."

They all laugh out loud. "Lima," says Alvin, "You are greener than asparagus piss."

2.

Dining car before dawn, not a spare bit of space on Boston train, Red awoken

after just a couple hours' snooze, across a bench, half underneath a dining table,

legs off the end & one arm dangling on the floor, briefly free

of zipping amphetamine rush of days watching back,

it only takes one slip-up once you get into these back-water hamlets they don't fancy

the look of polished business-suited Red, crackers may give you credit for the sense Satan gave a snake,

may well be saying, "You sure he works for the rail-road?"

Senses bolt upright though he remains flat on his back in the dark car.

It's the same man from before. He stands before Red, his Johnson unsheathed, shagging it with a flipping, underhand wrist motion, such as a man would use to shoot dice.

"Hey, boy," he says, panting. "I'll buy you breakfast." His neck is angled back, his mouth half open in pleasure, his eyes half shut.

He spurts on the floor.

"Aw, Jesus," says Red, burying his face in the seat back.

Nothing happens for a few seconds. Then the standing man says, "I'm Dick Post." He's restored himself. He removes a handkerchief from his pocket, squats, and cleans his come from the floor. He folds the handkerchief into his inside breast pocket.

Red only groans.

"I've got a business proposition," says Post.

Red knows. Everyone is always either making someone or being made.

"Submit it to my lawyer."

Post taps out a Lucky Strike and lights it. "I want you to know that I don't consider myself to be any better a person than you," he says, and even as Red is thinking, *no, not this rap again*, he continues: "In fact, there's probably no one on this earth who's worse than I am. I'm under no illusions. I know what I am. A man driven by his basest hungers." He drags from his cigarette. "But I pay handsomely."

"What the fuck time is it anyway?"

Post looks at his watch: "Four twenty-five."

"Christ."

"You don't ever like to make a little money on the side?" Post reaches into his wallet and pulls out a ten dollar bill, which he flips onto Red's flat, shirted stomach.

Red still lies prone on the dining bench, but he's removed his hand from his eyes. He grabs the bill, crumples it in his hand and backhandedly throws it back. Post catches it in mid-air with his glove hand.

"You know," he persists, "A lot of guys pay for a woman to do it to them. And that's all I'm asking you to do. Most guys would say that's not a bad way to make a buck."

Red feels sick. Breakfast gets served early on a train. In another twenty minutes, the set-up crew comes in. He sits up, rubbing his eyes. He wants to escape, rest.

"Wait." Post grabs him by the arm as Red stands up. Red pulls the arm away and jumps to fighting position. He towers over Post.

"Whoa, hold on," says Post. "OK, look. You're not interested right now. But keep in touch, right?" He takes out a piece of paper with an address and phone number. "This is my sister's place in the Bronx. Nice house. I'm going to be out travelling for a little while, but you can leave a message with her." He picks up the bill, smoothes it out and folds it beneath the note, handing it to Red. Red grabs it and puts it in his pocket. Something for a rainy day—you can never tell.

"No breakfast?" says Post.

"Tsk," says Red, and walks away.

3.

In Springfield a dance, typical countrywhite fellers comb up hair wet & flat,

their little fillies in their one good dresses, curled hair, & 1 or 2 hipsters in goatees,

maybe a lady in satin or black velour, but this ain't even Boston

& these are at best wannabes, too loud, eager, predictably

drunk by the end of the night without any real EDGE to it—

the band is bored, the stifflimb steps always the same—

Red hangs backstage until it's finished & does good business,

basically always the same business,

then it's back to Gotham for resupply,

worn to nothing, nowhere to really sleep on a train,

you just sometimes fall into a trance where you match up with the rhythm bud-a-thump, bud-a-thump,

but brain never actually shuts off or recesses into pure

dream,

   like the soldier marching through Europe cramped, red-
eyed, tired,

   movements automatic, sizzling from the constant small
pops of nearby danger,

   taken past feeling, not wanting to feel anymore—

   not able to shut it off either, feeling sensations acutely—

   or didn't you know that's what was meant by BEAT?

Red gets off the train and heads upstairs into Grand
Central. He should get over to Penn where he can get the A
uptown but he wants to try to fully wake up, walk around,
get blood moving. Been cramped in an aisle leaning against
suitcases too long. His suit vest is unbuttoned, pants creased
like washboards high on each side of the crotch from trying
to position his long legs anywhere they'll fit, shifting and
extending but never getting any closer to comfort. He does-
n't even adjust his clothes though his shirt tail is half out,
peeking from under his jacket on one side. He does no more
than to pull at the fabric on his back where it sticks with
sweat soaking through to the outside of his jacket. The fans
are going full blast high in the windows and ceiling corners
of the Grand Central Station lobby but ain't doing much
good. New York in August and hotter'n hell.

Out on the street the heat hits you full in the face. There
isn't even what you could call a breeze—just more hot wind
stirred by speeding taxis and sidewalk vents. Red's legs are
still tight from the train. He begins to stretch them out by
striding long and fast down the sidewalk. How his legs can
carry him—and he isn't even running! He puts the first leg
out in front of him and then when he pulls his body forward
to meet it rockets forward like a slingshot and his other leg
reaches out, sets, pulls his body along again. And the move-

ment feels so good after the train, after the uncramping, after the dull light of the station, here in the sun, that Red is soon flying up the street, arms as well as legs pumping. This city that moves like mad all the time and he's back in it.

"Hey! Hold up! Where are you going!"

Red looks around him for the first time. Park Avenue! Ritzy hotels, barbered poodles, limousines, strollers with goldknobbed walking sticks and spats, fur stoles not on whores but on wealthy gray women, servants stooping to open automobile doors standing at firm attention, eyes forward, and jewelry, even here in midday. Park Fucking Avenue!—where Red would avoid even setting foot most of the time and now where he's running full speed! And a cop now after him raising a baton—Red sees him over his shoulder, then looks forward again and as he does rushes full into a tall hollowcheeked whiteman in thickframed glasses whom he has to grab to keep from knocking completely to the pavement.

The two men look at each other each blank-faced. Then the cop comes rushing up and grabs Red and twists him by the collar against an iron fence.

"Hold on, there!" says the man in glasses. "Let him go!"

The cop shouts instead to Red, pushing his face against the iron:

"Why didn't you stop when I yelled at you to?"

"Let him go!" says the man again. "He's my butler!"

This has an effect on the policeman, who straightens and lets Red go.

"I wouldn't have grabbed him like that except he was running up the street like he'd just grabbed a purse or something," he says to the man.

"Well, he hasn't. So back to other dangers, officer."

The man turns to Red: "Come on with me."

With the policeman still there, Red has no choice. The man beckons toward a taxi and the two get in.

He gives the cabbie an address downtown then turns to Red:

"I think you can help me out."

"Sir?" says Red, not wanting to give any additional cause to a passing officer of the law, who's hovering outside.

"Yes, yes, you're just what I've been looking for."

"I don know, suh," says Red, laying on the Negro thick. "I think I'm loss."

"Nonsense," says the bespectacled man. "You're found!"

He motions Red to take the flipdown stool across from the back seat in the deep rear compartment of the taxi and facing away from the driver leans over to whisper to him. His accent is a croaking deep drawl coming through even in the low tones of the lips brought close to his ear as the two men lean over toward each other, putting the back of the large front seat between them and the driver's eyes.

"You're wondering for what reason I accosted you in this way. I wouldn't blame you if you cried murder, but if you give me a moment of your time and don't mind the excursion downtown for which you can be sure I'll compensate you, I have a proposition. My name's Bill. I've recently come into a reasonably large haul of guns and other contraband—syringes primarily—and I need a go-between to secure disposal. I don't know anyone in the market for these things uptown, though I'm sure such a market exists. My regular man Herbert—a mistaken epigram as he's anything but regular in all things except his vices—was arrested a few days ago on an unrelated matter. An all too common occurrence with him, I'm afraid. I had acquired the merchandise thinking that he'd be the one to handle it for me but now that he's determined to lay low for a while I'm stuck with it. Not knowing the ins and outs of the marketplace I'm in desperate need to be rid of the stuff. Does what I say interest you?"

"No, suh," says Red. "I don't know nothin 'bout that sort a thing."

"As I'm in a difficult circumstance I'll of course be willing to give you a very generous split on the profits as well as covering all incidental costs you may incur. Say fifty percent."

Red shakes his head and sits upright. They're speeding downtown and west toward Greenwich Village.

Without himself straightening, Bill raises his slender hand slightly as a sign for Red that everything is OK then turns his fingers slightly and motions for Red to move forward again. Which Red does to hear more whispering.

"I see what your suspicion is—that I'm a cop. Believe me, I keep a great distance between myself and officers of the law. Let me prove it to you."

He takes Red's hand and begins to pull it toward his beltline. Red resists but Bill calmly purses his lips and nods slightly to assure Red there's no danger.

"Do you feel that knife?" he asks. "Palm it in your hand and take it out."

Red glares at him but when the man nods Red does what he's told.

"Put it in your pocket."

Red looks up toward the driver and then mimics boredom, looking out the window. He opens the blade slightly, concealed against his hip. It's sharp. He shifts it to his jacket pocket.

"Go ahead and check me for other weapons."

Red reaches in and pats around his waist and back then

up and down his legs and inside overcoat pockets finding nothing.

"There," says Bill, voice a barely audible gravel. "Now do you think you can trust me? I'm unarmed and I know you've got a knife. Would a cop do that? I think not. I must be crazy to do it myself. But I do this as a sign of my trust in you. I think people are generally trustworthy unless they're in positions of power, in which case they become vicious as piranhas. I certainly would never have turned my back on that officer we were just so rudely introduced to, else he might have simply clubbed us both with his nightstick and made off, pretending the whole thing never happened. As a safeguard against fears you may still have, keep the knife until we've reached some sort of arrangement."

The cab arrives at an apartment address below the Village. "Let's go inside," says Bill. He hands money to the cabbie.

The apartment is spare—one room with a kitchenette, a ragged couch, two metal chairs, a square table with a radio and cases filled with books and another adjoining which Red can glance into through a half open door, seeing a bed night-stand and lamp. On the nightstand is a worn leather belt.

Bill walks to the table and puts the belt in the drawer of the nightstand.

Red looks at him. Having taken off his jacket, bruises are visible on the insides of each of Bill's bony pale arms. "Why do you want me to do this?" say Red. "You don't know me."

"I need someone. I think you'll do fine."

"But why did you pick me? Do I look to you like some kind of criminal?"

Bill looks Red in the eye. They have almost the same build—tall and thin. "Fella," he says, "We're all criminals."

4.

Later, Red's going over it all on a public bench off Amsterdam Avenue uptown:

"Man, the last couple of days I've had, you wouldn't believe. But this sounds like easy money."

"You talking pie in the sky again, Red?"

"Naw—for real. The man—a white guy—that I'm doing business with don't look like no rube that don't get what's for when he does his deals."

"White fella? You crazy, Red? How you know he ain't no cop?"

"Do cops shoot smack? This guy lives in a flat downtown and he's got a good sized habit from what I seen."

"I don't know about getting mixed up with a junky."

"That's the thing. If he didn't tell me his own self that he was a junky I wouldn't never have picked him for one. Never in a million years. You should've seen him fool this cop who was hassling me on Park."

"Park? As in Park Avenue?"

"Yeah, down by Grand Central."

"What was you doing over on Park?"

"That's where I met this fella. Anyway, I run into this guy and a cop starts hassling me when cool as ice this man tells the cop I'm his butler. And the cop goes for it. And you would too—guy just looks like he owns things—and not your fleabag landlord type neither. He could pass for old Rockefeller. Naw, this cat knows where the money's at, and that ain't no scat."

"If he's so rich and Park Avenue, how come he's got digs downtown? How come he needs us?"

"That's probably his extra place—the place he does his smack and runs things outta. These rich white folks, they know how to run their business. Anyway, he's got a whole damn supply store he's looking to unload down there."

"What of?"

"You name it. He showed it me. Guns, needles, all kinda things. Look like he ripped off a drugstore and a damn war factory."

"Sounds like he's riding pretty high without the help of no brothers."

"Naw, he needs us—he said he had me pegged the moment he saw me on the street."

"He stopped you right on the street? Man, I know he's a cop."

"Yeah, Red—and what was you doing strolling up Park? You hit the numbers?"

"Yeah, old Red was checking out properties for investment."

"You can laugh out your black asses for all I care, but this man's cool and there's quick money to be made. I think he's one of them white dudes that's trying to act black."

"Act black? What you talking about?"

"You know exactly what I'm talking about. Look around you, man. Everywhere you look you see these white dudes dressing up, all zooted out, or coming uptown."

"Why would white folks wanna be black?"

"Maybe they're after our women."

"They must be in for something."

"Maybe white folks want everything they don't got and the only thing they don't got is the nothing they've left us with. So now they want that too."

"I'll be damned if what you just said means a damn thing."

"My bet's that you'll be damned whatever you do from here on out."

"Whoo-hee, hear this boy? I think you're the one gonna

be damned, but first you'll get slammed. It's only a wonder you ain't been done already."

"Who's talking? Are you talking?"

"Now easy, Red."

"What, easy? You heard the boy. You got anything else in your mouth need to come out? Besides teeth?"

"Maybe."

"Hold on now, cats. Back up five feet."

"I'm only coming here with a hustle. I don't need no shit."

"And all I'm saying is you're gonna end up with a room in the Tomb."

"And I'm saying you can go fuck yourself."

"Easy, easy. Back up now."

"I just don't need nobody telling me how to run my god-damn life. Especially some know-nothing, hanging-out, waitin-to-hear, tell-me-when-it's-clear scared Negro like this one."

"Red, we're all tight here."

"Then he don't have to give me that shit, no how. This is straight up, it's cool. I'm telling you, it's cool."

"I'm game Red. You done alright by me."

"If someone don't want in, that's no skin off my ass."

"Easy, man. He didn't mean nothing by it. Did you now?"

"Red, you know you're my brother, man."

"I wouldn't put you out if I didn't feel it was right. But there's money to be made."

"Off white folks that want to be black?"

"That's funny. You're a funny man. Off white folks that want to be black. Maybe there is, at that."

5.

The day and time are set to meet Bill in a coffeeshop on 116th street—neutral ground between black and white neighborhoods where laborers and students, upstanding citizens, soldiers and criminals, kids and housewives come near enough to eye each other in mostly fear but occasional longing, fed up with the life they lead and aching for change but also stuck with who they are—ah, but it's an old story.

So when Red arrives with Alvin—who's bought himself a dark red pork-pie hat and matching double-breasted suit on credit and dropped the railroad slave since seeing Red and all his Harlem hustles—when the two of them look to find Bill, Bill ain't there and it ain't as comfortable as one would've hoped. Alvin and Red don't want to have to go in and spend money, thinking this would be taken care of by the rich white man and too nervous to just go in and order coffee and wait, this too suspicious seeming. So they continue to walk around outside trying not to peer in through the large glass panes, knowing this too can attract attention, then, doubting whether they can see everything from outside, Red goes in to the counter and buys a pack of Sen-Sens and looks around discreetly. Might he be dressed different today? No. Bill ain't there. So after strolling block to block and passing casually by but not wanting to have to go in and buy something else, since it's obviously a bust and kids and the iceman with his big metal cart are starting to look at them funny, Red finally agrees to what Alvin's been saying all along and they head back uptown.

"Shit, I should've known better than to waste a whole afternoon," says Alvin, sliding back his hat and mopping his brow with a handkerchief.

Red is tight-lipped.

"You sure it weren't no ghost you seen, Red? All pale

like that and scaring away cops?"

"Shut the hell up, Alvin."

"Oooooh—ooooooh—I'm the ghost of Park Avenuuuuue—"

"Alvin—I'm gonna shut you up!"

He steps out in front of Alvin blocking his path, gets up close and puts a knife tip to his shirt belly.

Alvin doesn't flinch but continues in his best radio Boris Karloff:

"You can't harm the spirit of the eternal undeaaaad—"

Red turns from fierce threatening anger to bent-over laughter in a second—a change rapid enough to terrify even Alvin.

They resume walking.

"Ah, fuck," says Red. "Maybe he was a ghost. I thought it was the junk that made him look so shitty, but maybe it was because he was dead."

"That do tend to make a man look like shit. Being dead."

Later—in the pool hall—it ain't so easy to keep laughing. Word is that the railroad may be getting wise and it's time to shut that operation up for a bit.

The heat is suffocating—everyone's taken their jackets off and are sweating through their short sleeved shirts. And the boys ain't helping any. It's becoming a sport to piss him off.

"Man, Red, I was counting on some change in my pocket. I wouldn't've, but you were so all fired up and convinced about this that I believed you, man. And look what it got me."

If it's one man you might deck his ass and that's the end of it, but when there's four?—so Red just sulks and hears it, thinks and looks down at the sawdust floor. He can't even make his shots fall and he's losing money he ain't got.

"Whole lotta nothing. Got us drinking foam by the glass 'cause we can't afford the bottle."

"Can't even afford the beer. Just the foam."

"And that ofay, that ofaginzy—"

"Ofaginzy! Ouch, daddy!"

"—he's probably off his head in some China parlor somewhere. One of those big talker types. Probably didn't have shit."

"I never like to get in with no junkies, neither. Just plain unreliable. No junky is ever holding aces. They may say so, but if you get a look it's all twos and threes."

"Naw, it ain't just junkies. You gotta watch when you do anything with anyone. I don't usually mess with no one ain't got introductions."

"That's just common sense, that is."

Red realizes that too—it was pretty chuckleheaded and they're probably lucky nothing worse went down.

"Especially you don't get involved," says Alvin, who despite the heat is still sporting the pork-pie, "With fellas talking such crazy bullshit. White men who wanna be black—shit. You know, they sit out in the sun all day and they don't get dark, they get red. They'd have a better chance wanting to be Injuns."

Three of them start making with the war dance: "Woo woo woo woo woo woo woo woooo."

"Where are they? They must be out riding the range. If there's all these white boys wanna be black how come they ain't none of them here uptown?"

"I see white guys at Minton's sometimes."

"And sometimes cruising."

"That's it!" says Red. He takes his cue and wipes all the balls to one side.

"Aw, shit, Red. What you doing?"

"Shut the fuck up. I got it. I know how we can get some green."

"Oh, shit—Mr. Racial Cooperation's got another idea."

"I was about to get some green, if you'd've let me finish with this table."

"I'm through listening to his shit—ain't no way he's gonna get my hopes up again for a wheelbarrow full of empty."

"Garbage truck full of empty!" Alvin turns to Theo, who's got rings on both pinkies and who's made the joke, and extends his hand, palm up. The two move their arms forward as if to slap together, then slide the hands back from each other so only the fingertips touch.

"One time, just one time," says Theo. "Show me it ain't a whole ship full of empty."

"Okay, you lofarios."

"What'd you call us?"

"You just loaf around all day—you're a bunch of lofarios. But listen, I got it."

"Well, you can keep it."

"Yeah, and I hope it ain't catching."

Red pulls out a small piece of paper. "You know what I got on this card? Aw—just wait here."

He goes to a phone booth over in the corner by the bar. And while all the others have been teasing him, they don't have any better ideas and besides, they're all curious. Everyone wants to see what Red does next.

He dials a number, clearing his throat as he does and mumbling a few words in a deep tone of voice.

"What are you . . ."

Red flutters his fingers and shuts up the questioner lickety-split.

127

On the other end of the phone, the sister answers.

"Hello," says Red in mellifluous tones, a flat white accent, "Is Dick there?" (Hoping he isn't.)

"No, I'm sorry. Can I take a message?"

"Oh, that's too bad. Yes, my name's Jack. I met your brother and he told me I could find him at this number. It's about some business. He mentioned there might be another man living there I might be able to talk to?" (Hoping there isn't.)

"No, I'm sorry, I don't know who that would have been. My husband and I own this house and he's fighting in the Pacific and Dick, my brother, is the only other person who lives here. He'll be returning next week. Would you like to leave a message?"

"Thank you, ma'am, no. I'll try another time."

And hangs up before there's any chance he might say something to screw it up.

"There you go, Alvin," says Red emerging from the phone booth. He comes over to the bar where his friend is getting another round of drinks.

"What you laying down, Brown?"

"High cotton country crib with only a single hen left for watchdog."

The bartender is suddenly near to them, an old bald-pate with half-lens reading glasses. He folds up his newspaper and lays it down, taking up and filling the glasses. "Hard day to keep cool," he says. "Why don't one of you boys put some mints in your mouth and blow on me?" He sees some of what's shaping up. "Now don't you boys get into no trouble." Which he regrets as soon as he says it.

"Why don't you lay off dishing up corn bread and get us our drinks, mammy."

The older man looks down at the glasses he's filling. Still, he can't resist. "It's funny what you see, reading a paper," he says. "I only just stopped fanning myself with it for one second, and there you go."

Nobody says a thing.

"Yessir, you can be reading about goings on in France and Hitler being just about done for and then you turn the page and it's something right in your own back yard."

"What's that, Pops? Did you lose your doggie?"

"Naw, ain't got nothing to do with me. And the name is Mark."

"That's the first sensible thing you've said, Mark. Got nothing to do with you."

"Suit yourselves. I don't want to butt in where it ain't none of my business." He sets a couple of mugs up on the bar, suds rising up and sweating down the sides. "But didn't I hear you boys saying you supposed to meet a white fella who never showed up?"

Says Red to Alvin: "If that dog that's lost is a bloodhound, I think I found it. It's got big ears and a big nose."

Mark is undaunted. "He lived downtown, right?"

"What do you care?"

"He didn't show up, right?"

Red says to the others, "I'm gonna plant you boys now and dig you later." And looking back at the bartender, "I need to find a fillmill that's got better noise."

"Suit yourself," says Mark. "I was just thinking, though. Wouldn't it be a pip if this here was the fella?"

He reaches over for the newspaper and pushes it around to where Alvin and Red can see it.

HONOR SLAYING STUDENT INDICTED
CHARGED WITH SECOND DEGREE MURDER
Dead Man Made Lewd Suggestion

A Grand Jury in Manhattan yesterday returned a second degree murder indictment against Lucien Carr, a 19-year-old Columbia University student who is said to have confessed to the murder of David Kammerer, a former teacher, who, he said, made an indecent suggestion to him.

Carr surrendered to police last week. Police did not at first believe the mild-mannered youth's confession. Carr is a sophomore English major at Columbia.

Coast Guardsmen later recovered Kammerer's body in the Hudson, some distance from the spot where Carr had pushed it into the water.

The District Attorney also disclosed that William Seward Burroughs, 30, of 69 Bedford Street, and John Kerouac, 23, a seaman, had been arrested as material witnesses in the case. Burroughs was released upon posting $2500 bail.

Kerouac was released from Bronx County Prison briefly on Tuesday, long enough to marry Miss Edith Parker, 25, of Detroit.

"Bedford Street," says Red. "That's where this dude lived! I was at that apartment!"

"This is the same dude? The guy who was killed?"

"Shut up! No, the other one. What else does it say?"

Bizarre Behavior.

One of the strangest aspects of this case has been the bizarre behavior of the defendant, Carr, and the main material witness, Kerouac. At his arraignment last week, Carr appeared uninterested in the proceedings, reading from a book by poet W. B. Yeets. It was learned that when the District Attorney questioned Carr, he responded with liberal use of polysyllabic words and frequent philosophical musings.

"It's continued inside the paper."

"Polly-sy-labic! What the hell's that?"

"Is that all it says?"

"No. It's a long article. If you stop interrupting me, I can read it to you."

"Here, give that," says Red, pulling the paper away and looking for himself. "Shit, 69 Bedford! That's the place I was at!"

"Read it out loud, Red."

"Okay, hold on. Okay. 'It has been suggested that the true motives behind the case may lie in the deepest secrets of a dangerous in-tell-ect-ual fringe movement. As for Kerouac, when bail was set in court for him last week, he whistled.

"'Homo-sexual. The dead man, David Kam-mer-er, 33, of 48 Morton Street, was a homosexual. He had long followed Carr in the hopes of enga-ging the student in his per-ver-sion. Kammerer met Carr in St. Louis, where Carr was a student in a phy-si-cal ed-u-cation class taught by Kammerer.

Carr and Kammerer both hailed from pro-mi-nent families in the St. Louis area. Carr said that when he entered Columbia last year, Kammerer followed him to the city, os-ten-sib-ly intending to take grad-u-ate work at that institution. University officials said that Kammerer never actually ma-tric-u-lated, however. Kammerer's personality steadily de-te-ri-or-ated during his year in the city, until he was little more than a de-re-lict, barely keeping himself alive by his jan-it-orial work, according to Carr's story, which was corrob-o-rated in this respect yesterday by evidence uncovered by detectives who checked up on the history of the older man. Never-the-less, Carr continued his ac-qua-in-tance with Kammerer. On Monday morning between 3 and 4 A.M. the two were sitting on the grassy bank below Riverside Drive, at the foot of 115th Street, enjoying a breath of the cool morning air, according to Carr, when Kammerer once more made an offensive proposal.

"'Used Knife on Older Man.

"'Carr said he rejected it in-dig-nant-ly and a fight ensued. It was then that Carr, a slight youth, fearing he would get the worst in a struggle with the burly former phys-ical education instructor, pulled out a Boy Scout knife, a relic from his childhood, and plunged the blade twice in rapid suc-ces-sion into Kammerer's chest. The bigger man fell heavily to the ground. Not knowing if he was alive or dead, young Carr rolled the fallen man down the grassy em-bank-ment to the water's edge. There he took the laces from Kammerer's shoes and used them to tie his hands and feet. He took off Kammerer's shirt and tore it into strips and tied them around the body, and fastened Kammerer's belt about his arms. Working with frantic haste in the darkness, unaware of whether anyone had seen him, the college stu--dent gathered together as many small rocks and stones as he could quickly find and shoved them in Kammerer's pockets and inside his clothing. Then he pushed the body into the swift-flowing river. After he left the area he toyed with the notion of joining the Merchant Marine, Carr said, but fur-ther re-flection convinced him that this was not the wisest course. Unable to decide what to do, he awoke first Burroughs, then Ker-ou-ac, pleading for help. Kerouac spent most of the next day with Carr and watched him bury Kammerer's glasses in Morningside Park, pro-se-cu-tors said.'"

"Shit!"

"Was those the guys?"

"That was a fucked up crowd you almost had us mixed up with," says Theo. "Murderers and butt-fuckers!"

"Yeah, Red. You sure he wasn't just after a piece of your pretty black ass?"

"I got a knife on me, too. How'd you like me to shove it up your ass?"

"Hey, hey," says the bartender. "Be cool."

"Man, Red. Can you believe this shit? I guess we know why this guy didn't show up now."

"This is messed-up shit all right. I guess we're lucky we didn't get mixed up with this guy before all this went down."

"Ofays," says Alvin. "One crazy fucking bunch."

Red joins him in laughter, and then they're all laughing.

"They want to be black," says Red. "They got to get them some pussy first."

6.

They cruise past the house in a car they've borrowed from Alvin's uncle on the pretense they're helping a friend move—it's a big old Packard out of which the old man has done them the favor of removing the backseat to give them plenty of room for boxes and furniture—"I know moving ain't no fun going up and down them stairways—I hope at least they got elevators—"

"Nope, no elevators," said Red.

"That's a shame. But at least it'll be easier with that back seat outta there. There's plenty a room."

Plenty of room for whatever they can carry out of Dick Post's sister's Bronx house in the fifteen minutes they'll give themselves inside and they see it's a nice one—not as enormous as some but not as rickety as others—as they drive past, although in the dark they may have some trouble with the steep incline from street to house—it's built up from the road in a neighborhood of such houses that get out of the noise of passing traffic by elevation, though the lots are not big and the houses close together like a line of high-top boots. The heist isn't tonight—tonight they're cruising the neighborhood to try to detect potential dangers and maybe see if they can tell how often the cops come by, though the Bronx is pretty sleepy and you don't expect to find houses locked. Alvin is driving since Red doesn't know how, but Red's instincts are alerted and he knows they're in trouble and tells Alvin to pull over as he sees a police cruiser turn the corner ahead—smooth Red is out of the car and waving down the police before they can suspect to pull them over, which they surely would if they had the drop.

"You crazy?" whispers Alvin.

"Shut your clamshell," says Red. "I'll do the talking."

He walks across the street to where the cruiser has pulled up.

"'Scuse me, officer. I think we're loss."

This said to preempt the question, "What are you boys doing in this neighborhood?" which now goes unasked.

Red works his speech into innocent nervous frenzy: "My friend here said he knew the way but we kept a-turnin' and a-turnin and couldn't find anythin' we recognized after a while and then it got to be night and we're still driving around out here and can't no way seem to find our way home . . ."

"Take it easy, boy," says one of the officers. "Where is it you want to go?"

"We was looking for my friend's aunt's house. She only

live a mile or two away from us in Harlem."

"Harlem? You boys sure are lost. Didn't you notice that you took a bridge across the river."

"See?" yells Red back at Alvin. "I told you we should'n-t'a taken no bridge."

"I didn't know dat was really a bridge," says Alvin back, catching the game.

It has the desired effect. The officers look at each other. One says to the other: "He didn't know it was really a bridge."

After getting directions back over to Harlem, Alvin and Red get back in the car.

"Okay, drive," says Red. "I figure these guys come by every twenty minutes or so and it probably won't be safe to come back here for a week or so. But by then they will have long forgotten about us and we should be okay."

The night of the heist goes smoothly. In the car, while Alvin and his brother King take off their shoes, Red unscrews a small glass vial and takes a snort up each nostril, then offers it to the others. Not a thing can go wrong, he's the slickest second story man in history—wheeee!—the coke has him bouncing up and down in his seat and punching his hand. OK, calm down. "Let's go," says Red, the leader.

It's nothing to slip in through the window and pretty much get the run of the house while Alvin circles the block for the ten minutes they're inside. The lonely sister living there—*the old bitch, we should wake her up, she probably wants it*—never stirs as they tiptoe room to room opening drawers and quickly calculating what's most valuable. They're out in ten minutes with all they can carry and, throwing it in the car, are gone. Cash, jewelry, an oriental silk rug, for which they get less than it's worth but, fuck, it's found money, right?

Alvin says to Red:

"OK, Daddy-O. Lesson number one. You don't steal *with* ofays. You take it *from* them. Got it?" He's still ringing with the coke. "They got it all anyway, so what they care?"

Soon, of a summer evening, Red is able to relax, to take a few hits off a reefer and stroll through Harlem without cares—attracting the attention of the young ladies with a new fedora he angles down over his eyes to where he must raise his head slightly to peer out beyond the block he's walking. And when he does—ooooh—it chills and delights the young ladies and puts them in mind of the same cool blue eyes of Frankie Sinatra. Red pays no mind—has it made in the shade of a glade—is a sudden glacier gliding down a sweltering summer block.

The last of the day's commerce is ending. The junk man leads his weary horse out of the neighborhood pulling a piled-high cart of metal, glass, and rags. Tank-like garbage trucks have clattered home on their solid tires, inching away on their chain-driving axles. The hurdy-gurdy man too is calling it a day; his monkey is no longer hopping to each passerby to beg for change but leaning quietly against the brick facing of a warehouse like an old philosopher. Mothers put their milk bottles out in the metal canisters to be picked up tomorrow and refilled. They sit on their stoops and watch the street sweepers in their chocolate uniforms and square-topped caps stow broom and shovel away and depart wheeling their hand-truck barrels of refuse. Residents are coming from their jobs or have already seen their washed-down porches dry in the late afternoon heat. Some have pulled out lawnchairs to ease into evening on the sidewalks. The only noise is voices: the cries of the children over whom they watch, the call and response of the preachers and flimflam men on busier corners.

Monk, Klook, & Christian bring the bop at Minton's—
taking tunes apart & put back together in ways that
don't fit but do, ping & pang & dink & doodle
in the right wrong places & Klook's with him on skins
out of control
till a new control prevails like a spinning wheel doesn't
seem
to be spinning at all, then seems to be spinning slowly
backwards, a different way of movement—
& sometimes Red hops a subway down to Union
Square—
an evening when families with young daughters go walk-
ing round, & the sidewalk speakers climb up
on milkcrates & crowds gather round to listen to the
true word laid down, hustlers just like him—
he likes the sound of their rapping in the night—
the twists and turns of their crazed words, worlds both
false and true but which no one comes forward to name
except these eveningsaints of the mind, another kind
of jazz & another kind of truth—
so strong it seems like a lie but instead tells the lies in all
the truths you assume, & the two flutter off,
end over end, above the skyscraper points,
Red's own mind unhinging in the deepening blue sky
dotted with orange and yellow electric lights . . .

The old men speak about history—a history they don't
teach you in the schools. The white man ain't so foolish and
the black man . . . well—the black man is too scared.

But it remains. Truth is truth and it don't go away

because no one's talking about it right that minute. Truth waits around for another to pick it up and speak it again.

Without this truth brothers and sisters you are blind to the real world, the actual workings of the world you inhabit blindly.

You are blind to your own lives. You are blind to the way you are forced to live. You are blind in the ways you spend your money. You are blind to the forces that keep you from earning a living wage. You are blind to where what little money you have goes once it leaves your hand. Then you get fed up and you hand your money to the man that sells you a glass of foam or the man that sells you a stick of tea. And that's the worst place to spend your money. Because behind the foam and the tea is the man that owns all the foam and tea and now he's got more of your money. He also owns your miserable tenement building and the factories and the profits on war industry and everything else you need just to live from day to day—your food, your clothes, your kids' shabby toys. That means he owns you. He don't put his brand on you or lay his whip across your back like in slavery times but he owns you all the same.

I am no different from any of you. I am owned and my family before me was owned. I've been treated miserably. My mother was treated like a burden on the world though she raised seven children and never stopped working. My father was killed. Six of his seven brothers died by violence. My ancestors were enslaved and beaten and tortured and raped and killed—my own mother was the child of a rape and then was raped herself as were we all by the white man's so-called "assistance."

But long long ago—long before a time we remember names of individual people—members of my long ago family lay in the close and fetid cargo holds of ships with only stinking air to breathe while they dirtied and vomited on themselves and listened to others crying and cried themselves or steeled themselves to keep from crying and began to smell death as the smell of sickness next to them became something incurable and festered and rotted and became stink so powerful it was killing to many to just breathe it in—and many surely must have died purely from the horror and hopelessness and circumstance of such things who had no illness themselves—

But whatever happened upon that long ago ship my family member lived and passed down and down and down and finally came to me—

I feel that presence—that refusal to die.

History. Do you ever think about history brothers and sisters? I find myself thinking of it more and more. I look down a street like this one and see not what is today but what it has been. History. The streets are paved no more once the vision comes upon me. No automobiles or electric lights but lanterns and muddy paths and signs with arrows pointing to the auction grounds. We know who was auctioned there. Trees standing where there are concrete buildings now and if you look closely you can see the bark worn off in a rough circle round a limb perpendicular to the ground. We know what act burdened the tree and what vain striving etched its mark on the skin. I see men in fine ruffles and three-cornered hats and powdered wigs. We know who it was did the work for these men to keep them in such daily finery. I see children growing up without pants or shoes, with only coarse sacks with holes cut out of them for head and arms, and we know who these children later grew up to be. They grew up to be our own families and to never know freedom their whole lives except to wish for it for those who came after.

I see this history, brothers and sisters, see this as clearly as I see any one of you. As clearly as you see me.

I may not know the whole of this history, but it is written in books. Now you may say how can the real history be written in books—weren't these the white men's books, in which they wrote only the history they wanted to be known? And I say back to you, yes, that is true. Yet one cannot write without writing the truth.

By the way a man speaks, so shall you know him. By the words that he authors, so shall his truth be spoken. To the unskilled eye, none appears but the lies and deceptions he wants us to fall prey to.

But look closely at the words, the words upon which the whole edifice of his untruths are built. Beneath, if you look closely, there is truth to be seen, an encrypted code to be deciphered which yields all. Because there is no hiding the truth with words from someone who knows—knows truly—how to read.

I cannot say I have completely mastered this ability myself. Indeed, brothers and sisters, I come before you tonight as a man who has not of yet decoded a single truth. The lamp outside flickers and little light reaches through to my cell. I have trouble making out the type. I rest on aching elbows and my leaning against the bars, which cast shadows across the pages. These pages are brittle and crumble at the touch. I have not yet learned how they are to be coaxed one from the next without disintegrating in my fingers. I have not yet learned to adjust to the poor light to tell where to be careful and where I may allow myself freedom to move unfettered. My eyes blur and water and strain. But the connections between hand and eye and impulse and motive and brain—these are sure. Once moving forward, there is no truth that will be denied me.

But where are we to find the time to read? And not only to read but to gain practice at reading so as to decode, to see the truth through the lie? I have my children to take care of. I have my job at which to toil and without toil there is no living. It breaks my back and it's all I can do at the end of the day to take down a chair to sit on the sidewalk. My feet are aching from these bad shoes and my legs and hipsockets from all day on my feet. From where are the moments of silent contemplation to come if this is a necessity of truth-seeking? If I had any extra time, I'd be using it to try and make more money for my family. Goodness knows, we could use more comfort, more security.

Yes, I hear you brothers and sisters. And you are right, there is no standing still in this world of ours. But I will never be a man who tells you to stand still. If you are to know truth, you must act in the world as well as observing it. If you are to know truth, you must learn to read while walking, while running, while jumping. We are not a people who can afford to sit—it is not our lot in history. If you sit down to read in the middle of the street, you will be run down by the trolley car. If you pause while running from the man bent on catching you, you will be caught and see the rope. No, brothers and sisters, I will never be a man who tells you to stand still.

Instead, I am a man who will tell you this: there are three possessions you must have if you are ever to improve yourself, if we as a people are ever to improve ourselves. You must have a book, and keep one hand free to hold it. You must also have a gun to protect yourself, and keep the other hand free to grab it when it's needed. And you must keep good shoes on your feet in order to keep moving.

Then, stride ahead in your good shoes. It will be awkward at first. Difficult, brothers and sisters—I will not say the work will be easy. It will take diligence and labor. But in time the wind you create in the moving speed of your stride will turn the pages at the exact rate you need to understand the words printed upon them.

America, you are the end of three months of man. For the third, which began when your head was turned, already has changed you, you nation of Finks. Let you rule the world. You are a dead hand. Man, in his courses, is on the other side: Capricorn is drawing the threads.

Charles Olson, "Across Space and Time"

DETROIT BLUES

1.

Jack walks into a Detroit blues bar.

The blaring steel sounds of factories are recreated with electric guitar and bass, harmonica, and loud thumping drums in the new blues music of Detroit and Chicago. Jack hears it before he goes in, but upon opening the door, it hits him full in the face, loud to the point of pain. Straight back through the crowd, he sees the band onstage. The man in the center, at the microphone, has a guitar slung over his shoulder and is making it scream, choking up the strings with a short beer glass. Three successive times, four, he slices down the fretboard to make sounds like the keening of a high-speed router smoothing in a spray of sparks the rough edge of metal fuselage for a bomber soon to be shipped out. Jack's eyes not yet having adjusted, the bar is dark except for this figure, spotlighted. The chrome on a harmonica, the white band on the man's black derby hat, the shine off his axe—these cry out in tandem with the music. Noise.

The sound breaks and the man takes the microphone in his hand to sing verses.

Jack is drunk.

Lemme tell you the story
How Jack got a wife
He watched Lu Carr
Ditch his killing knife
He woulda got out
But couldn't make bail
So he stayed locked up
In Bronx County jail

I said he stayed locked up
In Bronx County jail

A blast of noise again fills the air, the music now a repet-
itive, insistent four blues notes, up in the scale then down, in
call and response with bass drum, played again and again
after each utterance—

He called up his papa
With a tale of woe
But the daddy said "Son,
I'm far too po'—
You're a big boy now,
You gotta take your blame
You put a black mark
On our family name
I said you put a black mark
On our family name"

Jack shakes his head to clear it—it must be the booze,
the sudden assault of this music on his senses—or does he
hear what he thinks he hears? Is this music directed at him,
telling his story?

Gangsters and killers
Slept right next door
Jack just couldn't take it
One night more
A cell was his home now
A cell was his world
And the only way out
Was to marry the girl
Yes the only way out

Was to marry the girl
So they set with the lawyer
And the judge got it done
The money was sent
And the man got sprung
They moved to her mama's
In the cozy 'burbs
Jack couldn't stay there
'Cause it made him disturbed
No he couldn't stay there
It made him disturbed

Jack doesn't want to go home. He doesn't want to wake up tomorrow and have to do the same dreary thing over again. His only solace is in thoughts of escape, in reading, like a man still in jail. The music becomes the thudding in his chest. Blood, energy.

For a while he was crazy
For a while he was mad
He made his girl sick now
He made his girl sad
But he had to get out
He was gonna explode
Get back out to sea, yeah
Get out on the road
Get back out to sea, Lord
Get out on the road

Go and catch a falling star, thinks Jack. *Tell me where all the past years are.*

2.

Jack and Frankie Edith Parker Kerouac began married life living with Edie's mother in Grosse Pointe Park, Michigan, in September 1944. A month later, Jack left. Grosse Pointe—in the 1940s, as it is today—was Detroit's most exclusive suburb.

One of the worst race riots in American history took place in Detroit, in June, 1943.

The war was in its second full year. Retooled automotive factories made Detroit the nation's leading manufacturer of war materials. Nearly a million people migrated from the south to the northern industrial cities.

In 1942, 1200 whites demonstrated and burned a cross outside the Sojourner Truth projects in Detroit, a Federal housing development for black war industry workers. As southern black families arrived in trucks full of furniture and belongings they were attacked by the white picketers— Klansmen side by side with Polish Catholics wielding knives, clubs, rifles, shotguns, lead pipes, and stones. Thirty-eight people—thirty-three black—were taken to hospitals. Of the 104 persons arrested by police, only three were white. The housing project was postponed indefinitely.

In Los Angeles, in '43, Mexican teens wearing zoot suits were identified by the newspapers as hoodlums and at least one newspaper urged white servicemen to take justice into their own hands while on leave. Soon, vigilante gangs roamed the streets beating anyone in a zoot. Los Angeles was declared off limits to servicemen and the wearing of zoot suits was declared a misdemeanor.

That same year, on a hot night in Beaumont, Texas, white gangs raged, pulling black folks from out of their houses to beat.

It was a trend fast on its way to becoming a national epidemic. Franklin wondered aloud to his aides, *Should I make a statement about all this racial violence?* The president was physically weak, more ill than he wanted the country or the enemy to know. Part of the job of his advisors was to shield him from distractions. Besides morale, he had other reasons to fear making race an issue, needing the support of southern congressmen, who didn't want the war be used as an excuse for integration, which at the time they called *subversion*. Southerners held war bills for ransom. Thus, all the armed forces were segregated: Jim Crow moved from south to north and then from the US to England, which created separate facilities for white and black soldiers for fear of offending Americans overseas.

On American bases, the majority of which were in the south, no black officer could be promoted to commander, whatever his rank.

Sixty members of the 94th Engineer Battalion were marching along a highway near Camp Robinson, Arkansas, around this time when they were forced by white state troopers to finish their exercise in a water-filled ditch out of view of motorists. A post commander from Tennessee issued a bulletin declaring any white officer with the rank of first lieutenant superior to any black captain. At a base in Arizona no African-American officer was permitted to swim in the officer's pool. Members of the 92nd Division, a black rifle company, had rifles, but were not issued live ammunition until the enemy was in sight and the company being fired upon.

In Durham, North Carolina, a bus driver ordered a black soldier to move to the back of the bus and when he didn't, shot and killed him. He was acquitted by a jury that deliberated twenty-seven minutes. In New Orleans, police beat up a black draftee, Herman Lee, because he stepped out of line to say goodbye to his mother.

In Little Rock, a black soldier in the Negro section of the city was accused of being drunk. White policemen began to beat him up. A black sergeant, Thomas Foster, asked the police to turn him over to the MPs, who had jurisdiction over soldiers. White MPs turned their attack on Foster. He died later that night.

In Jackson, civilian police threatened to kill several officers, black soldiers were not allowed to walk in town, and an army lieutenant was reprimanded for making the statement, "all Negroes need to be beaten to death."

Should I make a statement about all this racial violence?

The Detroit riot was triggered by an auto accident involving a white and a black motorist on the Belle Isle Bridge, which turned into a fistfight. The rioting that ensued went on all that day and into the next. "I was waiting for a bus with a group of Negroes," said a black witness. "It was 8:30 am and we were going to work. Suddenly several squad cars pulled up and began throwing tear-gas bombs and shooting at men and women as they began to run. We hadn't been doing anything, and that's the God's honest truth." According to the Detroit Police Department's own report, fifteen of the twenty four African-Americans killed were shot by police. None of the seven whites who died were killed by police.

FDR never made a statement about racial violence in the US in this period, probably because he deemed such acknowledgment too much of a danger to national security. In 1942, again in the interests of national security, he signed Executive Order 9066, which relocated Japanese-Americans, approximately 70,000 of whom were American citizens— into detention camps.

The internments occurred in an environment of extreme

anti-Japanese feeling following the attack on Pearl Harbor the year before. Many American citizens of Japanese descent had their land, houses, and businesses repossessed as a result of their relocation.

Historians have long observed that the racist hysteria in the Pacific states that led to Japanese-American internments was accelerated by rival farmers and white produce collectives who stood to benefit by their competitors being forced out of business.

Relocation of Asian-Americans was profitable for them in much the same way lynching was frequently profitable for white property owners in the south.

3.

Photograph, early August, 1944. Lucien and Jack are just about to go to sea on their planned trip to France. Each has one leg up on the lip of a fountain on the campus of Columbia University. Lucien has a cigarette dangling from the corner of his mouth, his shirtsleeves rolled up, his eyes narrowed against the sun but also projecting self-assurance, dismissiveness, as if saying, "What can you tell me I don't already know?" It's a retrospective joke on the subject, as the viewer can now answer: "I know that within 48 hours you'll have killed a man and destroyed your future." After four years in jail, the next pictures we see of him show a man with a mustache, facial lines, and nothing like the earlier bravado.

In his t-shirt, Jack is athletic; he's fashionably déclassé, but one wonders if he wears the white pullover because of a lack of money for good dress shirts. He's more open, less posed; his cigarette is in his hand, his hand on his hip, like a laborer stopped for a moment in the middle of a job. The muscles of his arms and chest reinforce the blue-collar effect. From recordings, we hear that Kerouac never adopted the refined accents of the Ivy League kids he was meeting at this time. It's always "yeah" with him instead of "yes." With one of the hallowed halls of the University in the background, the picture could easily be of a sophisticate relaxing, out and about, taking in the sights with a poorer relation, even a favored servant.

The photographer was Edie Parker.

It's funny—a few weeks ago I thought I might not even see Jack again and I wasted a whole roll of film on pictures of him and Lucien. Then they didn't sail off after all. I called them a couple of bastards and they just laughed these shiteating grins. And now all that's happened—and we're married! Not that I feel really married. We've talked about it, Jack and I. It's so bourgeois, it's so much what everybody expects you to do. But it's kind of nice, too. Romantic. It's just all happened so fast, whisking out of New York and coming back to Grosse Pointe—that I'm not thrilled about. It'll give us a chance to save some money, I guess. That's one thing that New York wasn't made for, saving money. Here, you never have to spend money. Everybody we know has fully stocked bars, even beer on tap in their basements. They've never really adjusted back over since prohibition—at least that's the story. No one ever goes out expecting to spend money. That's something about Grosse Pointers—they own everything, yet no one's ever got a cent on them.

I'm going to get back to New York one of these days, though, and open my own hat shoppe, selling my own designs. My sketches got a lot of compliments from the art profs at Columbia. I love felt. I can sit and brush felt all day, and when you do it gets softer and thicker until it becomes lighter than skin. I love the mysteriousness of lace net falling from a gray velvet toque with a light spray of sequins at the crest. It's a sophisticated look, a city look. I've also got a whole array of colors: lime, cherry, royal blue, kelly green, champagne. These are the styles I'm most in love with. It wouldn't be that hard to break in—everybody comes to New York for fashion, and I have some contacts. After the war, people will want to dress up and will have more money to do it. And they're saying now that it'll probably be over in less than a year. I've got a good fashion sense—that'll serve me well in New York.

That is, if being back here in Michigan doesn't kill it dead!

It's not so much that it's boring here, it's also just SO CONVENTIONAL. I can't believe sometimes that I grew up here. I'm such a completely different person than who I was when I lived here. Mother doesn't realize it yet; she still talks to me as if I'm the same girl. Luckily, she's so involved with her causes that she never really looks too closely. Things just don't quite get through. She doesn't want to see who I really am. If my mother had been able to see how we were living in New York—people at all hours, sleeping on the couch or the floor, wherever, the door open to everyone, or staying up all night talking and having parties, not to mention the grass! But then again, even if she were to see it, it probably wouldn't register with her.

I think you could have an elephant standing in her living room and she'd walk right past it until it started doing its yelling thing with its nose and maybe getting up on its back legs and hitting its head on the ceiling. Then she might notice it. Maybe.

New York was just so packed with people. Detroit is crowded these days, but just about everybody's working. In New York, people worked too. God knows I did, in clubs and the dock warehouses. But there were so many people always coming into town or leaving for the war. Every day, getting to know interesting people who then leave and you listen to their whole life's story before they go, all their hopes and dreams, because they don't know if they're coming back. With some guys it's a line, but most of them are really scared, and far away from home already, and everybody is scared and excited all at the same time, and every night practically is an all-out, end-of-the-world bash. In Detroit, in contrast, everybody's glum. They go out to get away from working. There's no energy. That's what I miss about New York—constant energy! And I know Jack misses it, too.

What fun the apartment on 118th Street was—any moment a party could start. One afternoon we were just sitting around and John Kingsland comes by looking for Jane. He's still trying to steal her away from Bill, even though Jane's gaga over Bill, them both being so weird they just hit it off. Then Lucien and Celia come by. Then Jack Fitzgerald, maybe bringing back some book he borrowed off of Jack. Then Charlotte, my sister, just happening to be visiting that day. Then Jerry Newman with a boxful of jazz records, because Jack told him to bring them by some time. Before you know it, everyone we know is just "stopping by," and the room is just filled with people, at first completely unplanned then after awhile coming because they've heard something's going on. It's not like a party was a rare event on 118th Street.

"What kind of party should this be?" someone yells out.

Lucien leaps up on a chair, puts one hand on his chest and raises the other arm in the air like an old time actor and pronounces in a hokey British accent:

"Let's make it an artichoke party!"

So the icebox gets raided: poems taped up on the icebox

door go swinging in the air and falling on the ground as several people poke their heads in to see what's available. Allen nervously reaches between people onto the floor to rescue a masterpiece that's dropped. Half the others are flying this way and that and out the door. The rest can't be bothered. Jerry takes out some "hootch" and starts rolling joints and playing records from his "Hall of Fame." He's got it printed on the side of the wooden box with all his records that he's lugged up to our third-floor rooms: JAZZ HALL OF FAME. He's invented this Jazz Hall of Fame idea, which is of course just something he made up but which he acts like is a real thing: "Count Basie was just inducted," he'll say with a straight face. He spins a record, then goes back to rolling, only the dope cigarettes keep falling apart because right in the middle he'll jump up and say, "Dizzy Gillespie is God," or "Charlie Parker is God," or "Coleman Hawkins is God." "Which one is God?" I ask him. "Are we talking pantheism?" That was funny, he didn't realize he'd said it about every one of them. Meanwhile, Jane starts a big pot of water boiling on the stove, grumbling the whole time about having to look after "children" and somehow or other we all end up eating artichokes, baskets of artichokes, dipping them in cold mayonnaise and sour cream, and by the end of the night there's artichoke leaves everywhere you look, all over the tops of tables, like fall has arrived on top of the summer picnic tables and it's time to rake up the leaves.

Now, in Michigan, Jack mopes around here too, looking like I feel. Who wouldn't miss New York? But I get the feeling it's also because he's never really lived in a place like this. He respects my mother, but you can tell he thinks he doesn't know how to act here in this neighborhood. Swanky, was the word he used the other day, with his Bogart voice: *Yeah, dese are some shwanky digs ya got here, kid.* When he jokes about it it's OK, but he's quiet a lot of the time and I don't know what he's thinking. But it's not like he has it all that hard, really. All he does is sleep all the time. He's actually got it pretty easy. His job at Fruehoff's Trailer Factory—if you can call it that—is to go in at eleven and check the counts on the ball-bearing counters at regular intervals until seven in the morning. That and some sweeping up. Keeping track of things, being there in case anything goes wrong, though what he's supposed to do if something does go wrong is anybody's guess. As far as I know, that's the extent of it. So he just brings a book with him or his endless yellow pads and reads and takes notes and writes. Rough life! With a job as easy as that, you'd think it was his father that got it for him instead of mine.

Me, I get an assembly line job at Chrysler.

There may be more women working now with the war, but I hate it when I hear that the jobs women do in these plants aren't real jobs! Like hell! I was running a forklift for Liberty Ships when we were in New York—and by the way I'd like to see one of these guys do what I had to do each night as a cigarette girl. Where are the get-paid-for-doing-nothing jobs for women? That would be real equality!

But Jack, he's another grumbler. You'd think they had him individually polishing all the ball bearings himself the way he complains. You'd think they had him on a chain gang.

Ha! Jack on a chain gang!

"My parents don't own any factories," he says to me one morning as he's getting in and I'm about to go to work.

"Well, it's not a particular source of pride that mine do, but you have to admit it's helping us out now." I can't keep track of what-all my mother is involved in these days, particularly since the divorce, but we used to have a couple shipyards, hotels, and a couple factories, textiles and shoes.

"My mother works in a shoe factory, your mother owns one."

Grumble, grumble.

I think one side of Jack has always wanted to live in this kind of life. We have a rule in our house that every evening at seven we have a sit down formal dinner. Lace tablecloth, candles, full china service—it used to be we'd have a server, too, but since the divorce my mother only has Rita, the cleaning woman, come in twice a week. No matter what else we're all doing, dinner is at seven—that way we get a chance to see and visit one another "as a family," as Mother likes to say. It's been that way in my family as long as I can remember. Jack likes that. I explained it to him the first day we were here, so beforehand, he went upstairs and showered and shaved and came down neatly dressed for our meal; no tie, but an ironed white shirt and clean pants, very respectable. He really wanted to impress my mother.

At the same time, in the apartment Mother's living in since the divorce, there's only one bathroom, and Jack has chosen this as the only place in the house quiet enough for his reading. So all day long, Jack's in the bathroom.

Mother doesn't know what to make of him. Gramma reported to mother that he was a nice boy, but a sailor, irresponsible, you know, the usual stuff they say, girl in every port. Gram's been a real sport. I know she worries about me. I used to think some of the same things a couple years ago, before I really knew him. I wish Jack was able to let others see what I've seen in him. He has a beautiful soul. But now he's just being weird.

"So I guess you're really looking to make a go of the writing game," she says to Jack at dinner. "I didn't realize you were so serious about it until you arrived here and your industry with books showed me otherwise."

"Industry," says Jack, but his mouth is full. He finishes chewing, swallows. "That's an interesting way of putting it, ma'am."

"Well, I suppose writing is ultimately like any other kind of business," says Mother. "You have to work at it in order to become successful. But there have been a good many writers I suppose that have made that hard work pay off. Pearl S. Buck has certainly done very well, and my friends at the club have told me that Harriet van Arness of Pinckney has made quite a renown for herself."

"I'm sorry, Mrs. Parker. I'm not familiar with her."

"Oh, please, call me Isabel. Harriet van Arness is said to be excellent at bringing the area to life. We have a farm in Pinckney, you know, right near Henry Ford's farm. It's a beautiful area full of creeks and wildflowers. Frankie, you should make up a picnic basket and take John there and show it to him while we still have nice weather."

"We were planning to go next weekend."

"Excellent. It will be lovely. I can loan you one of her novels so you can see for yourself. She describes the countryside quite naturally."

"Well, I'm kind of in the middle of several things right now," says Jack. He's always nervous someone's going to tell him what to do and forgets he should just play along.

"It's very nice of you to offer, though, Mother."

"Yes, Mrs. Parker, thank you very much. For everything. I'm rather embarrassed that it's come to this, and I just hope I can do something to make you feel this hasn't all been a big catastrophe. I mean, allowing us to stay here. I will make it up to you, I promise."

"Oh, you are quite welcome, John. Newlyweds often need help when they're starting out and there's no shame in it at all. We've enjoyed having a man around the house. Haven't we, Lottie?"

Charlotte loves Jack. She would always look forward to Jack's visits when we were staying with Gramma, telling me what to wear and making a pumpkin pie, Jack's favorite. "No," she says. "Jack's company doesn't interest me at all."

Everybody laughs.

"It's not impossible to make a good living as a novelist," Mother repeats, as if she's turning a doubtful proposal over again in her mind.

"I just need more to write about," says Jack. "I'm going to get into the Merchant Marine this fall and see the world. A writer needs to live more than most people when he's young, so he'll have stories to tell. He needs to observe different people in different places, see the real world and not just take it second hand."

"Money doesn't always have to be the issue, Mother," I put in.

"Well, it doesn't hurt for a young couple to give it some consideration, though."

"I couldn't agree more, Mrs. Parker," says Jack.

Actually, Jack couldn't agree less. Jack fancies himself a rebel, but in certain ways, he's very respectful of authority. It's funny listening to them talk, because neither one hears what the other one is saying. It's typical of Mother to miss his comment about going to sea went right by her. But Mother's got her mind on certain things these days, like her letters to the editor. You'd think that living in a place like Grosse Pointe these days you'd shy away from drawing attention to yourself. But Mother has declared herself the moral conscience of southeastern Michigan. She's got her clubs and boards and she likes people to know her opinion of things. My father's more the playboy-type, and doesn't care much one way or the other. I think I inherited more of my personality from him. On the other hand, Mother's the old, New England, always-knows-what's-best-for-everybody type.

The first Sunday after we arrived, Mother went to church and Charlotte decided to go with her, so Jack and I were in the house alone for just about the first time since we got here. One or the other of us is almost always working on this new schedule. So I made bacon and eggs and Jack had the Sunday paper spread out all over the floor when he comes upon my mother's letter. He looks up at me as I come in with our breakfast plates he looks up at me with this wounded, vacant expression, like someone's done something terrible to him. Then he lets fly a flurry of words:

"I started reading this letter and it was your typical conservative, let's-keep-everything-the-way-it-is, there's-no-misery-in-the-world, Sunday school, whitebread, knee-bending marching orders—and then I see at the bottom it's signed by your mother."

"Well, that's the way she is, Jack."

"Listen to this—'In the act of defending our way of life against overseas enemies, we may be putting our way of life here at home in jeopardy.'" He switches to the deep radio voice of The Shadow, putting a crooked elbow up in front of his face: "And who might we ask is behind this sinister treachery, these myriad internal threats to all that is good and holy? The Shadow knows . . . hoo hoo hoo ha ha ha haaaaaaa.

"Baby," he says, picking his normal voice back up, "Your mother is off on a boat in the middle of a lake on this one. Listen to her: 'We have only gotten to where we are through belief in the purity of America. The War has demanded great sacrifices of us all, but let's not sacrifice who and what we are as Americans.'

"I wonder how it is that your mother knows so well the real soul of America."

As I put our plate on the dining room table, Jack's sitting Indian-style on the living room floor in a spread of newspaper, pulling distractedly at the cuffs of his Army surplus pants. But this only costs him a few seconds away from his meal. As the food aroma begins to take hold, he tosses the paper with the offending letter back into the mess and takes the seat at the head of the table for three eggs sunny-side up, four slices of smoked bacon, and triangle buttered toasts, the way he likes them.

One thing Mother's right about, the way to a man's heart is through his stomach.

"This is a pretty sheltered neighborhood," says Jack between mouthfuls. "I guess I didn't realize it so much until this week. Everything is so perfect here—lawns cut, walks immaculate, people dressed perfectly—everything mani-cured. It's like a morgue full of embalmed bodies."

The gruesomeness of this picture doesn't hurt Jack's appetite. He wolfs down the food like he's just gotten off a starvation diet, then stares idly into space, tapping his ring on the kitchen table; it's his unconscious way of saying to me he doesn't want to be here, that we shouldn't have been so quick to get married. Like it's my doing!

"You can't blame me for this," I say.

"What? Why are you starting? Did I say anything?"

"You didn't have to. I know what you're thinking."

"So I get blamed for what I'm thinking? How am I to control what I'm thinking? I wasn't thinking that at all."

I come to the table and sit beside him and touch his hand. My hands are getting to be like an old woman's with washing dishes and working at the plant. They're all dry and scaly. I hate looking at them. Everything has happened too quickly, after too long a wait. If it could have just happened in its own way, as it would have, it would have been so much better. We had talked of getting married a hundred times and we both knew that if it was going to work it would have to just happen. But there were right times that it could have and didn't. Not that I don't think the moment wouldn't have eventually come—I'm sure it would have. But now the right thing has happened in the wrong way and we're in the wrong place and for the wrong reasons. It makes me want to scream! But I push it back down—I don't want to ruin the one morning we have alone together.

"I'm sorry," I say. "What were you thinking of then?"

"Oh, just something that Allen and I were talking about a couple weeks ago. I'm trying to get back to before all this happened, to what I was thinking of, to my novel."

"It's not all bad, what's happened."

"No, not at all. But I took so much for granted in New York, that there would always be someone to bounce my ideas off of."

"Well, you know I'm interested in your work."

"I know." With a sigh.

"We don't really talk about books anymore. What are you reading right now?"

"*Notes from the Underground.* By Dostoievsky."

"I know who it's by."

"It's a work of genius."

"Why?" I ask as a leading question.

"Why? Why?" He's stuck for a second. "It's just amazing! The narrator is a man completely outside, or underneath, normal society. Totally estranged. But that's what makes it so real. There's not a false word in it. No concessions to the expectations of society or to the false conventions of literature. That's what the New Vision has to do, that's what Allen and I were discussing—we have to get down deep into ourselves, into that part of us that's untouched by the outside world, the eternal limitless irrational fire of the soul down beneath false rationality. There's a lot that's similar to what Spengler is saying, and Nietzsche for that matter, that the truths that society wishes to promote are in fact the greatest lies. Like—" he starts to say, then trails off.

"Like what?"

"Promise you won't get mad at me for saying this."

"Of course I won't. I want to help you as a writer."

"Well, it's sort of like what happened with us. If we could have gotten some money to get me out of jail without having to get married, we would have. And we could have kept going the way we were going. We were living in the underground. Subterraneans, was Allen's word. But the society tells us, 'No, if you want this, you have to give us that'— something in the society's interests, to make you conform, to bring you into the fold."

We saw Allen just before we left, a final get together uptown, with him and Celia there. Allen made a joke that he was worried about the way we got married. He said he thought we were great together and wasn't worried about us, exactly. "But you know why they got married?" he said to Celia. "The state made them. I'm worried they'll be fascists inside a year."

"Just because we got married doesn't mean we're going to change, you and me. I'm still the same girl. Eventually, we'll get on our feet and go back to New York if that's what you want. Or we can have a marriage where we live apart sometimes and get back together because we want to be together. That way you can travel and get material for your books. We won't be here forever."

"It's not just New York. I wonder if we'll ever get back. Like Thomas Wolfe, *You Can't Go Home Again.*"

"You mean us?"

"No," says Jack, "I'm not worried about us. But I am" he pauses—"suspicious."

I move over to him and he pushes his chair back from the table. I sit on his lap.

"What time do you think they'll get back from church?" asks Jack.

"Oh, there's still an hour or so."

"The maid isn't coming in today?"

"Nope."

I start to run my fingers through the hair by his ear and feel him start to get hard. He squeezes my breast and the feeling runs through me like hot water. He reaches for the dishes, puts the coffee cup and juice glass on the breakfast plate and leans down and slides them under the table, very neatly. Then he lifts me up onto it. Suddenly his face shows panic and he pivots toward the front window.

"Do you think someone will see?"

"Who cares? Besides, married people fuck even in Michigan."

"I hope the table can take this."

"If we break it, my mother can just put it on your bill."

The table won't break—it's an old oak table that's been in the Parker family for years. There really isn't much danger of being seen, either, or else I'd take him to our bedroom. The picture window in front is covered by two evergreen pines, one on each side. I remember, looking out this way, how we used to decorate the big spruce in our yard every Christmas when I was girl growing up where we used to live, only about a mile from here. We'd put lights all over it and the house, then hope the snow didn't turn to rain, which would make the strings short out. It was smaller than a regular indoor tree then, but now I bet it's over twenty feet high. Besides, I like the danger—it's like when we were first dating and used to meet at the Jersey shore at Gramma's and do it in the living room while she was sleeping. We also did it once on the deck of Dad's yacht while everybody else was sleeping. Now it's Mom's turn. Jack pulls off my underwear from under my skirt and undoes his pants.

"'There's little Johnny!"

"The writer's tool. Hey, what do you mean, little?"

"Ooh, BIG Johnny! Is that all for little me?"

He puts it into me and I wrap my legs around his back. I love the feel of his lower back and push his pants down with my heels so the backs of my ankles are against his muscles. He thrusts, then stops, stroking my legs up and down with his hands. He begins thrusting again, harder, and I put my hands to the edge of the table where his hands are now, pulling myself up closer to him. He grabs my wrists, slows down again to a stop. A moment later, he thrusts again. I concentrate on feeling him moving, pulling my bottom half off the edge of the table with my arms. His legs tighten and he moans, "I love you, I love you," and his legs buckle slightly. He leans on top of me and we hug, rocking slightly side to side.

"I love you too, honey pie," I say.

Ha! There's a doily under my ass!

Then . . . it's funny how the song comes to me. I'm happy—having done it on the dining table, it will be all I can do not to burst out laughing when we have our "sit down dinner" tonight! The irreverence of it all makes me giddy. But then, at the same time, some undercurrent begins working and I'm not even aware of it except for the melody in my head—

Away from the City that hurts and mocks
I stand alone by the desolate docks

—and without even thinking about it I have "I Cover the Waterfront" in my head. Our old song. It just shows you, your mind works on its own without you trying. So many times—well I suppose only really twice, but it seems like more—Jack has chosen this moment, right after we've done this, to tell me he's going away. It's not so much his going, it's the way it happens—immediately after he's gotten some. It's just insulting. The first time, there was no reason at all to go to sea. He would have been protected by Columbia's athletic program—they'd rather see the Germans land on Long Island than lose a halfback to the war. But that's Jack, always afraid of someone running his life. So I end up watching the sea—*Will the one I love be coming back to me?*

It's about eight or nine days after this that a second letter appears. I'm working this morning and when the alarm rings I reach over and turn it off. My mind plays one of its patented games on me: I dream that it's okay I'm still in bed cause really I've gotten up and am preparing to go to work and I'm doing this so well that I deserve a few extra moments in bed in the morning. Anyway, by the time I shake these cobwebs out of my head I'm running a half-hour late. I enter into my get-what-I-need-and-get-going mode. Jack isn't in bed, which can only mean one thing.

"Jack!" I whisper, but forcefully, knocking softly on the bathroom door. "I have to get in there. I'm late for work."

He opens the door with a sad little boy expression. He's holding a folded newspaper. "Does your mother like me?" he says.

"Of course she does. Jack, I have to get going. I'm late."

"There's another letter in the paper, and I think it's written to mean me."

"Oh don't be ridiculous, Jack"

"If she doesn't like me, I think she should just tell me to my face."

"Why, Jack? What does it say?"

"Here, look at it yourself."

This is the last thing I should be doing right now. "I don't have time to right now, Jack. I have to be out the door in fifteen minutes and I'm not even dressed."

Jack frowns.

"Look," I say. "I'll take it with me. Will I see you tonight?"

"No, I'm leaving for work at 4:30."

"I'll set the alarm early tomorrow so we can have some time in the morning. Could you put some coffee on for me?"

A quick gulp or two, a roll I take with me, thrown on clothes and I'm out to the trolley just as it's coming by. I grab a rail, shifting paper and bread in my hands, but a man is nice enough to give me his seat. I'm sitting in the bunched up crowd of commuters when I finally do look at the paper, still folded open as Jack handed it to me.

NEED POLICE FOR WAR AT HOME

The wars in Europe and the Pacific theatre aren't the only wars that patriotic Americans have to be worried about these days. We are also waging a war over the direction of our society itself.

More and more, idle youths have become a fixture in our public thoroughfares. You've seen them yourself, hanging around on street corners, wearing leather jackets, smoking cigarettes, or filling the pool halls and the coffee shops in the middle of a workday.

It's true that some of these boys are late-shift workers attaining a little much-needed relaxation. But that's not all that goes on!

Why do you think we have the problems we do today with crime and general immorality, if not due to the large numbers of these idle young men! Many are draft age. Why aren't they fighting?

Today's criminality goes deeper than most of us are willing to admit. This is a new kind of hoodlum, filled with foreign ideas and more concerned with intellectual fashions than right and wrong. Nightly, they scheme to bring a new type of America, one that is losing the Christian principles of industry and humility that made this country great.

As much as our society is threatened by the Axis powers, we are also threatened from within.

The answer is to use the same means to defeat this scourge as we use on the Germans and the Japs—to support a strong army for right, right here at home.

I never talk politics with Mother. I've never been interested in her "causes." I mentioned before how unaware she is of my life—well, I try not to pay much attention to what she's doing either. But Jack's right—this is a bit close to home. If it doesn't describe how we've been living here, it certainly could be true of New York. And the leather jacket—I'm sure that's what Jack saw as aimed at him: he's been wearing it ever since he got here and, well, let's just say it's a fashion peculiarity here in GP. But does she mean us? I can't imagine it.

"It's too bad that Jack's work schedule makes him miss our evening meal," she says when we're all at table. "I suppose it can't be helped." She's said something to this effect just about every night, but somehow it never really bothered me until tonight. Would she rather he didn't pay her back so that she could keep her sense of moral superiority?

"I see you've had quite a few letters in the paper lately, Mother."

"Oh, those. Well really they're the work of a committee; we alternate signing them. But, yes, our campaign has really gotten off the ground. We've had letters in all the papers on an almost daily basis."

"Daily? Do you think the problems are that bad?"

Mother puts down her silverware and looks fully toward me. I hate to use the word matronly, but it describes her to a T. Her hair is as perfectly done as a queen's and she touches her ever-present string of pearls as a way of guarding herself against some imagined horror. "Oh, goodness, yes. Much worse. Haven't you noticed?"

"Noticed what?"

"Well, how things have changed. Maybe it's because you're young you don't see things in as stark a contrast as people my age. But the changes that have been brought by this war have made that much worse changes that you could already see happening, though they were occurring much more slowly before."

"I didn't read this letter," says Charlotte. "What changes?"

"Really, I'm not sure if this is the time or the place to be discussing such things."

I feel my blood rising. "Mother, if you're going to insult my husband, we can discuss it right now."

"Oh," says Charlotte, an evil grin coming to her face, "This is better than I thought!"

Mother actually rises two inches out of her seat. "Insult

John?"

"Leather jackets? Foreign ideas? Do you mean Russian novels? That's what Jack is reading these days."

Mother regains her primness. "Oh, no, dear." Her expression now hints at a rather bemused smile. "What we were complaining about doesn't have anything to do with anyone WE know. I'm talking about the trouble we've been having. All these people moving here. Last year there was terrible rioting. I was afraid to leave the house. It was all over the radio. Gangs of hoodlums roaming up and down the streets, Negroes and southern hooligans."

"I think I should read this," say Charlotte. "Maybe it's someone WE know, huh, Edie?"

"But you should know, dear," says Mother, her expression becoming grave again, "I didn't mean anything about John. You know I like John. He seems like a very serious young man, and it sounds like he comes from good, hardworking stock. It's not particularly the kind of background I would have wished my daughter to marry into, and I must say I'm not particularly fond of how his father acted when John was in trouble, but love doesn't always play by the rules, and if you're happy, that's what matters most. Besides, Gauls have a long and distinguished history in the Midwest. Several of our best families come from French backgrounds."

I don't say anything and for a moment the only sound is silverware and swallowing. Charlotte finally pipes in to fill the silence:

"Is it a French trait to stay so long in the bathroom?"

We all laugh, the kind of long laugh that ends the discussion, if that's what we were having.

"Twa-let," says Charlotte in a heavy fake accent, wiping tears of laughter from her eyes. "Yes, that is a French word, come to think of it!"

It is a lot of hoohah about nothing, I suppose. Who knows how much of the letter my mother actually wrote, if it's done by one of her committees. I go to bed early and set the alarm for the crack of dawn, planning what I'll tell Jack to ease his mind. "No, it didn't have anything to do with you." But when I wake up, Jack isn't in bed. I check the bathroom and he's not there either, or anywhere else in the house. Probably he hit an after-hours bar in the city. Fine. All this worry over him and nearly getting into a fight with Mother and he goes out for a drink. It's Friday. I haven't been out myself in I don't know how long. Jack's right about one thing, it is terrifically boring here. Maybe I'll go out for a little while with Charlotte tonight and then we can all go out for a nice dinner on Saturday and go dancing afterward. By the time he gets off work Saturday morning, it'll have been two whole days since we've seen each other. This is what it's like to be married?

So after we both get off work Friday, Charlotte and I head over to the Rustic Cabin. It's the only place within walking distance that's worth bothering with and there isn't a dress code to get in. A regular beer and cheap cocktails place, a real, New York-style dive bar, wood molding all around chipped and repainted over and over, pool tables in the room adjoining the bar and a patio out back. No one cares who your parents are, or whether you're paid up at the Yacht Club.

Virginia's there. She's drinking V.O. and ginger ale, so that's what Charlotte and I have too. Ginny's probably my best friend in GP. Her father is the number one announcer for the Tigers, and they are always having ballplayers over the house. Ginny says she wants to seduce Hal Newhowser, who's actually our age and is the Tigers' top pitcher this year, and she could get him, too. She's perky, like a magazine girl, and she's a wiz with a ribbon and some fresh flowers for her hair. I've learned a thing or two from her. Oh, I'll say! She was my first "bad influence"—the first time I ever got drunk was from that well-stocked bar at her parents' house. They had everything! Still do. We sampled different things all night, mixed drinks and strange liqueurs, till we both got sick. She's that kind of friend—we've been through a lot together over the years. It's funny, though, now that I've been to New York, how easy it is to shock her.

"Ginny," I say casually during a lull in our conversation, "Do you know where we can get any reefers?"

"Marijuana? Have you tried that?"

"Tried it?" Charlotte and I exchange knowing nods.

"Edie practically lived on the stuff when she lived up by Columbia," says Charlotte.

"Really? I've heard it makes you crazy if you do it more than three or four times!"

"If that was true, I'd have my own padded wing in the mental hospital by now."

"What's it like?" Ginny's like I am, she'll do anything. So now she wants to find some so she can try it herself.

"Oh, you should try it sometime. It really relaxes you and makes everything seem really funny. It's effective as a pain medication too. After I had my abortion, I smoked enough grass to fill a trashcan!"

Ginny's eyes widen in surprise. "You had an abortion?" she asks at half the volume we've been talking, an eye out to see if anyone's listening.

I smile. "No. I was just joking."

It's not something I'm sure I can tell people. Someday. I do want kids, eventually. But what was I supposed to do? Jack was off on his ship and we really didn't even know each other that well then. I thought he was gone for good, that I'd been a "conquest." I even made copies of the letter he had written me and sold them from my cigarette tray for a dollar apiece as a "how-to-get-lucky" letter. That showed him. He'd written it to me and it was so beautiful, all about how if I wanted to find his heart I should search deep in the woods and when I reached the last stone in the path I should look underneath and I would find it there. Then, wham, bam, thank you, ma'am, off he goes. I know better how he is now, so I know he didn't mean it personally. It's just Jack, never wanting to feel tied down. I just wish he'd think sometimes about other people in the world. I don't think I'd want to have a baby with Jack even now that we're married. Jack wants one, or at least he was upset when he found out. But he doesn't think of all the changes it would mean to have a child. For him, too. He used to say I didn't think about all that marriage entailed, when I brought it up. But he's even more of a dreamer than I am. He just wants a little version of himself, a little Jack running around. I don't want to take responsibility for a child, at least not yet. I'm too young, I haven't really grown up yet myself. Nor do I want to, when I see what growing up means—babies are helpless, and they take all of your time, and you never get any sleep. At least I know enough to know I'm irresponsible. Luckily Gramma knew someone to go to in the city. It was over pretty quickly. Mother never found out—she would have flipped her wig! She never will, if I can help it.

We don't stay out real late. My heart isn't really in it without Jack and I want to be home—and not dead to the world!—when he gets off from work in the morning. I have a dream that we're back in New York. We're sitting in Central Park, having a picnic and high up above us in a tree there's a woodpecker. I've gotten a bottle of wine and chilled some asparagus and olives that we're eating with mayonnaise and Jack has gone over to a vendor and gotten us two frankfurters apiece with mustard and sauerkraut. It's beautiful out, not a cloud in the sky and Jack looking so handsome, though not dressed in anything special, just a plain white button-down shirt and chinos. But Jack doesn't have to dress up, just shave and comb his hair—he's a handsome man. I like his chin—it's a strong chin. I remember being suspicious of Jack when we first met, he was so good looking. He could have a girl in every port, were he a different type. In fact, he could sell you the Brooklyn Bridge, he has such a way about him that you want to believe anything he tells you. Luckily, Jack's not that way. Jack doesn't lie. He can't really hide anything that's on his mind, whatever it is for him at the moment, and if something comes out later, that's just because he wasn't thinking about it before, not because he was intentionally keeping it back.

Anyway, we're sitting down munching on our food and there's a nice cool breeze coming across the sheep pasture part of Central Park. We're going to go to the zoo after our lunch. But Jack is agitated. It's the woodpecker, rat-a-tat, rat-a-tat-tat.

"Sit down, Jack. It's just a woodpecker."

He tries to be calm and sit with me and enjoy lunch, but the woodpecker is too much for him, almost like it's pecking on him, like the tree is his spine and the tat-tat-tat just goes right through him.

"I'm going to climb up that tree and stop that woodpecker."

"No, Jack, don't. It's too high up." Not only that, but as I look at it, the tree is strange and dark, having a twisting trunk that recedes into shadow above. I can't even see where the bird might be.

"High up? I used to climb the main-mast of the George Weems when we were going back and forth to Liverpool, and that was much higher."

"No, Jack. It's just a bird. Can't you just ignore it?"

"I won't hurt it. You know I'm kind to animals, baby. I just want to have a conversation with him, is all. I'm going to ask him if he can move to another tree."

But I'm scared he's going to fall, or even if he doesn't he's going to leave me again. I know he always comes back, but I don't want to be left alone. It doesn't make any sense, so I can't explain it to him, nor does he seem to see the same tree that I do; he starts climbing up the tree and I yell at him, "Jack, don't, don't."

I wake up and Jack hasn't come to bed. I find him in the bathroom.

"Jack, there really isn't any reason for you to hole up in the bathroom to read. No one's up this time of the morning anyway, and I'm sure the living room couch would be more comfortable."

He's sitting on the floor with his back hunched up against the tub and legs crossed alongside the toilet. "This is fine," he says.

"Do you want to get some sleep? I was thinking we might go out tonight. Wouldn't it be fun to go out for a lobster dinner, like we used to in New York, then maybe dancing afterwards? We owe it to ourselves. We've been working hard.

"Yeah—and then it'll take us twice as long to save enough to get out of here."

"We can have fun cheap, too. We could go to the Rustic Cabin."

"We call different things fun."

"Oh, come on, Jack. Fun's fun. If you want, you can sit

me and Charlotte down for an hour before we go and we'll discuss Dostoievsky with you before we go out."

"Haven't any of your friends here read Dostoievsky? They probably have good gold-leafed sets of the world's major authors in their parents' studies. Unread in their entirety, of course."

"You've got a stick up your ass, Jack."

"Fine, I'll go back to what I was doing. Shut the door on your way out."

"Jack." This is so juvenile, having an argument with someone sitting on the floor of the bathroom, like it's him and the toilet against me. I just want to get him moving, out of this stupid funk of his. "I have to pee."

Jack gets up and without saying a word goes out through the hall and grabs his jacket from the closet by the front door on his way out, jacket over one shoulder, book in his other hand.

"Oh, fine, Jack. That'll solve a lot!" I yell, but he's already out the door. And I've probably woken everybody up.

I don't want to fight anymore. I can't wait until Jack makes enough money to pay back the trust and allow us to move out of here. But that'll be the rest of this month at least. Jack's bringing in a decent check now but we have to support ourselves and give some money to the household. Neither Jack nor I want to take more than we need from my mother, even if it takes a little longer to get out of here.

I wish I could just close my eyes and this month would be over.

Jack loves his breakfast and I don't see any dishes in the sink. I bet I'll find him at Janet's.

Janet's is kind of a partner to the Rustic Cabin, about a block down and just as beat looking and out of place as the bar. It's the kind of diner you'd expect to find further into the city, where people who don't have servants to cook for them can get eggs and bacon for thirty-five cents before going to work. It's not big; no tables, just a U-shaped counter with the soda fountain and coffee toward the front and the grill in back, Janet herself having a smoke while making your breakfast, but never dropping the ash from her dangling cigarette. I never used to appreciate places like this until I met Jack, but when we began dating we'd go to seedy diners like this and he'd do a running description of what everyone was doing and thinking as they cooked and waited on customers or waited for food. In fact, Jack tells me he fell in love with me when he saw me eat five frankfurters with sauerkraut the first time we went anyplace together. I'd never had it like that before; I never really went to diners like this before living in New York, just nice restaurants and club things with my parents.

Jack is there. I see him first from the window outside and he's got his back to me at the counter. He's watching the workers intently and it's almost as if I can read his mind reading theirs. Her name's June and she's pissed-off at that guy at the counter who never gives her a decent tip, sits forever after breakfast until he's gotten four refills of coffee and keeps expecting her to keep refilling it as soon as he downs each cup, even kind of giving her half a dirty look when he has to wait minute or two, or the way he'll use that newspaper, ruffling open with extra force when his cup is empty when a simple "Excuse me . . ." would do—no, he thinks he's too important to ever deign to actually ask for another cup. Well, two can play this game; I'm just going to ignore him completely and be damned if he gets another cup of coffee out of me without either being nice or leaving me a decent tip for a change.

I can't really be mad at him seeing him there so lonesome and sad. I go inside.

"Buy a girl a cup of coffee, sailor?"

He looks at me with his cocker spaniel brown eyes, bloodshot. He hasn't had much sleep. He grins a little. "Hey, aren't you the daughter of the man who owns that big factory in town?"

"Yeah, but it bores me, all those society types."

"I suppose it would get tiresome. But I don't know anything about that. I'm just a working man."

He takes a big mouthful of eggs. "I suppose you've got lots of admirers."

"It's true," I yawn. "Is it hard work, the work you do?"

"I can't complain."

"You look very strong."

We go home together.

Later, Jack props himself up on an elbow in bed. "You know, I bet I know what she does."

"Who?"

"Your mother. I bet her committee doesn't even write the letters themselves. I bet they get their factory workers to do it for them. Someone with so many people working for her doesn't ever really have to do anything herself, and I bet that's how all her friends are too."

"That's ridiculous, Jack. I asked my mother about that letter. She said it had nothing to do with you. It had to do with the riot."

"What riot?"

"I don't know. I guess they had some riot here sometime."

Jack rolls out of bed. I've been too negative with him. But I'll be damned if he's going to win again.

"Come on, Jack. What do you say about tonight? Can

177

we go out? I can't stand the thought of staying home on a Saturday night. It won't cost too much, and it'll be a lot of fun. We don't have to get lobster, we can order something cheaper. But wouldn't it be fun to get all dressed up for a night on the town? I can't remember the last time I saw you in a tie. You could wear that nice jacket of yours. My old college beau."

I talk him into it, finally. Charlotte has her own date tonight, so it'll just be the two of us, out on the town, which is nice. I can't remember the last time we did something like this—I almost can't remember anything before the awful business with Lucien and that creep David Kammerer and then Jack getting arrested. Anyone else would have called the cops in on HIM long before, especially after what he did with Kitkat. It was lucky Jack happened to wake up. Here he breaks into OUR apartment in the middle of the night, looking for Lucien, and when he finds no one on the couch except Kitcat he puts the window sash around his little neck and tries to hang him! What kind of person hangs a little kitten? It's just a good thing we found him so soon after, and even so the poor little thing cried and hid under the bed the whole day after we got him down. And we're supposed to feel sorry for Dave? He might not have deserved to die, but he was an A-number-one asshole. Lucien shouldn't have done what he did, but Dave pushed him a long way.

Lu woke us up that morning, coming in the door and shaking Jack. We were out on the front room foldout couch because it had been so hot—our best hope for a good night sleep was to catch the crossdraft between the two windows in the front room. I was still half-asleep but I knew something was up. The way Jack told me to go to the store and get eggs for breakfast when he knew we already had some in the icebox, without even starting to smile or let me know what was going on, that was creepy. And then I saw that Lucien had blood all over him!

"What's wrong? What's going on?"

"Nothing," said Jack. "Just go get us some food."

I wanted to say, "No one tells me what to do in my own apartment," and normally I would have, but I saw that this was the wrong time; the blood and Jack's look told me that. Jack told me later that he only didn't tell me then because he didn't want me to be a part of it too. It was bad enough he was involved.

It was a weird day—we spent most of it after Lucien left just trying to put things in our way so that we wouldn't have to talk about it. We saw four movies. Then, just when he finally started to tell me, that night, that's when the police break in.

These cops must have spent the whole day at the movies themselves! They break in the door and one yells: "Is this a dope den?"

I couldn't help laughing, but Jack was petrified. They handcuffed him right there. This was serious! I don't know what I did then, but I wasn't laughing anymore. And just then, as we're going out the door, John Kingsland comes by, looking for Jane, who somehow slept through all this. Jack just looks right past him and so I did too—we didn't want to get him involved. But poor John, he turned white as a ghost. He didn't know why the cops were there, but naturally figured that it had to do with reefers, and who knows, he might have had one tucked into his sock himself. So he caught on right away and says, "Excuse me, do you know where Joe Johnson lives?"

I don't know where he came up with the name Joe Johnson, or why the cops didn't think anything of it.

It was surreal. There were photographers downstairs

waiting to get a shot of the big criminals. None of the pictures made the papers when they found out it wasn't the big marijuana den they'd hoped for. I mean, we smoked it, but the way these cops were looking around, it was like they expected to see drugs everywhere. I don't know what they expected to see, but they seemed kind of disappointed by what they found—just me and Jack, and we weren't doing much of anything.

Now we're here. I guess you could call this the honeymoon. And this is what our "honeymoon" has become—going out to dinner on a Saturday night is a luxury.

But it is nice. It's only when we get all dressed up that I see how low we've let ourselves get. I put on the skirt Gramma gave me before we left New York and a pretty red-striped blouse, a French sailor design. But the humidity makes my hair stick up all over the place. I need to go to a beauty parlor soon, if we can spare the money. I should drop a hint to Mother, and get her to pay. Jack's clean shaven, which is a treat, as he's only been shaving every second or third day or so. And he looks so handsome in his jacket and tie, like I knew he would. I feel suddenly like we're real people again, not just factory workers or interlopers in Mother's house, but people with their own lives who can go out and do what they like to do.

"Mind if I stop for a moment at the liquor store?" says Jack on the way down to the trolley that'll take us into Detroit.

"What for?"

"Well, it'll be cheaper if I keep a pint in my pocket and pour my own drinks."

"Not at the restaurant."

"No, probably not at the restaurant, but maybe at the club we go to later on. We can buy the first round, then pour

our own after that. We'll have to get ourselves a new round here and there to keep them from being too suspicious, but it'll be a lot cheaper this way."

Jack buys a pint of Seagram's and as we get to the corner, unscrews the cap and takes a quick slug.

"Hey," I say. "Give me some of that!"

What a fun night! Once we get to the restaurant, we decide to go for the lobster after all. Jack's a stitch! "The boys in the pen told me about this place," he says in a perfect Bogart voice, hunching his shoulders. "Yeah, said it was Lucky Luciano's favorite spot in Detroit." We get a bottle of champagne. And in between, we're handing the pint bottle back and forth under the table and swigging from it. We're blitzed before we even get to a bar. We try to go dancing, but it's too much, I'm laughing too hard at Jack, who keeps making jokes and doing different voices—it feels like we're a roaring twenties couple getting sloshed on bathtub gin and doing our best to try to Charleston, making complete fools out of ourselves but not caring in the least and doing it all in our best clothes, like happy-go-lucky young millionaires.

"So, Scott, shall I call around the limousine to take us home?"

"Oh, Zelda, you know how that oaf's slow driving taxes my patience." "Yes, Scott, but you don't want to end up sleeping another night in the gutter. You know what a stiff neck it gives you."

"Are we going to quarrel, Zelda?"

"No, Scott, let's have a drink!"

Jack puts me in a cab after awhile because I'm completely legless.

The next thing I remember is the doorbell ringing and a hard knocking on the door. I hear it distantly several times before it hits me. Jack isn't here! There's someone ringing the doorbell and pounding the door. I jump up out of bed and the room whirls sickeningly. My head feels like it's packed solid with steel wool and my stomach like its floating in a jar of laboratory solution. Jack! Mother's surely at church. I throw a robe on and walk quickly to the door.

"Sorry to bother you, ma'am. Are you Mrs. Kerouac?"

"Yes."

"I picked your husband up downtown. He was snooping around one of the mills down there, but he told me he was Mrs. Parker's son-in-law so I thought I'd better just bring him back over here."

"Thank you, officer." My stomach starts to roil, but I hold it down. "I'm sorry if he was any trouble."

"Well, he's pretty snookered, so he didn't put up much resistance. Let him know, though, that he could have gotten into a lot of trouble. People are pretty worried these days when they see someone snooping around that's not supposed to be there."

Jack looks like I feel, plus some dirt for emphasis. He's not even acknowledging this conversation, as if unconscious, wobbling to stay on his feet, the policeman half-supporting him. His pants are torn from the crotch halfway down one leg and his jacket and one of his pantslegs are all muddy. I don't know if he's actually asleep, or half-asleep, or faking out of humiliation.

But when we get to our room, Jack has revived.

"What a strange night," he slurs. "You wouldn't believe what happened to me, what I saw."

I flop on the bed and groan. "Tell me later. Let me sleep."

Jack ignores me. "Let me start out right. The night—it was weird out, Shakespearean weird. Magical."

I'm face down on the bed. Every word is a teasing out of

the steel wool and a sloshing of the solution, excruciating. "Can't it wait, Jack?" I plead.

"I'm sorry." Then a moment later: "But it was just so crazy! Just let me tell you. You don't have to say anything. Then you can go back to sleep? Okay?"

He's not going to let me go back to sleep until I let him tell me. I groan assent.

"I was down at the river, where your mother's shoe factory is."

"Jack," I roll over to face him. "You didn't try to break into Mother's company, did you?"

He half closes his eyes and pushes his palms down in an exaggerated gesture for me to calm down and let him tell the rest of the story. I can see now he's still drunk, though it's not something you can hear in his voice.

"I simply observed, sitting on a ridge which ran down a gully slope at the bottom of which was the fence surrounding the factory. Factory road. The road of the sad majestic soul. I sat, feeling the early breeze of morning on my cheek. And then, then I saw something! The shadowy figure of darkness in his cape! Or didn't quite see him, but knew he was there in the wind getting cold and whistling ominous. Wheeeew," he whistles. "It was just like I was back in Lowell, growing up—water, factories, wind, and the evil spirit lurking there behind it all with his sinister laugh—like we used to play at while we were kids, but didn't guess at the reality of the evil we were in fact subconsciously perceiving, which gave grave life to our innocent games."

I wonder how long he practiced that sentence!

"Grosse Pointe is nothing like Lowell, but here, Detroit, this is what I knew growing up. The same desperate tragic heart-rending sadness of my youth, which most of Grosse Pointe will never know. They'll never know it in the houses of this neighborhood at least, in these kitchens of comfort. I felt this weird witchy breeze, the presence of that evil with a scent that was nothing so much as embalming fluid. And it was coming from here, from these mansions, from Grosse Pointe Park and Woods and Shores and what-all.

"So I turned into the wind and shouted back at it: 'You're nothing but a bunch of stinking funeral homes! You're nothing but a bunch of funeral homes for dead people!'"

"So is that when the cops picked you up?"

"No, not then. Let me finish. I was sitting down there feeling this enormous sad echoing flow of nostalgic deep blueness, when I look over at the factory and see a single light on in a corner window on the second floor, a single spotlit cubicle in the cadaverous hulking deathhouse. From where I am, it's almost exactly even with me, but far away, the gully below separating us. I can make out the form of a man hunched over, doing what I can't tell. I have to get closer to see him. So I start down toward the fence, and it's too deep for me to keep my balance—they're built that way to keep people at a distance, I realize. But I get there, sliding part of the way. Then there's the fence. It's chain-link, with barbed wire at the top, so I have to be careful. But I get over it safely. I caught my pants going over the other side, but no big deal. Now I go up a little rise and I can see a little better, but while I'm closer, I'm further below, so I can only see the top half of this guy, and even less as I go toward the building. His face is in shadow and he's doing something—I still can't tell what—but he's the most forlorn man in the world, I can tell that, laboring on in the wee of night as the world sleeps its sound sleep of feather mattresses. It's weird—I couldn't see him, but I somehow knew him nonetheless, just like I knew what the wind meant. Working alone in that empty shell of a factory in a single lit office, and not in the main plant either, but in the corner, a man who is as lonely in the middle of the day rush and buzz of bodies and talk as he is right now, so it makes no difference to him if he works in the middle of the night or the middle of the day. He has no past or future, just his office, the office of the lonely man and outside whirring the laughing shadowy fiend whee hee hee hee hee ha ha.

"So I wasn't going to get any better a look where I was, but it wouldn't really improve as I got closer either. But I just had to know what he was doing and I saw at the building's corner a gutter coming down and I figured if I could just climb up that gutter I could look into the office."

"Jack!"

"I know, I know. It wasn't the *smart* thing to do." He pauses for a moment, as if puzzled by his own behavior. "It was just . . . irresistible."

"OK, Jack. Is there much more? I'd like to get some sleep."

"Not much more—but wait until you hear! It was getting to be dawn about this time and I get about fifteen feet off the ground when a police cruiser comes by and sees me and the cop gets out and points a light at me and shouts for me to get down. And as soon as this happens the light goes out above me in the office and there's no more sound. But just before that instant, when the cop car just pulls up, I hear inside, barely but unmistakably . . . typing."

"Typing?"

"He was typing."

"What was he typing?"

"You know what he was typing. Letters for your mother's committee."

"Oh, Jack!"

"I'm sure that's what he was doing! It's how she has it set up, to cover herself, so no one knows it isn't her that writes them. The others involved, too, I bet, have similar arrangements. They have to have them done in secret. How better than to put workers in empty office space at night after the factory has closed down. She probably gave him instructions to keep the shade drawn, but he is the type of man who needs to at least see the night sky. The window gave out on the side the moon was hanging lonely in the sky. A lonely man, a man as lonely as this, takes comfort in the presence of the moon, his companion in the empty night of death!"

"Don't you think that's a bit dramatic?"

"Mark my words. This man is writing hundreds of letters for your mother, and probably for others with even more power, not just in Grosse Pointe or even in Michigan, but all over, the owners of all the factories, the politicians, the powerful men who dine with Dr. Sax in the dark castles of sinister eternity."

"Oh, Jack, is that what you think of Mother? That she's some evil mistress of the dark powers?" Even wanting sleep I can't keep myself from laughing.

"Mark my words. There's a much larger evil that your mother doesn't even realize she's part of."

"'Okay, Jack. I'll mark your words. Now can I go back to sleep. I'm dead, and if I don't catch up on sleep now, I won't make it through the week."

But I know then what's coming. It's too quiet and my own feeling of cold evil starts to come into the room.

"I have to tell you something else, Edie."

I've heard the tone of voice before. Drunk, sober, or hungover, I know when Jack's leaving.

"But we were going to go back to New York together

before you got on a ship."

"I just can't stay here any longer. I need to get out into the world and get back to writing and living. I feel like I'm dying here—like I'm having the life sucked out of me. The longer I stay here, the more impossible it will be for me to recover. I have to write, and I can't do it if I stay here any more. I have to get out."

I won't do it again. "Then that's it, Jack. I'm not going to think of myself as a married woman if you leave again."

"Edie." Jack gets in bed with me, tries to put his arms around me.

"You're getting dirt all over the bed, Jack!"

"I'll drop the sheets off at a laundromat. But just listen to me.

This has nothing to do with us? We're married. You're my wife. My life's wife. You're a part of me, wherever I am. But I can't be a husband to you like this. I have to follow my calling. I can earn a living for us, but for now I have to get the materials I need to write. Six months, then I'll be back for good and we can go to New York."

I can't help it. I start crying, which makes me half scream the words I say back to him.

"So I'm supposed to stay here for six months with my mother and sister while you go enjoy yourself?"

"I have enough to give your mother money back for the bail, and if I can just borrow a little to get me back to New York where I can get on a ship, I'll send it back after I get paid. Then you can go back and live with Joan if you want."

"Yeah, so your friends can keep an eye on me. Is that the plan, Jack?"

"Edie, you're making this more difficult than it has to be."

"Oh, I'm making this more difficult. It's me. You stay

out all night, get brought home by cops, go on about my mother being some sort of villain. . . ." I can't finish the sentence, say he's leaving.

"I love you, you know."

"I know. I know you do."

My father has a friend who'll loan Jack a car by the end of the day. It will all be accomplished very efficiently. Monday morning, he'll be gone.

Monday, I'll call in sick.

I'll see him again in New York.

But this is my life, too. I can't just wait around. I shouldn't.

Jack's been talking, but I can't listen to him anymore. It's the same speech I've heard a thousand times before. One day we're going to settle down and have bunches of kids. Live on the same block as all our friends and sit around on the front porch, talking about old times. He'll be a famous writer, everyone we know will be famous. It will all be lovely and we'll laugh and drink bottled beer to the setting sun. This is what I'm supposed to still be around for, one of these days.

I don't know who he's talking to. It's not me.

He does love me, though. I know that. I just wish he knew what it meant.

I've been lying away from him, but when I turn back I can see it in his eyes. The poor, lost boy.

Come to me, Jack. Make love to me once more before you go. You stupid sonofabitch.

4.

Jack walks into a Detroit blues bar.

This isn't integrated. Jack's the only white man to open this door tonight.

One time when he got on a boat bound for Europe it went down the coast first and good thing, the bosun was a big queer who wanted to make him, he was absolutely sure of it, so while he'd intended (again) to go to Paris and perhaps search out his long lost Breton ancestors he ended up jumping ship in North Carolina where he looked up and had a drink with Thomas Wolfe's brother, an aging man in the white suit of a southern gentleman. The next day, looking around that part of the country, at the rolling meadows and white fences of plantations, he heard the deep blues singing of a black man walking who knows where. Jack fell in behind him and followed on dusty dirt roads some three or four miles. It was a long trip to be making on foot but the man didn't seem to be in any hurry, and it blew Jack's mind. Jack raced everywhere; everyone in New York raced everywhere; even back in Lowell, where no one had any particular place to get to (and did they have any more to get to in New York?), everybody was always late for somewhere, going someplace else, hustling, even drinking their beers in a hurry. Everyone in the northeast raced everywhere. But this music itself was slow, not the frenetic speed of be-bop always riding with the tis-ta-ta-tis of the high-hat cymbal but a deep down singing which came as if out of a cave or the hollow of the depths of a human soul, and even when the tempo made it fast the music itself was deep, like a cavern formed in rock by the constant eroding drip of pain year after year. The man's song never seemed to get anywhere; there was no part of it you could call the beginning middle or end, though sometimes it did seem as if a new song had begun, a new tune being sung, but the borders between songs were never quite clear. Nor was he ashamed of being heard. Unselfconsciousness. The meandering of a man free to feel and express himself, without looking to see what others thought about it or him. Had Jack ever felt as free in his life, to simply do as he wanted, when he wanted, without thinking about how someone else would look at him? The man would sometimes stop singing, but then he'd just continue on again with the same song when he started up again: where he stopped and started actually singing did not correspond to where the songs began and ended; as likely as not the man would stop upon seeing a rabbit scamper off into woods as he approached or to nod to a hand in the field he was passing by. The first hand they passed also nodded to Jack, and Jack back to the hand, worrying at the same time that the singing man in front of him would in this way be apprised of Jack's presence and turn around, but Jack then knew that the man in front of him knew of his presence and still didn't turn around. Never did, all while Jack followed. Nor was it fear or lack of fellow-feeling that prevented him, Jack felt. Jack saw in his mind two pieces of wood drifting downriver lazily.

He tried to make out words. But the words were bent to the purposes of the song and its singing and became more purely music than any attempt at speaking or singing words. The feeling in these utterances came through in the sound of the voice, the pacing, the cries and murmurs. Jack now wasn't thinking only of the man and his song but also, and perhaps more, about what he would say about the man and following him when he got to his notebook or his typewriter; in other words—and this was now true of everything Jack did—he did not simply observe and experience walking behind the man listening to his song, but at the same time spun his own tune in his mind in response, a response that frequently entirely obliterated that to which he was listening in favor of the music he was creating within his own mind. Nor was this a process of which Jack was unconscious; he realized, more than once, that he was no longer listening to the man but pretending to listen and instead listening to himself describe how he was listening to the man, selecting phrases for when later he might be able to write it all down. So he began to think about the act of this pretending, his recreation of what he was experiencing even as he experienced it, and then realized, to his even greater dismay, that now he was no closer to the man singing and the experience of listening, but at a second remove even more distant. "Listen to the man," he said to himself, in just these words, seeing even the quotation marks around them as he reprimanded himself, imagining reprimanding himself and the necessity of gaining entrance to the authentic . . .

With all of these self-conscious movings of mind on this lazy day, it was no surprise that the beginnings and endings of songs were ungraspable; and while the day and its movement were lazy, and he was now in the lazy south, it takes more than one day to adjust yourself to a new rhythm, so while lazing along imagining himself adjusting to the rhythms of a southern black man's lazy blues song while travelling nowhere at all, Jack was simultaneously speeding along in his mind in his work and determining how the lazy experience would fit into it and become part of his larger project which in turn was an extension of his ambition to devote his life to writing and be aware of everything around him and record it all or as much as possible and the speed of reactions and vocabulary and insight needed to reach such a massive goal and undertaking and spinning as a result all manner of plots around the man, around himself, around the landscape. The fields were largely empty, except for cattle and occasional horses. But they held thousand-soldier battles, Army officers on mounted charges, death, labor, fields of black men and women with hair tied in rags, a little pickaninny boy walking beside him dressed in only a sack asking for candy, elaborate *Gone With the Wind* plantation houses entertaining men with perfumed mustaches calling on pretty southern belles in satin gowns in huge ballrooms with buffed maple, no, cherry floors, and garden terraces blooming with fragrant magnolias, and then the same houses falling board by board into ruin or set afire by rough men at war who'd lost everything themselves and now were resolved in hearts rusted by hatred to destroy everything in their path, led by Sherman, who'd already had them rip up rail lines, chop down weather vanes, wreck water wheels, cripple horses, drown livestock, take iron bars to chandeliers, pocket jewelry, bugger it all to hell and back.

As by the same process, right now, throwing aside a drained pint bottle and entering a Detroit blues bar, Jack finds himself walking down a road in North Carolina.

He comes forward into a crowd, which half-parts before him. Men look at him, some in shock ("White man in here?"), others laughing, poking each other in the ribs, two or three smiling his way. Each face is almost familiar to him. Then he sees someone he's sure he knows. Not personally, but he's seen him around. In New York, maybe Greenwich Village. A tall, light-skinned man with distinctive red-orange hair, in baggy lavender pants cinched at the ankles and a matching oversized jacket too loud for this workingman's bar where everyone else is in short-sleeves and dungarees. He's loudly regaling a small group, waving arms to make up for words drowned in this veil of sound, making great theatre out of continually checking a pocket watch attached to a long chain that loops eighteen inches down and back from his beltloop to his jacket pocket. The jam breaks and the song goes back into blues verses, deeply intoned but fuzzed nearly out of recognition through the amplifier. Jack edges closer. This group is near the bar, so he's going in that direction anyway.

"Don't you brothers Lindy-hop? What is all this noise? You brothers call this music? Where's the dancing? I hear this guy singing about fucking but I know a lot more of it actually happens when you get them bitches working up their blood with a good Lindy-hop."

A young man, maybe a couple years younger than Jack. Jack keeps trying to catch his eye. The man of course sees Jack—it's impossible not to in a place like this, where a white man would be crazy to go.

"You brothers would do well to catch my act in Harlem sometime. Now that's music. And in between, you got me dancing licks onstage to make the girls drip honey. Hey, here's one—what's the difference between your sister and a U-Boat? Give up? Troop ships sometimes escape U-Boats."

Jack bellies to the bar. The bartender comes over. They shout to be heard.

"Hey, man, what's this music called?"

"Nothing but the blues."

Jack isn't sure what he's said, but doesn't want to fight the music. "Bourbon, neat. Hey, wait a second." Jack checks his money supply. "Send that guy over there one from me, too."

"You got it."

The man pours one for Jack in a thin stream from the pointed tip of a labelless bottle, then moves a few feet over and pours another for the man whose voice has no problem being heard above the din. He keeps talking, reaches over for the glass and makes more theatre out of drinking it, holding the glass at arm's length directly overhead, tilting his neck backward, opening his mouth wide and with a quick flip of the wrist upending the glass. The whiskey pellets down on his face, a third of it splashing away but two-thirds going right down his throat. "Warms my belly," he says, slapping his stomach, which even through the layers of clothing creates a thin smack of muscle on muscle.

Jack leans over and pokes his head through the group. He must be drunk.

"Hey, don't I know you?"

The tall man looks at him off-handedly. "Ever been to the Lobster Pond in New York?"

Jack doesn't have a better answer. "Yeah, I think so."

"Aw, you'd know it if you'd been there. I'm the Master of Ceremonies and everybody knows me, Detroit Red."

The others smile at Jack. They're rubes, though one or two are fancied up a little with feathers in their derby hats.

"What I owe for the drink, Daddy-O?" says Red to Jack. He pulls his arm out from behind his back and twirls a large gold coin in the air between his fingers. Jack can't tell what it is—it's slightly bigger than a dollar. Red grins wide and, the men parting away from Jack slightly, he allows his hand to glide across the air, the coin flipping around like a moth, light winking off its spinning edges. "Do you think this is enough?" Red's eyes watch the play of the coin in his hand, past Jack's face and up over his head, whereupon Malcolm closes his hand in a backward fist then opens it for all to see. The coin has disappeared. "Aw, man," he says to Jack in mock anger, "You weren't fast enough!"

The twirling coin flutters to Jack's stomach—where it meets the bourbon and a sudden anxiousness about where he's wandered to in his night-long ramble when he should be at work—and boils up into his head. Suddenly he can't breathe. He's cold from sweat but at the same time finds the closeness of bodies suffocating him in dense, muggy fog in which he feels himself turning over and over. He has to puke.

He falls slightly against the bar, manages to turn around, makes his way out the door.

"Blew that man's conk right off the stem," says Red.

They don't meet again for another year, until just after the end of the war.

5.

Most of Malcolm's family lived in and around Lansing. His mother no longer lived there. She was up in Kalamazoo.

First there'd been Wilbert, a good, quiet, responsible boy. Then came Hilda, who always helped her momma with the cooking, the wash, the tidying up and the babies. Then the three rambunctious ones—Philbert, Malcolm, and Reginald. Philbert was good at boxing and Malcolm was the one he practiced on, but that made Malcolm quick-witted. Reggie used to tag along with Philbert and Malcolm like a hungry little puppy dog. Finally came the little ones—Yvonne and Wesley and Robert. So much government issue food the kids thought Not to Be Sold was a brand name. So little else they considered fried ketchup bread a delicacy. Such poor luck in that family, rabbits could rub their own feet and get away.

As things got to be too much for Momma, the sour-grease-cooking smell became a visible yellow tar on the walls and windowsills, and dust and animal hair matted there. Kids with same size feet fought for warm shoes once the snow came. Ice zig-zagged on the insides of windows in the morning. Wilbert never came home except to sleep and pour some water over his head before going out to his other job. "Such a good boy, I'm sorry, Wilbert," Momma would say to herself when the clouds broke in her mind and the world was clear for a moment. Then the wind would shift back the other way. "Social workers came in, pushed me over and stole the coal for the stove and broke its door, so that any heavy walking might spill hot coals and torch the whole place. Social workers got me with this child here, cause I ain't been with no man since my Earlie died. Social workers saw Earlie kill that rabbit with his bare hands and throw it at my feet and roused the klan to meet him at the railroad tracks. Social workers secretly mix pork into the food they give us so I end up having to throw half of it out. Social workers put sugar in the engine of that old car which was just brand new last month. The sun shone and the crickets buzzed too loud and we ended up with the sheriff out here banging on the door. Now every day is cold and cloudy and I don't have a husband anymore to keep me warm at night. That's what social workers do."

Finally, social workers detonated a bomb under the house that sent everything and everyone flying off every which way.

Philbert was even more alarmed when Malcolm came back in a dark pinstripe gabardine suit than when he used to come back in purple and yellow with a hubcap-sized hat on his head that had to be tied to his collar by a string in the back for fear it would blow away. Malcolm told Mrs. Swerlin, his old foster ma, that he was now in international finance. The only part of dandy left in him were fingernails neatly manicured and coated with transparent polish so that they shined like his teeth. He kept an emery board in his pocket to keep them free of nicotine stains.

Time was, Philbert would have punched Malcolm out, the way he kept fucking up and covering his trail in shit. Instead he told him to quit smoking cigarettes and eating pork.

"Pork? You wearing the same monkey collar as

Momma's old preacher?"

"Hadn't thought of that. Maybe Momma knew something after all. But no, brother, I've found the black man's natural religion, the one that the white man's lies have kept us from for 600 years."

"Back up forty-five feet else your spiel gonna dig my heel, bro. The God rap goes back in the pocket of your slack. I'm skinned for that noise."

"Will you stop acting the fool for one minute? This is serious. Hilda and I are driving out later in the week to see her, and I think it would be good if you came."

"All she care, I could be the Yellow Kid and you could be Old Black Sam the Sham, she wouldn't collar us from some floor mechanics. 'Sides, I got places to go, people to see, legit. Got my spotters peeled for gone talent."

"Running a game?"

"Naw, no stuff. Shoe talent, to lay down sand and make it jump. Do me right, I ain't down for that shit. This is strictly uptown. I'm slinging a show back in the Apple, at some strong digs. If it works out, I'll be able to sell out to Hollywood by next year, two years tops, and then I'll have the life of Jack the Bear, no more of the slave. Gotta find me some real fresh Susie-Qs, some real green bananas, see if they're in New York they've already been discovered and get their own kick. But Detroit, see, that's untapped. Plenty of talent here just waiting for someone to hook them up."

That's about when the old Philbert would have punched Malcolm's pimp ass out. But he'd learned patience and self-discipline, as well as the language of liberation.

"I'm not telling you this to disapprove, but to help save your life, brother. There are many lies in the world, but there's one big lie, and revealing that lie means finding out who you are and who your people are, like I found out who

197

I am. You think you are free, going here and there, but you are in the shackles of the race of white devils. Only you can deliver yourself from bondage, and you can do it only by following the Honorable Elijah Muhammad."

"I've been gone longer than I thought! You've turned into one of those crazy religious niggers!"

Philbert felt a rush of chemicals across his back, filling up the muscles in his arms. While not budging an inch, his body seemed to swell larger. His voice, backed by anger, but so cold and restrained, took the image of a flimsy gate holding back a huge bull bent on tearing Malcolm apart.

"I am not a nigger."

Malcolm had been known to whistle "Don't Sit Under the Apple Tree" with guns pointed at him, but he found this impressive enough to shut his face.

Philbert had always been good at boxing and Malcolm was the one he'd practiced on.

But that made Malcolm quick-witted.

All Philbert and Hilda and Aunts Ella and Sassie could wish for was that Malcolm get slapped in jail before someone got tired of his mouth, his trickeration and his lies and shot him. And that he wouldn't take Reggie down with him.

His mother didn't care one way or the other. She was in Kalamazoo.

She, Louise, played checkers sometimes and often crocheted, listening to Jack Benny or Amos and Andy in the community room. Or she'd sit and stare at a blank white wall, pharmaceuticals running laps through her blood. She had been a pretty woman in her time, had what they called high yellow coloring, and her bearing was upright and regal. Her voice carried the musical cadences of her native Grenada. Her light skin contrasted with long, silky black hair, and as a child she'd been nicknamed Pocahontas. She liked the name, because it told of another princess who'd lost everything to the hands of robbers, save her dignity. She was educated, and tried to pass some of that on to the children, the desire to learn, to find out about the world. She read to the oldest ones when they were quite small, and all of them had done well in school at one time or another, which shows you they had the potential.

Now a dream kept recurring for her. It was strange, it referred to no one she knew personally, yet kept coming back, again and again, perhaps because it bound up many things she knew in one shorthand image or composite world. Or maybe as it was a message from some vast beyond, an attempt on behalf of some great intelligence beyond the clouds to tell her something. At times, as she came in and out of consciousness, moored to nothing except the confinements of physical space and thus able herself to drift away, she entered the world of her creation to such an extent that it became as real as anything in her life. The clouds and fog would burn off to find her on a large island plantation, like where she'd grown up, but also different. The master was an old, gray-haired white man in a wheelchair, who would be rolled out on the large portico each morning to get his air. He'd been a very kindly old man, who'd once been hearty enough to call everyone over to him each Friday afternoon to sing him songs as the sun went down. Her old aunts had even told her of a time when the old man had been hearty and hale and worked the fields side by side with his hired hands. He paid them, which made him an exception, and made all his workers the envy of laborers for miles around. Or so she'd been told, anyway. The Friday singalongs had happened when she was a girl and pleased her to no end— she had a fine, deep voice, even as a child, which blended with the others in gospel chorus so sweetly that in short order she'd been allowed to lead, with the rest of the singers backing her. But after a time, the old man was too weak even for this, and all they saw of him was when he was wheeled onto the broad portico. This glimpse was distant—by this time they'd already be out in the fields. Once verdant and lush, the crops were having trouble. Vegetables and cotton hardly grew at all, and got ravaged by weevils, while weeds grew overnight to your waist. The soil parched open in cracks, aching for rain. None came. The fogs descending seemed deprived of moisture, or at least of enough to sustain life. The overseer, who now had no one looking over his own shoulder, blamed the workers for the poor yield. But it wasn't their fault—the land itself seemed to be turning barren. When she was close enough to the main house to see the old man's face when he was brought out in the morning, his jaw had gone slack and a line of drool fell onto his shirt. He had shrunken within his own clothes, which now appeared several sizes too big for him. "Eyes front!" snapped the overseer, who tolerated no looking away from the work and used any excuse to blame them for the plantation's new troubles. He was a knotty-muscled, fireplug of a man, whose face was marred by a large, red birthmark, which ran from the left side of his forehead and spread diagonally across one eye to surround half his mouth. Strangely, the birthmark seemed to grow larger and more hideous over time, and every time she saw him she was reminded of the pirate ships and limbs replaced by sharp metal hooks she'd read about in storybooks. The money paid them by the new man, a young one who needed to get outdoors more, such was the pallor of his skin, was now taxed to supplement equipment purchases, so they received only half of what they had in the past. Meanwhile, the prices of cloth and small items of necessity had risen steadily and the meals they were provided grew smaller and smaller. Oatmeal that had once clung to a spoon turned upside down now ran off before you could get it to your mouth. They got no better meat than was being given to the dogs.

"Master must not be being told what's really going on," someone would say at night from his bedclothes in a dark room where twenty slept on straw ticks and tried not to sneeze, for one sneeze would get everyone going.

"Master's dead. He can still get his eyes open, but he can't speak a lick."

"No, he ain't. He always told us he'd take care of us as long as he was alive."

"That's what I'm saying. We ain't be being taken care of because he's dead."

Her mind would move to the old patriarch's bedroom. His bed was a four-poster with a billowy cotton canopy and veils on each side to keep out mosquitoes. Daily, new freshly picked flowers were set in a vase atop an expansive mahogany table, inlaid with pinstripe swirls of yellow oak. Around this table were beautiful straight-backed chairs of the same mahogany frames, with plump cushions on the back and seats covered by red shiny velvet on which no one had ever sat. One hundred gold tacks pinned the material into each chair at tiny, perfect intervals, the material tucked perfectly even at the rounded joints. They were the most beautiful chairs Louise had ever seen, and she never thought of them without her eyes starting to tear a little. But the tears never forced her to stop thinking about the chairs either. Their beauty made her sad, but also comforted her and even elevated her spirit. She didn't know where or when in her life she had actually seen these beautiful chairs.

The man himself had shrunken in size, but his weight had settled into the chair, and getting him out of it was an effort that required three men, who, while brutally muscular all, approached the task so gingerly they seemed to believe that if they pulled directly on either of his arms the man would pull apart like rotten fruit. They got him upright, then another came forward, fell to his knees, and as the others slipped the suspenders off the man's shoulders, pulled the man's trousers open and slipped both these and his undergarment down to his knees. The man's genitals appeared, three shriveled walnuts. The attendants lowered the man to a sitting position in their arms and carried him to his bed, two maids in black cotton with white aprons pulling aside the veils, another from the opposite side turning back the sheets. They sat him at the edge. A piece of shiny, coated canvas lay atop the mattress pad and after one on the maids sprinkled talc over it, the men arranged themselves on opposite sides and shifted him onto it. Throughout all of this, the man's expression never changed. His eyes were the faded blue of the confederate army, glistened over with fluid. A white thatch, finer than his hair had been in his youth, it still had enough stiffness for a few strands to stick up. This the maid covered with a tasseled nightcap.

Louise came to. She blinked her eyes. Around her were the other people in the home, all gowned in hospital white, most older than her, a few younger, slumped in easy chairs or standing, walking around in isolated circles.

The voice of the president warbled from the radio.

America I'm putting my queer shoulder to the wheel.
Allen Ginsberg

1.

A sleepy-eyed man can be my death.

I don't mean heavy-lidded, a don't-care gangster. There's a look, and it's helped by youth, of one so beautiful that it's the smile of first awaking, a ridge of sleep still blemishing the cheek.

The sleepy eyes smile, they don't know how beautiful. Or pretend not to.

They are so young. Younger than their physical years!

To know one's own beauty—we always assume they know it themselves, but how could they? To be confident alone is not to know the ache of the other side, an ache becoming more prominent with age. And that's assuming confidence, not subject to clandestine suggestion and designs.

No, beauty does not know itself—that is to say, its effects.

The sleepy-eyed smile goes to the heart, is so innocent. It can be broad day and still the effect is of the blanket pulled to the chin and the eyes blinking sweetly in the light.

And so you can be lulled to sleep. Sleeping, asleep, you are vulnerable. You can catch your death and never even feel it.

Does a bullet hurt?

No. What you feel is your heart exploding. Not literally, but what does it matter as the frame begins to crumble? You feel its impact, one hard on the next, but they are just rain-drops on the roof of a building on fire.

How do I know?

I was shot once. That is, on one occasion. I was shot at

four times. Two missed me.

One grazed my shoulder.

The last—the second in order fired—was nearly lethal. It missed my actual heart, but took the top half of my right lung by the time it had been removed by surgeons.

So now I am often liable to be caught short of breath.

You'd think that I wouldn't act so breathlessly, take such chances.

You'd think so.

2.

For the record, Doc, the name's Post. Dick Post. Christened Richard Adams Post, IV.

I couldn't have chosen a more appropriate name for myself. I was never called Richard, except by my father in anger. I've always been Dick. That is the public form of my desire, the meaning of a name made secret by means of its public nature. The expression of a man's desire and fulfillment—its swollen intrusiveness, its spitting—is so offensive that therein lies its eroticism. It is nearly always hidden. Even for me, a man who takes chances in order to be fully the man I am that gives me pleasure, there is an overwhelming degree of hiddenness. In fact, the more overt I am, the more hidden. Even when I show myself to strangers, even when I sneak behind someone on a bus and leave evidence of my presence that they will later find on the back of a pantsleg, I am for that the more secret, the more anonymous, for no one has seen me. It is in that instance as I've chosen it. And when I do reveal myself, it is when I can be assured of anonymity, with those who have no recourse to the authorities, or in places where I can slip quickly into a crowd and be gone.

My boner is my rigid self and calling card, but I will not

be found by those who want to find me. I know all they want is to exterminate me.

It was time to get out of New York. I had made myself seen once too often.

I knew the police were after me, and that they had a good description. I had been much too indiscreet. Right in the center of Washington Square, for Chrissakes, for a gaggle of witnesses, and then swift pursuit by a nearby flatfoot. Not swift enough, not this time, but I was slipping, like I wanted to be caught.

I did not. I knew if they got me I'd be a tar baby for anything they wanted to throw. They would call me before the law and whip me with years, years among real criminals, companies of hoodlums, and laugh if it meant my death. No, laying low on my own or hiding out at my sister's place in the Bronx would not be enough this time—I needed to get out of town, at least for a while.

At the drugstore on 14th and Lex, I knew, was a rideboard. I would go wherever it pointed.

How could I know that it would point me toward my destiny? How could I know that to go away would be to bring me back to myself, and comfort?

How could I know that, of all places, Bloomington, Indiana, would prove my secret home, the home of my secrets?

How could I know that the emissary of my savior would go by the unlikely name of Wardell Pomeroy?

3.

There was a college kid staring at the corkboard, probably about fifteen years my junior, pulling cards down one at a time and holding them to his nose.

I tipped my hat to him. "Anything smell good?"

"That's what I'm checking for—the rose of my future."

He was tan, with muscles like a young colt and short, dark hair combed to a crest atop his head.

"Looks pretty bleak," he said, now flipping through a small stack culled from the twenty or so on the board. Most were offering little more than pay for transporting furniture to Jersey or Westchester. "Pretty bleak, I say," he crooned. "I want to go west, and I want to go today, right now. This is the best they got."

With one of his powerful forearms, he extended me the card. "Cornfields," he said.

"You look like a ballplayer."

"Was a halfback at Columbia."

"Graduate?"

He put a solemn hand to his chest. "I'm opting instead for life education."

The card indicated we'd be transporting a piece of equipment to a University in Indiana in a Willy's Overland, a kind of Army-style, general purpose vehicle.

"I suppose those are crossroads," he said, emphasizing half-rhymes as I examined the card. "Destiny's lode at the crossroads."

"Crossroads?"

"Heartland. A man can go east or west, north to Canada, south to Mexico, diagonally to aching desert or cool, verdant forest. Not much there, but a lot of where you might be going."

"You don't sound like you're headed anyplace particular."

"Just the places I haven't seen, Mr. Bean."

"Sounds like a plan. Mind if I tag along?"

"I insist on it." He thrust out his hand. "Jack."

"Dick."

"Jack and Dick for trek or trick," he sing-songed again. I wasn't sure if he was drunk or just goofy. He stuck out his thumb and gestured back over his shoulder: "I got a buddy who is the craziest, high-lifeingest, most happening dude on the planet, who'll be going with us. He's parking cars downtown right now, but free to go as soon as the man gives him his pay this afternoon."

"And this fellow—" I looked at the card—"Pomeroy, makes four. Looks to be some sort of scientist."

And I swallowed hard. The equipment was to be picked up from a building at NYU, no more than a hundred yards from my follies with the law the day before.

"Hey, do you mind meeting me uptown after you pick up the goods? I've got to clear out some junk from my sister's house. She's moving out to the country before I'll be getting back, and—"

I didn't finish the sentence, because I knew this was a hopeless suggestion. This card was my best ride out of town, but he'd gotten to it before I had and was likely to simply abscond the moment it was possible, with or without me.

I waved my words aside before he could say a word in reply. "The hell with it," I said. "Let's just get out of here."

Just act natural, I thought. Be cool. After all, who's gonna expect to see me back so soon? Who would expect to find me in the company of clean-cut collegians?

4.

Billy Backus had been a ballplayer. I was assisting in the training room at Weston Prep that Spring, and I'd rub him down after games. Nothing speeds seduction along like mineral oil. Soon I was taking him in my mouth. He was worried. "You don't understand. If Coach or anyone else finds out, I'm finished. No Harvard, no scholarship, everything I've worked for, gone."

"They wouldn't do anything to you. You're the star. They'd blame it all on me. And I'd take the blame. Don't worry," I said, "I'll protect you."

He had a pushy, bastard father who'd made him instinctively distrustful of anyone who offered him help. He suspected a con game wherever he looked. I think even as he had his fingers in my hair, even as his legs trembled and buckled, he was thinking I was somehow his enemy.

He couldn't have been more wrong. I loved Billy Backus.

At the end of the term was the Chancellor's Darby. I got on his back in the piggy-back race, riding him, bouncing in time with the rhythm of my mount like a jockey. I still had a boy's body then, slimmer in the arms and legs. I weighed one hundred and twenty-five pounds carrying most of my textbooks. My crotch was tight against his back, my erection nestled in the crevice his big shoulders made of his spine.

We won the first heat, lined up to await the second. He looked at me and laughed. As non-suggestively as I could, I kept my hands over my groin.

He had beautiful white teeth and a sleek, hard throat, and his eyes, lovely, were half-closed in pleasure.

That snapshot will remain mine through the fires of any hell I end up burning in.

We began the second heat. I felt a droplet of come at the end of my cock, and I untucked my t-shirt from out of my shorts before jumping up on his back. We took off, and I felt him establish his rhythm and matched it, my hands cupping the top halves of his chest. My cock felt like I was inside him.

I came as we reached the finish line, and the whole world of bright colors—green grass, baby-blue sky, white cottoned boys and our headmasters' ceremonial gold blazers—burst and flared like a camera flash.

We finished second by a nose. We crossed the limed stripe at the end of the field and Billy collapsed in joyous fatigue. I panicked as soon as we were uncoupled. I bounced to my feet and, doubled over, sprinted for the locker room.

I reached it, an empty tiled room, everyone outside at the festivities. I was covered with my own warm spunk, which had soaked through underwear, shorts and t-shirt to ooze slimily across my belly. I had to bury these in my locker, fast, and hope to find clothes that matched them to put on. I rubbed myself off with the sweaty back of my race shirt, buried it quickly away and had new underwear and shorts back on when Billy charged into the room.

"What are you doing?" he shouted. He wasn't angry. But neither was he acknowledging what had just happened. He just looked at me, blankly. "Come on," he said, "Hurry up. We're in the run-off for third-place."

I was confused. Hadn't he felt what I had? And then it hit me. He didn't know. I had fucked him and he didn't know. We had never done that. Billy didn't think of himself as a queer, and thought about what we did as boys having fun, like splashing at each other in the trout stream. He knew it was wrong, but somehow since he was doing it, believed it had to be innocent. I had never suggested his bumhole, or mine.

But I knew something now. It was true! You could have sex with someone without them knowing!

Of all the discoveries in my life, this was one I made entirely on my own, one I've never told anyone, Doctor, until now. It changed me more than anything I might have learned at school or from anyone else.

I put on a new shirt and went out to race again on top

of Billy. Again he ran hard and I matched his tempo.

We did take third.

The position they call Show.

5.

All I can say is that I hope these walls are as soundproof as you say, Doc.

Ward can tell you the next part as easily as I can, how we met up with him at the automat on 23rd and decided we should get the equipment first and then pick up Jack's friend, so we'd be able to get out on the road faster. We could spend the night out on the other side of Jersey and then drive into Bloomington today. No, that isn't quite what happened, I know. That's what we said at the time, though. The best laid plans, eh, Doc? I didn't know I'd end up doing anything different—I was just concerned with making my run.

I know it's no surprise to you because you know him, but when I first saw Wardell my jaw dropped. If ever there was a man who was meant to be a movie star, it's Wardell. Tall, dark, and handsome—I'm not surprised that you utilize his talents the way you do here. He put both me and Jack completely at our ease from the moment we met him. And if I were casting a leading man to star in group sex demonstrations, I'm sure I couldn't do any better, especially given what I take to be his great proficiency in that department, as well as his excellent technique. Do I find him attractive? Who wouldn't. But no, he's not the type I would ever approach. My heart would be in my throat. I know I must impress you as a man who operates without fear, but I can assure you that isn't the case. Like I said, I get short of breath, because of the shooting. It kicks in whenever I see such an Olympian as Ward—my nerves would make it impossible for me to get out the first word.

But I had seen him before at this same automat, talking to this man or that. I never realized before what he was up to—getting more stories for your study.

That automat, I agree, is a very good place to meet the types of men you're interested in.

We had the Willy's with him, and we took it down to a back parking lot of a brick building about a block from Washington Square. I was very happy to discover how out of the way we were from the crowds of promenaders near the arch and the fountain.

The equipment we were to transport was not what I expected. Who would have imagined such a thing? An anatomically correct model of an adult woman, made entirely of glass.

She was heavy, too—had to be careful, but ungainly, so that there was no easy way to move her a great distance quickly. It was all Wardell, Jack and I could do to get her down the four flights of stairs to the back entrance.

It's funny that I keep saying "she" and "her." But that's how she struck me from the first, as a creature with her own identity, beautiful and Amazonian, and absolutely perfect in contour, a wonderful specimen for your researches, I'm sure. I am certainly aware of what men admire in women, even if it isn't my particular preference. I have been envious, in fact, of women and their inviting bodies, the reclining mounds and softness that beg to be fucked.

Though I agree with you, most women are essentially cold. Or as you say, too repressed to enjoy sex as easily as men.

We had the model in the very back of the Willy's now, and Pomeroy stuffed newspaper in around and over her to protect her from shocks. Jack sat in the back seat, and

Wardell and I took the front. It was almost three, time to pick up the final traveler.

I agree with Jack—he will be a great subject for your study as well. It seems like all that guy Neal thinks about is sex.

Jack had been talking a blue-streak about this guy since he'd found out about your study. "Let me tell you. He needs to get out to Frisco to get back together with his ex-wife, and he's leaving his wife here for a while to do it. One woman is never enough for my boy Neal, or even two. If he doesn't make ten women on his way from coast to coast, I'll eat Dick's hat. And he's got a dangle on him like a murderous anaconda."

Pomeroy was enthused. "Great! Perhaps when we get to the motel tonight, I can take down his history."

"If you want to hear about every sweet honey Neal Cassady ever got into, you might have to take up residence there permanently. But he'll also get you to Indiana sooner than you expected. Maybe we'll just ball the jack all the way to Indiana, because Neal Cassady's talent as a swordsman plays second fiddle only to his greatest talent. He is the world's swiftest and most skillful driver."

Ward turned to me. "I hope you'll be interested in giving us your history as well."

"Sure," I said. "We'll see what happens."

I was still worried. We were still in New York. And for all I heard, I didn't think it applied to me. I knew you wanted to know about sex; I didn't know you'd want to have anything to do with perversions. How could I know that what was criminal to most people was something you would call, though I think you go a bit far, heroic?

"Do you ever interview guys in prisons?" asked Jack suddenly.

"Sometimes," said Pomeroy. "Why?"

He didn't answer. Maybe there were more secrets to this college kid than I'd suspected.

6.

I've never seen a cowboy outside the movies, but as soon as I saw Neal, I knew that's what I was seeing. He was lean and weathered as a fencepost. He bounded across the lot as soon as we pulled into it. Jack reached across the back seat and swung open the door with perfect timing, as Cassady suddenly left his feet and dove in headfirst, managing to hook the door with his ankle and pull it closed behind him, all in one motion. His head was in Jack's lap, and he spun over so that he faced upward as a gush of words came immediately out of his mouth.

"Unless y'all want me to drive. I been driving sixteen straight hours, since eleven last night, but in these confined spaces you can't ever really drive, just zip and park, zip and park, so there's nothing I'd rather do than to get this sucker out on the open road and gun her, you understand!" He sat up and looked behind him. "Hey! Who is this little filly? Come on, sugar, don't be shy, let's have us a little peek." He hadn't stopped moving since he'd come in sight, and now, bouncing on the seat, he twisted his hips in mid-air so as to land on his knees facing the model, his back to us. In a moment, and before Pomeroy could object, he'd stripped the newspaper covering off her chest.

"Whoo-hoo! That's one nice set of titties, maybe the nicest I've ever seen, except for one time a little Spanish girl in I believe it was Albuquerque and those had the advantage of being attached to one of the warmest honeys or I should say heinies it was ever my pleasure to know, but these are all clear and round and bee-oo-ti-ful, and look at the way those pert little nipples stick up in the air like she just wants to be made right there in the back of the car here in the middle of Manhattan!" He pinched one of the nipples approvingly.

"Gentlemen," said Jack, "May I introduce you to the most happening man in all of Manhappen, Dr. Cassady. Dr. Cassady, these are Doctors Post and Pomeroy."

"My excuses, distinguished sirs," said Cassady, flipping back around to us before we could even get a word in and extending his hand, though I could see Pomeroy was somewhat worried at the rough handling of what he thought of as expensive scientific equipment, which we'd all treated very gingerly till now. "I'm very pleased to be accompanying you on this trip out into the heartland, though if you ask me we ain't going nearly far enough, no, you don't really see America until you get to the High Plains, and from there on you get the real wide-open spaces, but even though we're stopping a good thousand miles before where we may want to get to, I appreciate the opportunity to help you transport this lovely cargo, and offer my services as driver forthwith, which will make us real good time, sirs, I assure you, excellent time!"

Pomeroy shook hands with him. "Ward Pomeroy."

"Dick Post," I said.

"Pleased to meet you, Neal," continued Pomeroy. "But please, I must warn you, the anatomical model isn't a toy. It's scientific equipment designed to model coital processes, and is important to our research. Please be careful. In fact, you'd do me a great favor if you weren't to touch it at all."

Neal rubbed his chin thoughtfully, "I see, I see. I didn't mean to do any harm, and I promise to be careful. But Jack told me the research you were doing, and that made me all excited—Kinsey, eh? like the whiskey?—and then seeing this little glass girl you got back here, well, I've yet to see a honey like that that I didn't want to strip her bare first thing, but you're right sir, this isn't fun and games, it's science, the sober pursuit of knowledge." Neal took a breath, then leaned forward a little to Pomeroy, confidentially, "But I don't mind telling you, at the same time, Ward, knowing the line of work in which you're engaged from talking to Jack here, that this little girl, glass or not, has given me a boner the size of Toledo!"

I don't think any of us could help glancing down at Neal's crotch, especially with the advance notice we'd had. What Jack had said appeared true—his pecker was popping out down his pantsleg, terminating at a knob outlined against the dungaree material, as close to his knee as to his beltline.

Pomeroy was impressed, and smiled toward Neal. "Neal, I think you are a man after my own heart. I felt an erection coming on myself when we picked her up in the laboratory."

Jack now burst into laughter along with Neal and Ward. "Believe me," Pomeroy continued, "That's one of the great advantages, when you do the type of work I do in Bloomington, of being able to wear a lab coat!"

Pomeroy now turned to look at me as well as the others. "Dr. Kinsey is interested in all aspects of human sexuality, and so I want you all to know you can be as free as you wish to be in discussing all manner of sexual expression, assured that what you say will be held in the strictest confidence and heard in an absolutely non-judgmental environment."

"Did you hear that honey-pie?" said Neal into the back seat. "I think I'll call you Lulu, because you are certainly some kinda Lulu, you are. Just look at those fine American breasts just sitting there, Lu and Lu, each one asking for a man's undivided attention!"

7.

Neal stuffed his small ditty bag in the last open crevice under the back seat of the Willy's and Pomeroy drove us out of the city. "Just gimme 45 minutes to shut these worn-out old peepers of mine and then I'll be good as new and ready to take on whatever driving duties are called for." Cassady lay back down with the back of his head in Jack's lap. He was still wearing parking garage overalls.

A lull in the conversation was enough now to send Neal immediately to sleep. He was already snoring. Jack looked down at him, and didn't seem to mind. For awhile we were all quiet except for this droning.

I myself broke the silence. Who was this college kid? I was thinking to myself.

"By the way," I said to Jack, "I never did get your last name."

"He is Jean-Louis de Kerouac, Canuck extraordinaire," proclaimed Neal, without opening his eyes.

"There's no 'de'," said Jack. "That's the aristocratic prefix. Just Jean-Louis Kerouac. A line out of humble Breton serfdom."

Neal began snoring again.

"That reminds me, Ward," said Jack, "I've been meaning to ask you—Pomeroy, I like that name. What is that? Who were your father's people?"

"I didn't really know my father," said Pomeroy.

"Oh, I'm sorry," said Jack.

"No, that's alright. Not having ever known him, I can't

really take offense on his account."

"I'm interested, though," said Jack. "If you don't mind."

Pomeroy smiled, eyes forward on the road. We were traveling no more than 45 miles per hour and had to slow down to 20 or even stop in each little town we passed through. The towns were still pretty frequent, not far outside New York. We'd already seen a lot of new buildings, new construction, large gas stations and restaurants, like tendrils of the city coming out into the country. "How can I mind it when people ask me questions? I'm going around the country asking people about their sexual experiences!"

"Yeah, I guess that's true. So do you know anything about your father?"

"The name, I believe, is Scottish. But all I know about my father is that he's from out West somewhere. California, maybe, some time in Texas, Oklahoma. I even heard stories that he rode the rails for a while."

A loner on the railroads, I thought. Not an unfamiliar idea. "I wonder what your father's sexual history would have been like," I said.

"You know," said Pomeroy, "I think that might be part of what draws me to this work, now that you mention it. I'm a happily married man, but I've always wondered what it would be like, sexually, to be a drifter. What it would be like to have a string of nearly anonymous partners. I hope you don't mind, but my work with Prok—that is, Professor Kinsey, Prok is what we call him—my work on this project has made me see the desirability and necessity of being utterly frank when talking about sex. I don't mind telling you that I think of my father quite often in doing this work. Seeing as how I have no picture of him in my mind, I see myself in his shoes when I think of him. I'm travelling the country much as he must have, but in a much different capacity, so I have to maintain a professional distance. I think of what it must have been like for him, as a drifter, meeting women in boxcars or in small-town boarding houses, women who are utterly naive yet powerful in their sexual energy. Nothing holds them back, they're willing to try anything. I've interviewed such women, yet felt constrained because I'd educated myself out of that class and couldn't approach them. Not to mention my responsibilities to Prok."

This speech was enough to rouse Neal again, who snorted awake and shouted, "Whoo-hee!," startling us. "You and me both, Ward, you and me both! I was just now starting to get that glass filly in back, so unashamed and so lovely showing her features to maximum effect, out of my mind, when I heard you and I guess I must have been dreaming, because I was sitting in a little Mexicali dive with that little lady from Albuquerque I was telling you about before, who was just what you were just talking about, with her big brown eyes swallowing me up right there at the table, and her brown bazookas tied up in a teensy little cotton halter and the hot scent coming off of them going right into my chest and then on down into my dick, and I was just about to get down into the good part of the dream when I realized I was hearing you talk about your old father the railroad man, and man, I've been on the railroad, it's just like that. Man, whoo, I've had enough of talking about it, Ward, what do you say we stop at the next little Jersey town we see and find us some fun-loving honeys and do a little research on our own, hey, Ward?"

We weren't far enough away yet for my comfort. "But it's not even dark yet," I tried to counter.

"There's never a right nor a wrong time for doing the horizontal hula, my friend," said Neal. "No-sir-ee, Bob. And

I can tell my man Ward here is a swordsman, ain't that right? So between Jack and both of us, they'll be plenty of action to go around. You've got all of those young mamas who've just come off their shifts at the plant—I betcha we'll find any number of gals around the laundromat and the hair parlor looking, or maybe not even knowing they're looking, but if you say the magic words they'll come running into your arms, I've been there a hundred times, boy, a hundred times! We just gotta get somewhere! What's coming up?"

"That would normally be something I'd be up for," said Ward. "But I really do have to get to Bloomington, and we should try to get a little further along. By the time we get there tomorrow and unpack the model, I'm not going to be able to get much shut-eye as it stands now. I want to get in at least a short nap before our debriefing session."

"Debriefing! Yessir, Ward, debriefing—I like the way you think," said Neal. "But I've got this all figured out, and maybe we can get in a little debriefing session before we get all the way out to Indiana, yessir. Listen to me now, Bloomington is approximately 700 miles from where we are right now, maybe a little less but we'll call it 700 to give our-selves the benefit of the mathematician. Currently we're driving at a top speed of 50 miles per hour, minus all of the little towns we have to go through, I'd compute this to be an average of, say, 40 miles per hour, which cogitates to a near-ly 18 hour drive, all things remaining constant, maybe 17 and a half, given that towns are now becoming less prevalent as we leave the urbanity. If we stop for a bite to eat we'll get there about three or four in the morning. But, and no offense to your driving, Ward, I can see you've got a nice feel for the road, I bet I can get this Willy's cooking up to a constant speed of 65 miles per hour, maybe 70, which these babies can do if you slowly coax them up that high, and maybe I can even get under the hood to loosen up the governor a little more and make us fly, because an extra 15 miles an hour over the course of our journey equates to four extra hours, which is more than enough time for us to hook up with a couple of pretty country honies in the next town and make them. And Ward, mind you, I'm still highly aware you should note of that fragile little creature in back, my little darling Lulu—don't you worry, when I take the wheel I will be nothing but kind to old Lulu, as I have never been anything but nice to women and thinking only of them. Believe me, I can see a pot hole coming a mile off and it's nothing for me to cruise along at 70 miles per hour and still give everyone concerned the smoothest ride imaginable, zoom through these little towns without slowing down much and not even put one little hairline crack in Lulu's pretty little heinie. Cause she's already got all the nice sweet cracks she needs, far as I know, boy howdy!"

"Neal is a very good driver," Jack repeated.

"Don't you need to get some sleep before you drive?" I asked Neal. "You've been up all night."

"Sleep is for pussies," said Neal, winking. "Meow!"

The man of science was himself starting to give way. "Well, I suppose I've already been burning the candle at both ends and another night without sleep won't really kill me either. You don't think it'll hurt the engine?"

"The road is to the engine as sweet pussy is to red-blooded American men like you and me, Ward. This here vehicle wants as much to get laid as any one of us, wants to let it out and go go go! There will be no question of running out of steam and we won't lose any time, either, I promise you." Then after we're through in this little town you can sleep all the way to Indiana if you want."

I leaned over to Ward. "You aren't really thinking of

doing this, are you?" I said.

But it was too late. We were pulling into a little town called Dronett, with a quaint little Main Street and the five o'clock sun painting long shadows from flags adorning the storefronts.

8.

Billy grew increasingly cold toward me, increasingly violent, increasingly worried, and he less frequently apologized. I became his slave, because he still liked blow-jobs. He might disappear and ignore me for three days or four, even a week if there was an athletic outing. Once I remember finding an abrasion on his cock, he had been beating off so furiously while avoiding me. He needed me and hated his need.

I gave love but took none. Or, rather, took a love that was not given. Does love precede desire, give it its form, or take up a form already present to try to fulfill its dreams? Or does desire precede love, the body's need fixing itself upon an object, and signaling the mind to start creating stories about it?

I had to put up with Billy passing me by in the halls without glancing at me while I still had the tingle of his come in my mouth.

We were now seniors, and Billy was actively making his plans to leave. His family had friends in high places. He talked about one day becoming a senator, after his college football and baseball careers concluded. His father called him three or four times a week and told him who to cozy up to, who to smile at. Mr. Backus had good friends among the trustees, servants among the school administration, untold numbers of spies. Any one of them might have tipped him

222

off about his son's unhealthy friendship.

Near the end of the fall term Billy had already obtained his spot at Harvard.

I wasn't nearly as well connected as Billy, but my family had money and my grades were good, so I applied there as well. I didn't tell Billy that was what I was doing. He never asked. It never really occurred to him that when he moved on, he might not completely separate himself from his former life. I didn't really know why I was keeping my plans a secret from Billy—I half-thought that I was saving the good news of my acceptance to surprise him, and that when we were back to the way we had been, for brothers who had shared what we had shared could not long remain estranged, we would celebrate together and thereafter always remain friends, *semper fidelis*. But I also feared telling him—that I would somehow make him angry. He was so tense, so worried, not only about me but about his future, and I would be doing myself a disservice if I didn't also mention the times when I soothed his fears rather than adding to them. I believed in him completely. I knew that one day we'd have separate families and careers, but I also expected we'd always have our friendship.

I was a pale young fool. I didn't know the way the world worked, how important it was to someone like Billy Backus to maintain a white and unsullied appearance. How money could be its own detergent, and how I was nothing more as far as Billy was concerned than the first hints of a discoloration that, left untended to, might develop into a deep, red stain.

He was about to have his life scrubbed clean of me.

None of this process of stigmatization is anything new to you, I know, Dr. Kinsey, from having heard you talk. You are no stranger to how a man like me is marked and hunted

223

down, how any injustice against us is justifiable.

But I knew none of this then, as I prepared for the end of the fall term and Christmas, 1927.

The Christmas Gala, a formal dinner and dance with local bigwigs and some of the girls from our sister school, was to take place before we went home for the Winter Recess. This was of course during prohibition, and I'd never drank alcohol. I knew that some of the more outrageous boys did, but I was normally quiet and studious.

Somebody got to the punchbowl. That wouldn't have been so bad in itself, but then there were also a couple of flasks being passed around secretly, hand to hand under the long banquet tables of the hall where the event was being held.

A hipflask got to me. Just then, Professor Johnston, one of our professors, came by our table to wish us Merry Christmas. I capped it and put it in my pocket. It belonged to Ringley, a large, red-faced, crew-cutted boy who was always in the middle of any antics that went on at Weston. But I didn't see him around now, nor was I able to pass it along to any of the others. I nipped from it—it tasted awful, basement rum of some description—and poured a little more in my punchglass. I didn't know anything about alcohol, how much was too much, but it didn't take a great deal to overindulge. I was suddenly light-headed and goofy. I forgot I even had the flask in my pocket.

I looked for Billy. I suddenly felt tremendous waves of love for him come over me. I wanted to find him and proclaim in front of everyone what we were to each other—lifelong best friends, the best kind of friends, who would do anything for each other.

Billy was talking with Coach, Rev Hindley, and some of the football boosters at the head table, where the Chancellor had toasted us to begin the evening. In the season just ended, Billy had scored the winning touchdown in the final game. Everything he did seemed mythic, larger than life. And I was the one who took his cock in my mouth.

"Billy," I yelled, still ten yards away.

Billy purposely didn't look up, and kept talking. He had such an easy way with people, words falling dreamily from his mouth, his head tilted at a slight, personable angle, eyes soft and gleaming. Rev Hindley smiled my way, tolerant of my youthful enthusiasms even if I was being rude by interrupting.

I came to the front of the table. Billy wouldn't meet my eyes, so I addressed myself to Rev, a gray-haired man in dark clothes and minister's collar.

"Isn't Billy beautiful," I said, loud enough for Billy himself to hear, and probably much louder.

"Yes, he is," said Rev, nodding in appreciation of God's splendor. Then a dark cast come over Rev's eyes and he looked at me askance. He stood up from the table. "Let me talk to you for a moment, Dick."

I remembered now—the flask! I felt sick and dizzy. Rev came around to my side of the table and took me by the arm.

As soon as he grabbed me, my stomach roiled and I bent over and began vomiting on the polished, inlaid wood floor.

The flask was discovered. I had ruined the event and would be in trouble with my parents and get extra detention, to be sure.

But I was unprepared for what actually happened.

"Expelled?" I shrieked when I got the news from my parents upon arriving home.

A letter had preceded my arrival, and was in my parents' hands as I debarked the train.

I had been a bad influence on the entirety of the senior

class, it said. Culminating in the debacle of the Christmas Gala, my behavior for months had been so debauched and reprobate that the school had feared even broaching the subject with my parents, for it would lead to disclosure of incidents so horrible that they were certain the crisis should only be revealed when I was back at home and they could speak with me about it face to face. There was no offer of readmission upon contrite apology and reformation of my character. I was too dangerous an influence, and had already nearly caused the ruin of at least one of the other students. Purely and simply, I was out.

My parents were flabbergasted. My mother cried. My father was beyond anger, utterly dumbfounded and confused. I had always been a good boy, never in trouble. I felt terrible, as if I had crushed their lives instead of my own, wasting their money, spoiling their dreams.

"What in heaven's name have you been doing up there?" my father asked me.

What could I say?

"I haven't been doing anything. The flask belonged to another boy, and besides that night, I've never been in trouble at Weston."

"Oh, and so I suppose Chancellor Stewart is simply inventing these allegations for his own amusement."

"Maybe he is."

The school being recessed, my father called the Chancellor at his home. I was not privy to their conversation. But soon I was scheduled to see a psychologist. There would be more of this to come over the years, as my parents tried to cure me. I cured myself when I learned to simply lie to everyone and keep my tendencies and desires fully hidden.

9.

"I'm looking forward to seeing your powers of persuasion in action, Dr. Cassady," said Ward.

Neal didn't register hearing this. He had now put one leg over the middle of the front seat and wedged the front of his body forward so that he resembled a hurdler captured photographically in mid-stride about to smash his way out of the Willy's. His face was scant inches from the windshield, and he eagerly peered around front, left and right down Main Street, chattering, "Lemme see, lemme see, lemme see, lemme see."

I was not immune to the testosterone energy now filling the car. While before I'd been worrying about making good my escape, now I realized I was worried about nothing. No one was following me off the island of Manhattan. Now I was more conscious of my throat feeling hollow, missing cock. With all of the shenanigans of the last few days, it had been probably a week since I'd given any head. Memory leaves its imprint on a body, and I was beginning to feel the empty form of what I wanted—a tickle, a desire. I would need to separate from the others and go on my own to find it. Somewhere in this town, if there wasn't a man just like me, wandering and looking for some action, a mirror image of myself, there might likely be found at least a rentable substitute, a nobody who wouldn't mind getting his rocks off with my encouragement.

"You know, guys," I said. "Why don't you just let me out right here. I think I'm just going to walk around town a little."

"Really?" said Ward. "You don't want to tag along and maybe see a little tail?"

"Ah, man, Squaresville," said Jack. "Dick the stick."

"Meow," went Neal again. Jack hugged him around the

middle from the backseat and the two began to wrestle, Neal's front foot kicking the roof.

"Really," I said. "You can just let me out here. I saw a little gift shop back a little ways, and it reminded me that my aunt's birthday is coming up and I forgot to get her something."

We were in front of a dinette. We agreed to rendezvous at the same spot at eight p.m., unless we ran into each other earlier.

I knew I wouldn't be greatly missed.

Still being light out, it wasn't the ideal time to go cruising, but I had to take what I could get.

I walked a half-mile back to where Main Street began, where the emptiness of the state road began sporting houses, shops, and flags. I came to the large, wooden sign that read, Entering Dronett, with the Mayor's painted on signature beneath, and knocked on it. I turned around. OK, I thought, Let's see what this town has for me.

Most of the shops had closed. Truthfully, the place was dead. Families were reconvening indoors to sit down to dinner. There weren't even children around.

But I'm not really one for children. I was looking for something hard. A teenage boy might suffice, but what I really wanted was a stranger, an anonymous man.

At the other end of the street, I saw my three comrades come out of the dinette. I ducked in an alley between two brick storefront buildings. I saw them get back in the Willy's, which they'd parked where I'd gotten out, and drive off.

I was counting, I realized, on Pomeroy to keep them to their plan. The other two would probably just take off if it was them alone. And to be left in stinking little Dronett would be about as exciting as having my own hand as a lover the rest of my life. Not to mention the danger of not yet having made a full getaway.

Yet I wouldn't be able to obtain what I wanted in their company either.

Soon, I was back at the same dinette where they'd let me off. I went inside.

The place was empty except for a counter girl and a cook in back. I sat down and ordered a cup of coffee.

Through the cut-out wall separating the dining counter area from the kitchen I could see he was just what I was looking for. I ordered a ham sandwich to watch him work.

Unshaven, he was slightly bald and the front of his white shirt was stained with grease and wet spots of sweat. His right forearm, exposed by a rolled up sleeve, had an anchor tattoo and the letters USN. I didn't see a wedding ring. As for his left arm, he didn't have one: the sleeve on that side was folded in a neat square, pinned at the shoulder. He was muscular—his neck bulged as he reached for the knife and brought it down on the sandwich he'd constructed with one quickly moving hand. Chips and a pickle added, he handed the plate to the waitress, who handed it to me.

"Thank you," I said to the waitress.

"You're very welcome."

The cook said nothing to either of us, but turned around and began scrubbing a grill I could not see in the back of the kitchen. His back and shoulders worked.

"Excuse me," I said to the waitress. "Did you happen to see three men come in here a short time ago?"

"Yes, as a matter of fact they just left just before you came in here."

"Did you happen to catch where they were going?"

"Yes—I think they've gone up to Henry's. It's a road-house about two and a half miles outside of town."

"Two and a half miles? Darn it."

She gave me a sympathetic smile. She was a poor crosseyed creature who, while not yet that old, wasn't attractive either. It was no surprise the three hadn't dawdled long here.

I figured a town this size would hardly have a taxi service. "I don't suppose there's a place around here I could get a taxi."

"No, we sure don't have one of those here in Dronett. They have one over in Jeffersonville."

"I'd really like to catch up with them as soon as I can." I searched for some plausible reason. What I wanted, of course, was to get the cook to drive me over there. To get alone with the cook.

"In fact, I need to," I said. "They have my medicine. I have a heart condition. If I don't get it soon . . . ." I wasn't sure exactly what to say would happen to me, but leaving it open implied all manner of horrible fates.

"Oh, dear. Oh, dear."

"Can either of you quickly drive me over there?"

It was a fifty percent gamble, and it paid off. Pam, the waitress, didn't drive. Since it was dead, and since they'd be closing up anyway in about an hour, Tony the cook could take me.

I ate half the sandwich and left sixty cents on the counter. We went out to his car, a beat-up old Ford. Good—he'd like the money. He started it up with they key, shifted it into gear on the column and simultaneously maneuvered us backward out from behind the diner, then forward onto the road.

"Did that happen in the war?"

"Yep. Guadalcanal. We were hit by a Jap bomb. I thought I'd gotten away with only a little scratch, but my shrapnel wound got infected with seawater or some jungle garbage before I could get to a medic and they couldn't get rid of the infection." He bit his lip grimly. "Least it wasn't my right arm."

I nodded and unbuttoned the top of my shirt to show him my own wound, my nipple on that side gone and the skin pulled into a thick, pink, hook-shaped pucker.

"Pearl Harbor. My war was over pretty fast."

I always say Pearl Harbor. If I said Normandy or the Battle of the Bulge, I'd get asked how it healed up so fast.

Of course, to say the wound got me out of the war before it even started isn't, strictly speaking, a lie.

He turned out onto Main Street. I was starting to feel my heart pound, and my breathing get more shallow. Heart medicine—maybe that was what I was after.

No. It wasn't about my heart.

It was nearing time to make a move.

But before I could say anything, Tony spoke.

"OK, Mac. What's your game?"

My breath stopped. "Excuse me?" I choked out.

"I might only have one arm, but there's nothing wrong with my nose. I smelled you for an operator the moment you walked in." He sneered. "Heart medicine. Right."

OK, if he wanted direct, I'd give him direct. I took a slow breath, got it back to normal.

"I'm a queer."

"Jesus Christ. I knew it." He straightened and tensed up at the wheel. "If I didn't have to keep this hand on the wheel, I'd give you what for, fella."

"Wait. Don't get sore. Keep driving a little ways and just hear me out."

I took out my wallet and pulled two twenties.

"All you have to do is get your cock sucked."

"I ain't no queer."

"No one's saying you are. Are you telling me you don't

231

like blow jobs?"

"I ain't no goddamn queer, I said."

"There's no need for namecalling. You're just like any guy. I never heard of a guy who didn't like getting his cock sucked. You're not queer, but you wouldn't really mind my going down on you. You can close your eyes and imagine anything you want. Look, here's forty bucks."

"Stick it up your ass. You'd probably like that."

I pulled another twenty. "Sixty."

He looked at the money, three silver certificates on the front seat between us, then back at the road. "Fuck you."

"OK," I said. I took the bills and put them in my pocket.

He began as if to pull over. But he didn't.

"Eighty," I said.

He came right back: "One hundred."

"One hundred," I said back.

"And I never see you again in this town the rest of my life."

"You got it."

"Because I'll kill you."

We drove up a little further. "This is the road to the roadhouse. Did you still want to go there?"

"If you don't mind. After."

He didn't say anything. We took another side road a little ahead, which took us into farm country, red barns, fields, patches of woods. We were on a dirt road now and slowed near a stand of pines. He turned the Ford onto a tractor path off the road and drove us to a little shack.

"My father's place. He died a couple of months ago."

"I'm sorry."

"Thank you." He stopped the car and looked at me. "I suppose a fella can't . . . " He stopped and reconsidered whatever he was about to say, then fixed me in the eye.

"Queers make my skin crawl."

"Lean back," I said. "Close your eyes. Think of a woman."

He reclined, and I opened his pants, not speaking for fear of ruining his illusion. But a hundred bucks—I was going to take my time. His member was hardening as I touched with my fingertips. He was large and uncircumcised, a tiny bit of moisture at the opening of his urethra. With thumb and forefinger I gripped his shaft and put the crown between my lips. I licked down the front of the shaft. He moaned involuntarily.

"Faggot," he whispered hoarsely. "Faggot."

He tasted, besides the slightly bitter taste of his come, salty from sweat, working on a hot day. But no residue of sex smells. Just cock.

I slowly brought my mouth all the way down until he filled the back of my throat. I started and fought off the reflex to gag, my throat muscles spasming. I was also erect, and had one knee off the seat so that I was grinding my shaft, still in my pants, against the seat.

He put a hand on the back of my head, not violently. "Suck it, faggot. Eat my cock."

He came, exploding and choking me, semen filling the backs of my sinuses and cutting off my air for a moment. I pushed into the seat cushion hard and came myself, like dying for a moment, everything black and shivering. *Le petit mort.*

He readjusted his pants. Half of the bills were underneath me, so I shifted back and he gathered them up. I took out enough money to make it one hundred and he stuffed it in his pocket and drove me back down the road and up a county road to the tavern, not saying a word. The sun was setting behind us and it made the chrome edging on the hood of the black Ford glisten.

10.

I pushed open the bulky tin-plated door to Henry's.

It took my eyes a few moments to adjust to the darkness inside, and before I did, I heard Jack hail me from within a wall of loud jukebox dance music, "It's Philip Marlowe! He's found us!"

"Luckily I didn't just wait for you guys, but made my own inquiries."

"So, Marlowe," said Jack, hunching his shoulders in imitation of a movie bad guy, "How'd you get mixed up with Eddie Mars?"

I got short of breath for a second. "Who?"

"Eddie Mars. After you fleeced Joe Brody's gat you went after Mars. It's what I woulda done. It's what everybody in Los Angeles County shoulda done for the last twenty years."

I got that he was doing a routine, though no one seemed to be following it any better than me. There were about a dozen people in the bar, and a half-dozen women had gravitated toward the newcomers in town. Ward was dancing clumsily with a small brunette. Meanwhile, Neal was romancing a tall blonde, his arm over her shoulder, leaning against a wooden beam, moving his head in and out in sly whispers into her ear. Jack now resumed the position he'd been in before I entered, which was to take three empty beer bottles from a round table before him and attempt to juggle for the delight of two more women and a man in work coveralls sitting between him and me. "Lookee here, Marlowe." He picked up the bottles and began them spinning in the air. The table began counting: "One, two, three, four—" but that's as far as they got as a bottle eluded Jack. He quickly stuck out a foot and impeded the fall to keep the thick-necked bottle from breaking on the floor.

Beneath the smell of beer and cigarettes was a clinging

odor of sour milk. There was a creamery nearby and the day shift had gotten off a couple hours before.

"Boy," said Jack, "That was close." He made a stagy gesture of wiping sweat from his brow. "If I break a bottle," he said to me, "I have to buy everyone a round."

The song ended, and Ward came hand in hand with the brunette over to the table. "Well, gentlemen, we should probably get back out on the road."

"Ward!" said Jack. "Warden Ward, poor Dick just got here out of the hot sun, and right away you want to make him turn around and get in the hot car?"

"Oh, don't stay on my account," I said.

"Come on, Dicky-boy," Jack pleaded. "You have to have at least one."

Ward had meanwhile turned to his girl and they met in a long kiss. This was a happily married man?

"Yessir, Warden!" shouted Jack. "Time off for good behavior! We can't go now, we're just starting to have fun!"

Ward and the brunette broke their embrace, but still held hands. Ward turned to me in profile, addressing Jack as well. "No, we have to get going. This was a great idea, and I told Sue that I'll be back through this town fairly often, it being right on the way."

"Yes, yes, yes, yes, YESSSS!" came Neal in now. "We are all set to go. Fellas, Dick, this is Doris, and once we get to Indiana, soon to be the new Mrs. Cassady! She's coming along with us, there's enough room, we'll go three across the front and four in back, because we need to stop off a little ways from here and pick up Doris's sister, Francine. That's OK with you, ain't it, Ward? What's a little extra crowding in the car if what you get crowded with is something so nice and warm and lovely as my Doris here, or her sister Francine, of whom I've heard such excellent reports, ain't that right, Doris?" Doris didn't get a chance to say anything, because Neal was off again: "Cause as we just agreed, just now, we're not ever gonna leave each other's company, it's decided, for now and always, isn't that right, sugar? One of you boys is sure to find Francine just as lovely and as permanently indispensable as my little old gal Doris, whom I feel I've known ever since I was growing up on the dusty avenues of Denver, and so whose face I already knew before we ever entered this here palace of pleasure, yes, yes, YESSS! And now let's get out on that open road! Zoom-a-zoom-a-roonie!"

Neal separated from Doris, put two hands out in front of him as if holding a steering wheel, and crouched down as if he were peering over it. He shifted a fantasy gear with his right hand and took off, wildly stepping around the bar, turning in and out between patrons and tables filled with drinks, but not brushing a single person or table or object, though seemingly daring himself to come as close as possible to wrecking everything he could. Completing a circuit of the bar in a half-minute, all our eyes on him, he came back to Doris, put his arm around her shoulder and leaned her backward in a long kiss, a maneuver executed with such speed that, as one of Doris's legs caved backward and her other kicked into the air, the shoe on this foot shot up, caromed off the ceiling of the bar, and ended by clanking against the front door.

"Come in," said Jack to the knock, and everyone laughed.

Again to my surprise, Ward was going for it. I had figured he would at a certain point assume an uptight, respectable position. True, it didn't seem as though he'd been drinking like Neal or Jack, certainly not as much as Jack, but he'd obviously had one or two, and didn't seem worried that his trip was imperiled. Doris now had squirmed away from Neal and was conferring with her friends at the table. The gist of this seemed to be that they were to pick up her paycheck at the end of the week and drop it by her mother's house. Her friends seemed skeptical about the whole business. A fourth woman's head was down on her arms at the table, and I thought for a moment she might be weeping. Doris bent down to her and shook her arm and she sat up, wobbling in her seat and nearly falling over.

"What?" this woman yelled thickly. "You're going where? You're leaving?"

"It's OK, Agnes. We'll be back."

"You're never coming back!" she wailed in a sick, drunken words extended like a diseased song. "Never! Neeeeh-verrrr!" She started to get up from the table, with great difficulty. Doris and her friend tried to help her, but she pulled her arms away and sneered at them. "No, go away. Don't touch me! Fuck off!" Standing, a quick change came over her again and she lost the sneer and tears welled in her eyes. "You're leeee-ving? Why can't I leeeeeve?" She turned in my direction and, while her eyes didn't seem to focus on me, she took a quick step and fell onto me, grasping me around the torso. Her legs again gave way, and she hung on me, looking up into my eyes. Her own eyes were red and bleary and she smelled like wine piss, in addition to the curdled milk; sweat soaked her hair and pasted it against her forehead and one cheek. "Why don't you take me with you?" she pleaded. "Don't leeeeve me heee-yurrr."

The reek doubled in force when she opened her mouth and forced it onto mine. I tried to peel her off of me, and the man and woman from the table helped. She was small, but wiry, and wouldn't give up her grip, yelling, "No! No! Noooo!," each cry a blast of sewer exploding in my face.

Finally, they pulled her away and, though she kept trying to break their holds, the two of them locked her arms, one on each side, holding her.

I was worried about what she'd taste from my mouth, but her senses obviously weren't one hundred percent intact. I took a quick swig from an open beer.

This episode prodded Ward to renew the push to leave. "We better get going," he said, with the clear meaning that it was not just a time schedule that concerned him, but escape, as if he'd just seen a version of all of our potential fates and his inability to control the downward spiral. He gave one last kiss to his brunette, winked, and turned for the door. Jack took a quick swig from a beer as he, Neal, and Doris followed. I was ahead of them; behind us were more pleas and wailing I couldn't flee quick enough.

"Ready to go, go, GO!" shouted Neal as Ward let him in the driver's side door.

"Now, you're sure you're OK to drive?" he said to Neal.

"Ward, sir, I am the very model of care and responsibility, as whenever I take on a task I see it through with the utmost concern and sober-iety."

"Thus negating any infringements on his judgment alleged by the pollutants in his bloodstream," added Jack with a nod.

"Sit in front with us, Ward. Doris can go between us, and then when Francine gets here she can sit in back between our two gentleman bachelors, who may then vie for her charms."

"And vie not?" added Jack.

"I think I'd rather sit back here and keep an eye on Lulu," said Ward. Jack took his place in front.

Doris's home was back on the same road I'd been driven up, then down a side dirt road about a mile. It turned out that she'd already called her sister from the bar, urging her to be ready when they arrived with suitcases for both of them. A length of rope was produced, and these suitcases lashed across the top of the Willy's, which now looked more than a little like the Okie caravan in *The Grapes of Wrath*. Francine was wearing a faded sun dress and had a floppy straw hat tied behind her, and she handed Doris another armful of clothes. In the harsh porch light, lines in Doris's face were visible that had gone unseen in the roadhouse; her sister was a year or two older. "Francy," said Doris, half out-of-breath with the pace of everything, "This is Neal, my fiancé. Introduce her around, won't you, sweetheart, while I'm in changing?" And she darted into the boxy white one-and-a-half story farmhouse.

"Ahem," said Neal. "Allow me to make introductions between my newly acquired family member soon-to-be and my comrades here of both long and short-standing." We all shook hands and exchanged pleasantries, but now the jolly mood was being rattled by a shrewish screaming in the house.

Francine smiled weakly at us. "Ma doesn't really like this idea."

Indeed not. Doris came bounding out the door, the back of her dress not yet zipped, and as the screen door slapped shut behind her it was half-opened again by a pot hurled against it from within the house, and more invectives screamed from within. The corner of the door screen was pulled out of the frame, but it was hard to tell whether this had just happened or if it was the normal state of affairs. From upstairs, a child's crying could now be heard.

"Zip me, honey," said Doris, and Francine obliged. The mother came out the door, a middle aged bag in an apron and curlers, just in time to see us pile into the wagon again.

The motor had never been cut, and Neal threw it into gear so fast that the tires shot a cloud of dust into the air and a rat-a-tat of rocks in the general direction of mother and household left to come to terms with what had hit them.

We all quickly rolled up our open windows to try to keep the dust out, but no sooner had we done this than the combined perfumes and unguents of the sisters, worn in abundance in an attempt to finally overcome the dairy reek, made me feel like I was suffocating under a mountain of rotting flowers.

"Hiya, everybody," said Francine, sitting between Ward and me. She was fairly loudly snapping licorice gum, and keeping her mouth open enough to tell its color. I hadn't detected what was so cloying in the perfume smell until I saw the black wad on her teeth and realized. Licorice.

"Oh, I'm sorry," said Doris, turning back toward us and starting to introduce us. What stopped her was that at this moment Neal came to a sharp curve as the secondary road ran back into the highway and, despite the stop sign, sped through, turning the Willy's hard right, making tires squeal on the pavement and the top of the wagon feel for a moment like it was going completely over. We all fell left, and Doris, who was off-balance, slammed face-first into the steering wheel with an impressive thwack.

"Aww!" she cried.

"I apologize there, Darling," said Neal. "You just better do your talking facing forward until we are well-established on our resumed journey Indiana-way. I promised Ward that we'd make up some impressive time once I took the wheel. Hey, let me see if I can get any bop on the radio. It's not the most promising territory here, but sometimes they surprise you."

Ward had recovered his easy demeanor from his brief

alarm in the bar, but had to shout a little over the static now coming from the radio as Neal ran through the dial. "I appreciate your doing the driving, Neal. But we should be in pretty good shape, time-wise. In fact, I'd take it as a personal favor if you knocked the speed down about ten miles per hour, to make sure Lulu doesn't bang her head as well."

"My name's Francine," chirped Licorice-breath.

I rolled down my window and stuck my head out. What was I doing with these people? What was I doing, period? I get a check from the family trust each month, and I'd just given away about a third of it for head. I could feel my own semen, drying sticky on the hair of my belly. Undershirt and shirt tucked into my pants, there wouldn't be leakage, but it wasn't a particularly comfortable sensation either.

"No, I'm sorry," said Ward, ever the gentleman. "I was referring to our pet name for a piece of scientific equipment we're carrying in back."

"Are you a scientist? What, like Boris Karloff?"

This made everyone except Doris laugh, and Francine cackled above us all like a too-tightly-wound jack-in-the-box.

"Hey, stop making jokes," whined Doris, her hand still up against her face. She pulled it away and grabbed the rear view mirror to look at herself. "You gave me a shiner, you jerk!" she shouted at Neal, and as she turned his way, you could see she wasn't exaggerating. "And I'll be lucky if I didn't get whiplash to boot!"

"Yes, Neal, I really think you should slow down a little," Ward repeated, now a little bit edgily, Neal having ignored his previous request.

"Yes, well, I'm sorry, all," said Neal. "But if you're going to drive, or do anything, there's one way to do it, and that's to do it so there's no doubt about it. If you're driving, you've got to drive, if you love a girl, you love her, I only know one way. And we're making good time—we'll be hitting the Pennsylvania border now in no time."

"Neal the lead-foot, the pain-in-the-head foot," rhymed Jack. "He knows time and makes it in no time. Racing the wind." I wondered who the hell he was talking to.

"Let me out!" yelled Doris. "Francine, you're coming with me."

"Let me see that, Doris," said Francine, ministering to her sister. Doris turned around and uncovered her face, which even in the growing darkness we could see was bruised.

Doris turned her head away from Francine. "Did you hear me? Let us out."

"No can do, sweetheart. We are westbound which is the best-bound there is and making time, making time."

"Dean," said Ward. "Why don't you find a place up ahead to turn around."

Dean craned his neck around for a second and met Ward's eye. Then, without a word, he slowed the engine only slightly before flipping us completely around in about a heartbeat's time. Now we were going back the way we came.

Francine sat back against the seat between Ward and I. "She's got a little boy," she whispered.

We got back to the house, untied the bags, and after some hugs, smiles and tears were back on the road.

I was feeling like we had done a good thing, bringing the girls back home. It had been Ward's doing—Neal might well have wanted to, in effect, kidnap the girls, now that they were in the car with us. We were heading west again, somewhat less crazily, Neal and Jack looking for a passable radio station in the front, when Ward said to me:

"I was telling Neal and Jack how important it was for us

to get as many sexual histories as possible, and they've both consented to providing theirs. Do you think you could give yours to me or Dr. Kinsey as well when we reach Bloomington?"

I liked him. I wouldn't be helpful in your study, I thought. But I liked him enough, felt comfortable enough with him, to want to tell him why. Tell him the truth.

"I'm a homosexual," I said.

Ward's head bobbed backward about an inch and his eyes widened slightly. Jack also turned around toward me from the front seat as he and Neal lost interest briefly in the radio.

"That's wonderful!" smiled Ward.

11.

The picture I get in my mind when I remember Harvard University is full of colors—broad expanses of deep green grass, quiet gray trees lining pathways around and past red brick buildings. Historical and stately, sure, but everything also fresh and spring-like.

This is subjective, of course. I haven't seen the place in almost twenty years, and I was only there for a week.

I didn't attend the University. My father thought it best I begin working in his business, importing and dealing in Oriental rugs. Both my parents are dead now and the business was long ago sold, but for the year after leaving Weston my life was the property of that business and my parents. I worked a solid year without a vacation. I spent Christmas eve in our showroom, reciting Persian lineages to lethargic millionaires. In May I was due a vacation and, more importantly from my parents' point of view, had earned it. Surely

I had fallen in with a bad crowd at Weston, or been unduly influenced by fey and unwholesome professors.

In truth, I had never stopped thinking about Billy and my inclinations had only become stronger. I hadn't had sex during this time, but I was daily fucking myself with various objects. As a result my bumhole often felt like someone had snuffed out a cigarette there. But that didn't stop me. I had also started to fantasize about exposing myself in public, orgasming in the crowded anonymity of the city, which would be like having contact with others and privacy at the same time. I hadn't yet crossed the line, but my hard-ons in the middle of crowds, my reaching into my pocket to touch myself softly and slightly by the fingertips thrilled me. It wouldn't be long.

But I'm getting ahead of myself. In May it came time for my well-earned rest. Telling my parents only that I was spending the afternoon at a museum in Manhattan, I hopped the train to Boston. I found Harvard and its green grass and sat down on the steps of the big library, considering my next move. I had no illusions about how Billy would feel about me. After all, even if others had done his dirty work for him, I knew he'd been glad when I was no longer there to be a distraction in his life. But I also knew that people were made of many parts. If I could just talk to him. He was in a different place now, a place where his life wouldn't be so controlled and restricted. He was away from home, and so much of his former life had been dedicated to getting him to Harvard. Now he was here—maybe he could now relax and simply be himself, not worry about what others thought of him.

He might now be free to return my love, I thought. It wasn't impossible. I should at least, I thought, give him the opportunity. If he wasn't interested, he could tell me so himself and that would be the end of it. I wouldn't pressure him.

I just wanted to see him, to talk.

I could go to a baseball game and see him play, see him anonymously first. I could sit in the bleachers. I picked up a schedule—but the team wasn't playing a home game for the next three days.

I went to the Registrar's office. I was a friend visiting from out of town but I didn't know where he lived on campus. Billy Backus. I didn't even have to lie, though it felt like I was lying.

My daily life was already becoming so full of lies that it was second nature to me to spin off some false story to cover what I was thinking about, doing, or planning to do. That's why saying things that weren't in themselves lies had taken on such a color of dishonesty for me. To say something true but which concealed the lies behind it seemed even more false, a lie which lied about itself.

I had his address.

I booked a hotel room, signing the register with the name Joe Combs. Earle Combs was the name of the Yankee centerfielder, who had always been a favorite of ours. He played shallow centerfield and dared batters to hit the ball over his head. Waite Hoyt would throw high fastballs and Herb Pennock would hang soft curves and batters would hit lazy flies and deep drives to the dead stretches of plain in centerfield in Yankee Stadium, where Combs would chase them down. It worked year after year, with Ruth and Gehrig knocking the ball out of the park time and again, straight down the lines.

I went to a Red Sox game in the Fens. The Red Sox who had traded Ruth and now swept up the basement of the second division. The only curiosity on the team now was Bill Wambsganss, who had once completed an unassisted triple play in the World Series, when he was with Cleveland. The joke was that he might do it again with the Sox, because any-one lucky enough to catch a ball on that hapless team wouldn't dare trust throwing it to somebody else.

But I was elated even to watch bad baseball away from home. I was on vacation! I had worked hard through school but then had been denied the opportunity to graduate with my class. Now here it was, a year later, and I had my free-dom. My delayed graduation. Perhaps I would go to college. Perhaps here, if I had cleared my name and shown by good behavior that I was not a problem student but had my own ideas and ambitions. I think at the time I was thinking about training for the diplomatic service. I knew Latin, French, and some Italian, and we knew some people. Or if not Harvard, somewhere else. Perhaps Columbia.

I was getting my nerve up. I would approach Billy calm-ly, as an adult, not mooning in adulation. As a friend.

I slept the night in the hotel, trying to settle into this calm. I masturbated, but without any special thrills, just a straight jack off to calm myself for sleep. In the morning I had breakfast in the hotel restaurant. I would find the dor-mitory where Billy lived, walk around, get up my nerve.

I walked out of the hotel.

Walking up the street toward me was Billy Backus.

I tried quickly to turn away but he had already seen me. I have better eyesight than most people, and tend to see them before they see me. But Billy had the eyes of a jungle cat.

He turned me around by the shoulder and in the same motion threw me against the brick facade of the hotel. "Goddamn you!" he screamed. "What the hell are you doing here?"

I couldn't respond. Already I had acted guiltily. We looked at each other for a full second, him livid, me speech-less. My elbow had gotten a stinger from hitting brick. He was bigger now. He was clean-shaven, but had let the top of his crew cut grow out. Hatless, his hair flounced across his forehead as he sneered in my face.

"Stay the hell away from me." He looked around, then lowered his voice. "You homo. I swear I'll kill you if you don't stay away."

And just like that he was gone, running back the same way he had come, too fast to even look at anymore.

If I had been smart, I would have gotten the bag from my room that moment and gone right to the station.

But he still had those eyes.

Why are we attracted to one person and not another? Part of it has to do with access, of course. I fell in love with Billy because the fates had thrown us together at an intense, vulnerable moment. But thereafter, why had his face stayed in my mind? Why is it there still, when there have been any number of others I have been intimate with, who looked nothing like Billy? Why does that certain look still slay me?

That look. Its youth. I have stayed within the law as far as making advances towards young boys has been concerned. At times I've had to stop myself. I've seen Billy's face in some very young boys. It's a contrast between sleep and waking, between the vigor of young, athletic blood and the quickness with which it wears itself out. I have even gotten hard at seeing a boy-child yawn. That's just between you and me, Doc. And let me keep that clear—I take chances, but I don't cross this line. They would lynch me. Lock me up, throw the key in the Hudson, and let the gangsters take care of me in jail.

Got that, Doc? I don't cross the line.

Billy was a year older, but he still had his child eyes. Still sleepy, lids drooping down.

I walked around Cambridge for a while, heart beating

fast. I went back up to the hotel and lay on the bed for most of the afternoon, as if in shock. But I didn't leave town.

The next day, I went again to the ballpark. I was afraid to go back to the campus, but the green outfield grass of the ballfield was the same lush green of Harvard Yard. I lost myself in green, remembering of course our Darby race, but also just mesmerized by its thickness and deep color. What a horrible person I was, to so horrify the person I loved most in the world! He saw me as nothing but a cancer, a tar pit he had to steer clear of in order to enjoy a successful life. I wonder how he thinks of me today. Whether he feels in the least guilty, or whether he's kept his self-righteous view of me as a dangerous vermin that deserved extermination.

Back at the hotel was a telegram:

"LEAVE IMMEDIATELY RAT. DON'T RETURN. YOU'LL BE SORRY IF YOU DON'T FOLLOW INSTRUC-TIONS."

It was signed, "BRETHREN."

I was scared, but I couldn't make myself leave. What would I be going back to? Little but loneliness and long hours. Couldn't we just sit down over a cup of coffee and visit with one another? Should I send him a telegram back? This was before people necessarily had phones in their rooms or even houses, and I doubted I'd be able to locate Billy from the hotel phone. Simply going to his dormitory was out of the question. And yet how could I simply leave? I hoped we'd run into each other again accidentally, and I could call home and tell them that, yes, I was safe, I had simply decided to get out of town for a little while and was having such a good time that I'd be back a little later than I'd originally expected. Yes, everything was fine, I'd say. Don't worry. Then I could stay long enough that the initial shock would wear off and when I happened into Billy the next time things would have cooled down. Maybe then we could have our coffee.

I ate dinner in the hotel restaurant. I went out and bought an evening paper, reading every inch of it, scrutinizing even advertisements and radio listings, trying to occupy my mind.

I think I saw a double-feature matinee the next day, or did some sightseeing, I can't remember which. Maybe I even managed to put danger out of my mind. I couldn't really conceive of actually being attacked. But as I was walking home, about a block from the hotel, that's what happened. Night had just fallen when an old time Oldsmobile, one of those low-riding gangster cars, pulled up next to me. Two men grabbed me and pushed me into the back seat.

One sat on each side of me in the back seat. The one on the left shoved a gun up into my ribs. A third man was driving. They were costumed identically: derby hats pulled down to their eyes in front, hankies tied over their noses and mouths Western bandit-style, and pairs of comic Vaudeville glasses: black plastic rims and white, bulging eyeballs.

"Who are you? Where are you taking me?"

"Out of town," said the one in front.

"Nobody mucks around with a brother here, pal," said one of the thugs next to me.

"You had your warning," said the other.

At this, the driver shook his head violently side to side, turned and gawked at me. The fake eyeballs, on long springs, bounced from out of the glasses and bobbled ghoulishly. He turned back as quickly again to the road.

In the dim street light, I recognized the driver as an old nemesis, the red-faced punch-spiker from my final party at Weston.

"Ringley?" I said.

"That's right, Dickie. But you're going to wish you hadn't recognized me. Tie him up, boys."

One of the two pulled my head down toward him and the other reached for my hands and tied them behind my back. They sat me up straight again and wrapped a blindfold over my eyes.

We drove for what seemed like an hour. Every time I tried to ask a question, I got nothing more than a simple, "Shut up," or, "You'll soon find out." After a time, I could feel the car leave the main road. I heard crickets. We went slower, turned left and right, bumped along on varied terrain. "Where are you taking me?" I asked yet again. Finally Ringley said, "Right here." In a few more seconds the car rolled to a stop.

"The last place you'll ever see. Once you see it."

Needless to say, I was petrified.

Still with the blindfold on, I was pulled from the car, then pushed ahead. I could feel I was walking through grass, and I smelled the piercing odor of farm manure nearby. I stumbled, was yanked up and pushed on again.

I was stopped.

"Richard Post," said a voice I knew to be Billy's. He was disguising it, trying to make it sound deeper than it was.

"What do you want?" I screamed. "I'll go home."

"There was time for that. But I know I can't trust you. Gentlemen," said Billy, still bellowing, "Take off the blindfold."

One of them said, "Hey, Bil—" But he stopped himself.

"Take off the blindfold," came the command again.

"Wait. We said we'd rough him up a little, but . . . ." He trailed off.

Someone removed my blindfold.

My eyes couldn't focus for a second. I shook my head.

The only light was from a third-quarter moon high in the sky. I could make out Billy now in the darkness, about fifteen yards away, dressed elegantly in a slim-cut, double-breasted suit. He also wore the bulging eye glasses, but on his the eyes had been painted solid red. He looked like an emissary from hell.

He pointed at me a small silver gun.

"Billy, don't, don't." We were all saying it, me and the others.

"You guys scram," said Billy to the others. "You're all done here. Not you," he said to me.

"Billy," said Ringley, immediately to my left. "Come on. Fun's fun, but—"

"Scram," yelled Billy.

They took off back to the car.

It was all very well-planned. They were going to disappear, then slowly sneak up on me again from behind in the dark and surprise me. There wasn't to be any shooting. They were just going to make me soil myself with fear, then send me on my way, never to be seen again, feeling lucky to be alive. But Billy had changed the plan. He wanted me dead.

Why? I didn't know that night, and it took me many years to figure it out. Eventually you arrive at the point in your life where you can understand what happened to you when you were a kid. I wasn't the only one with a secret. I started to think about what this meant for Billy. He wasn't worried so much about me, about what I might reveal, as he was about himself, who he was, in wanting to keep that secret. Billy could tolerate me alone—it's okay when someone else is inverted, is strange, corrupted. But if it's you yourself, that's a different story. I reminded Billy of what he himself was and yet which no one could do anything about. Including himself. He could bury the truth about himself, he was burying the truth about himself. But now I had come back—the part of him that was supposed to be dead. The part of him which threatened everything.

You ask me for my opinions on this, so I'll tell you. From what I know about men, and I think I know a lot, I'm certain that Billy has found a way to live in the world without his secrets being known. Most men do. It's only the odd ones like me that have revelations, that break out of the confinements of what's expected of us and seek out what we desire. Every man learns how to keep secrets, to keep one part of himself separate from the world so that he himself hardly acknowledges it exists. I've given a lot of thought to this. It begins with a boy's first erection, the thing he's never seen before that's part of his body, that he knows no one must ever see except in very special circumstances. It is the horror of the world, the thing that must be most kept out of sight. And so he conceals it, and conceals that part of himself. He goes about in the world, develops a public persona, and this public part of him never acknowledges the other side, defined as it is by complete denial of it. And yet every man, certainly including heterosexual men, wants it to be seen. It is what makes a man feel most alive, most like a man. I'm sure Billy has made a great success in life and that he's had many lovers. I don't know if any of them have been men, though I wouldn't be surprised. The walls have a way of crumbling down. You go along in the conventional way, you see and talk to people, and then one day when you think you have it all under control, like a charging bull, your cock takes over your life again. It's part of who you are.

He fired—blam!

I don't know why his first shot missed. Maybe firing a pistol was one of the few things Billy wasn't good at. Maybe his hands were shaking. Maybe he fired too soon—premature explosion. That's even kind of funny, given the circumstances. Or maybe he was too far away or wasn't yet convinced he wanted to do what he was doing. The fear of exposure must have worked him into a blind rage.

Isn't it telling that Billy didn't fear murdering me so much as having the truth about him told?

He ran up closer to me and the others scrambled toward him to get the gun away. I had fallen to my knees, and was shocked that I wasn't dead. That thought was followed instantly—blam!—by an explosion in my chest. Blam! Blam! I heard two more shots go off.

I spent two years recovering, and of course have never completely recovered. I can't today run the length of one short city block, or from home plate to first base. But every cloud has its silver lining, I suppose. The lack of oxygen I get gives me more intense orgasms. Auto-erotic asphyxiation—well not complete asphyxiation, obviously, but to the point of near unconsciousness—is easy for me to perform. I know my shortness of breath well enough to be able to control it for greater pleasure.

When life gives you lemons, right?

I've done what Billy wanted. I've never seen him again. Nor have I ever told this story. I've kept his secret. Until now. Which I do in the interest of science.

12.

The remainder of the trip here would have been uneventful, had we not run into some bad luck around noon the next day, just across the Indiana line.

Dean was still driving, ripping into and out of each new town, barely bothering with lights or signs and probably leaving any eyewitnesses too stunned to actually get us into any trouble, when unexpectedly he stopped at the single traffic signal in a small town just waking up.

An old timer in a Tin Lizzie pulled up behind us. And no sooner had he stopped, poor fellow, than a local kid rammed him from behind and pushed him into us.

The impact wasn't hard, but a look of horror appeared in Ward's eyes. Simultaneously, Dean yelled out, "Lulu!"

Lulu had gotten it alright—even wrapped in blankets, the impact had caved in her entire side, with hairline fissures running up and down her entire length.

"She's ruined!" cried Ward, looking at the shards. "Ruined!"

The old man was in a bad way. The kid hadn't been drunk, he'd just made a stupid, kid mistake. The Willy's wasn't damaged—just a ding in the back bumper. But it would be a while to straighten it all out.

The police arrived.

"Da Cops," said Jack. "No, thankyou."

"I'm with you." We drifted a safe distance away and began walking.

Among the usual storefronts—garage, diner, a dress shop, a haberdasher—was a very strange clothing store, one I've never seen anything like before. It seemed to be a men's shop, but it sold only hats and shirts—no slacks, ties, belts, underwear or socks—and particular kinds of hats and shirts. For instance, there were no dress shirts I could see, or any kind of man's hat—fedoras, derbies, what have you—except for ball caps. The only kind of shirts they had were t-shirts; nor were they white t-shirts. They seemed to be advertisements. Available in any color imaginable, most or all had messages on them, be they simply words, or words illustrating pictures, or insignias of professional sports teams.

The window facing the street announced the name of the store: *Revolution!* With the exclamation point.

Jack and I looked at each other wordlessly, then went inside.

There were more oddities inside. One was a metal rack featuring rectangular pieces of thick, colored paper with statements on them:

No Sell Out
Remember The Scotsboro Boys
Africa Has A History
Fuck Tarzan
Butterfly McQueen Not My Mammy
Fight the Power
Separate But Equal Ain't
Pay Reparations For Slavery's Crimes
Your Uncle, Whitey: Nathan Bedford Forrest

—as well as others I can't recall. Larger messages appeared on the walls, as well as paper posters, mostly colorful head shots of Negros with names beneath, none of which I knew, though a couple of which seemed vaguely familiar. Paul Robeson I recognized. I wrote some of the names down on a piece of paper I had in my pocket, so fantastic the pictures and names seemed, like something out of a dream: a balding man with round eyeglasses, identified as W. E. B. DuBois; a dark man in military regalia, Marcus Garvey; a beautiful young man with fine features and the exotic name Touissant L'Overture; another man I had heard of—proudly bearing a round mass of kinky salt and pepper hair, Frederick Douglass. He had been a slave who came north, I remembered, helped by the Underground Railroad. But this was as close as I came to recognizing any of the significances of what these people, names, and statements were supposed to mean.

A Negro behind the counter, a little younger than me, with a wispy beard and penetrating dark eyes, looked my way and smiled. A block-lettered sign on the wall behind him read:

REVOLUTION
Sanders X, Proprietor

"How are you folks doing on this fine day?" he said, directly to me, but aware also of Jack, who had wandered around to the back of the store and was out of his direct line of sight amongst other bizarre wares.

"Fine, thank you." I waved at the rest of the store. "Are you Sanders?"

"Yessir. Sanders X."

"What does the X stand for?"

"It doesn't stand for anything. I just call myself X."

"Is that your middle name? Like Harry S Truman?"

"Not much like Truman." He gave me a sly smile. "I guess I haven't yet found the name to call myself, so I use X."

"It's a very unusual selection you have here." I reached over and grabbed one of the colored rectangles. It had a thinner, smooth sheet of backing to the message on the front. "What is this used for?"

"They're for your car." He took it from me and showed me how the backing peeled away. "It's sticky underneath, so you can affix it to the bumper of your car."

"For what purpose?"

"To fly the colors, my man."

I started to get a creeping, worried sensation. "So what

kind of store exactly is this?"

"Just what you see. T-shirts and stickers."

"No, I mean . . . ." I was looking for how to broach the subject. This was Indiana, and this was the Negro man who claimed to own this store. And the store—well, I guess I was worried for the man's safety.

"Have you had any problems?" I finally said.

"Problems?" he asked back.

"You know. With the locals."

"No, I'm afraid I don't know."

"I don't know," I said. "Selling what you sell here. You know. Some people might have some problems with some of these things."

"So are you saying that I don't have the right to have my store? Is that what you're saying? My shirts and stickers got something wrong with them?"

"No, of course not. A man has the right to have any kind of business he wants."

"But you seem to expect that I would be a target because of the things I'm selling here. That it would be normal for me to expect some kind of trouble."

Jack now came from the back of the store, holding a crumpled rag of some sort in his hand. He laid it down on the counter, and I realized it was another shirt, but this one made of an American flag that seemed to have been burned in parts and sewn back together.

"What the hell is this?" said Jack, seething.

"It's just a shirt," said Sanders X, his temples pulsing. "Man."

More of a scene might have occurred if, at that moment, Wardell had not come to the door to tell us that we were free to leave and that he was anxious to finish the trip.

Strangely, I thought again of Tony with the one arm as

Wardell came into the *Revolution!* shop and there were more words, but unfortunately I didn't listen to them, drifting out the door, suddenly unhinged instead into random possibilities, reinforced too by body memory—I still felt Tony's hard thrusting in the small muscle ache in the back of my throat whenever I had casually swallowed since our encounter in his father's driveway. We had gotten together and committed crimes, when neither of us had any thought of the other upon awaking that morning. Yes, I had lured him into crime, but the law might treat him harshly too, depending on who might have discovered us and how. It would have been hard for him to convince anyone that he wasn't responsible, struggling to put his pants back on at the same moment. Missing one's pants robs one of a great deal of credibility. But no one did discover us, and so, unlike I had with Billy, we got off free, unjudged, unhurt. Now you know, Professor Kinsey, and yet you will put the knowledge to different use. You say that others will learn from Tony and me in the magnificent book you are in the process of compiling. But in other circumstances, Tony and I would both be jailed. And then there was his arm to consider. Why had the shrapnel found his arm and not his heart? How and why had he come to work at a diner in Dronett, New Jersey? Why was Indiana different from New York, or New York from the deep south? What else had Tony experienced in his life, by accident or by others design, that made him take out his cock for me? Where else had he lived his life? Because you can make offers of money—even large amounts of money—without being taken up on them. You can have others decide to use the new information they've received against you, maliciously, even if they have nothing to gain by it.

A bullet had missed my heart, but my heart reacted anyway, differently. I was born different as well, and that had been both beautiful and accidental.

I can't deny what the world has made me, nor would I want to. I will always love what I love and, loving it, could not want to change.

Maybe I'm talking this way because I haven't yet really caught up on sleep, and it makes me dreamy. But I hope you can follow what I mean, Professor.

We went back outside to the car. Neal had somehow found two adolescent sisters to talk to on the sidewalk. They had merely (merely?) happened along. We dislodged him from them. Our mood had come pretty far down. Jack was still angry about Sanders's "desecration," as he put it, of the flag. I listened, though I was more worried for the man himself than for the flag, which generally seems to do fine for itself. I also felt bad for Wardell. He was still upset with himself. This was the entire reason for the trip and I could see Ward was blaming himself for stopping in Dronett earlier, as if his poor judgment in taking his mind off business then had somehow resulted in this accident. I don't think Ward is used to things not coming out quite right—and, to be sure, Lulu was one of a kind, a remarkable specimen. I hope you are able, in the end, to salvage some of the pieces and fit new ones, that you can in some way fix her so that you will have gotten something out of our trip besides our histories.

But even if Lulu can't be repaired, when I see this laboratory and the scope of your research here, Doctor, I know that this will be only the smallest of setbacks in the course of your great work.

I have to smile. So much of what you do and say surprises me!

What a strange thing it is to have made a scientific interest of passion. I'm not saying I disapprove, not at all. But it does seem to lead to some strange behavior. For instance,

Ward was telling me after we left off the girls from Dronett that it couldn't have gone any further between him and his brunette from the bar anyway because he didn't yet have your permission.

"Permission?" I said.

"Dr. Kinsey must preapprove all sexual contacts undertaken by his staff."

"Really?"

"Yep. But he's good about it. I've called him once or twice, in a pinch."

"Does he ever say no?"

"Sure. If he thought that it would interfere with my marriage, or any of the marriages of our team, he would deny approval. Prok is a great believer in marriage. The sex study started, actually, as a course on marriage. What makes for a successful marriage, how couples with long, happy marriages have managed to stay together, those sorts of things. Prok believes that complete sexual openness is good for a marriage."

"So do you tell you wife about all the women you've been with?"

Ward flashed that movie star smile. "There's some things Prok and I don't view in quite the same way. Or let's say there's things that Prok and my wife don't view in quite the same way."

I must say I've also been surprised that your questions, once we started this interview, were of such a personal, intimate nature. It's hardly what I would have expected from a scientist of any sort. You've got a mouth like a sailor, Doc. Do I enjoy sucking as much as being sucked? Have many of the men I've been with been circumcised, and how does that effect my pleasure? Have my experiences extended to include boys who have not yet reached sexual maturity? (And as I've

260

told you, I've never touched a very young boy.) What have I observed to be the signs of arousal in pre-pubescent boys? (Again, I don't know for sure, but I can guess.) Have I ever had sex with a woman? Did I enjoy the experience, or was it distasteful? (Yes, no.) At what age did I have my first erection? What is the most times I've ever come in a single day, and what were the circumstances? (6. It was just a normal day that took off, I guess.) Have I used various apparatuses to increase the breadth of my sexual experiences—cock rings, leather harnesses, whips, handcuffs, dildos, drugs? Had I ever intensified my autoerotic experiences by cutting off air or tight clamping my nipples? (As I've told you, I have, frequently.) To what degree have I explored the territory where pain becomes pleasure, or the two become indistinguishable? Have I had affairs with married men, men who otherwise blended in with mainstream society, who keep their socially unacceptable desires secret and thereby successfully negotiate a double life? (Yes, of course. Most of them are this way.) Do I frequent prostitutes and have I ever myself been a prostitute? Have I inserted objects into my penis? When exposing myself to others, how often have my actions been reciprocated, and do I have a general sense of how often my witnesses have themselves become aroused, or whether their protestations were merely the conditioned responses of citizens in a society where most people's true inclinations must remain suppressed? Has my number of partners increased or decreased over the years?

I'm tired. Has this been all my life has been about?

Let me put it this way: I've chosen this life, but I wish I'd had better choices. I know you are interested in varieties of experiences, and I've had those. But the beautiful remains constant—rarely seen in full but offering glimpses. The eyes half-closed riding a wave of pleasure. Eyes half-open smiling at the sun, in the morning, across a field. Smooth face and a few chin whiskers. The smack in my mitt of the ball he's thrown. The smack of an ass. Touch football on the school-yard, touch football in a bed. A cool night when no one's looking though you can't be certain. You don't want to be certain. Blankets and petroleum grease and losing yourself, your own eyes rolling up behind your head, the thrill of slicking and indulging a perversion. OK. But also, and maybe more, the quiet afterward, when you have it. Blinking, feeling it all come back to you. A bed of leaves and its loamy smell, and you're half in the ground.

It is a little death you come to. Beauty is. Wouldn't you say, Doctor?

OK, I guess here I'm the expert.

But really, it is too much for you to keep insisting I'm a hero. And for you to have made up this certificate for me after Wardell called ahead—it's very kind and entirely unexpected. "To Richard Post. In honor of a lifetime nobly spent bravely fighting repressive norms in the field of sexual expression. Our greatest respect and admiration. Institute of Sex Research. University of Indiana."

It's incredible, and more than I deserve, truly. Is this actually the University President's signature? I'm speechless.

I'd like to be of more assistance to you, if I can. There are some things I can add to what I've already told you. No, I have no problem staying in Bloomington for a short while.

I'm happy to help in any way I can. Really, I never would have imagined it possible that there could be a man like you, Dr. Kinsey.

One more thing, Doc. I don't know whether this is an appropriate question but, well, what the hey. Do you ever get any interesting Negro men coming through here?

The following people read and responded to this novel in ways that helped me bring it forward over the ten years since I began it. The book wouldn't exist without them: Nicolette de Csipkay, Marta Werner, Jeffrey DeShell, Bob Pelton, Alan Bigelow, George Saunders, Sandy Faiella, Joseph Lease, Stephen Paul Miller, Daniel Nester, Brian Lampkin, Marten Clibbens, Greg Roper, Steve Morgan, Neil Schmitz, Florine Melnyk, Chris Fischbach, Eric Miles Williamson, Harold Jaffe, Ed Taylor, and Tod Thilleman, the courageous publisher of Spuyten Duyvil Books. Lynette Herron has made countless photocopies for me. Thanks to all, and hoping I'm not missing too many.

Finally, I am indebted beyond measure to the many wonderful writers—poets, historians, journalists, musicologists, activists, thinkers, witnesses, and participants, too many to list!—that I read and researched during the writing of this novel. This book is theirs as well.

Geoffrey Gatza

Ted Pelton is the author of a collection of stories, *Endorsed by Jack Chapeau 2*, and a novella, *Bhang*. Recipient of an NEA fellowship in Fiction in 1994, he founded the fiction press Starcherone Books in 2000, and continues to be its Director. A graduate of the Masters in Creative Writing at University of Colorado, Boulder, with a PhD in American Literature from University of Buffalo, he is currently an Associate Professor at Medaille College of Buffalo. This is his first novel.

SPUYTEN DUYVIL

All Spuyten Duyvil titles are available through your local bookseller via
Booksense.com

Distributed to the trade by
Biblio Distribution
a division of NBN
1-800-462-6420
http://bibliodistribution.com

All Spuyten Duyvil authors may be contacted at
authors@spuytenduyvil.net

Author appearance information and background at
http://spuytenduyvil.net